CLOSE ENCOUNTER

It had the rough shape of a
so forth. But it was more t
deformed, each a different le
a slightly different way. But
away from. Scrambled som
flesh, the face brought to m...
the Arizona desert, with fire and falling steel all around . . .

"They do that when they've been badly injured," Steve said, keeping his voice level. "Lose their cohesion."

"So you're sure it's Chitauri?" Admiral Garza asked.

"I'm sure," Steve said.

"Sampling matches existing specimens of recovered Chitauri tissue," Justine said.

Garza stepped closer to the strapped-down body. "Well, this one's a ways past injured," he said. "We killed it on the base perimeter last night."

"Then you can expect its shape to scramble even more," Steve said.

Justine walked around to the other side of it. "How many of these have you seen?"

Steve remembered starships falling from the desert sky.

The Chitauri opened its eyes.

Steve felt the adrenaline shock like a punch in the chest, his super-soldier overdrive kicking in. The Chitauri snapped the straps holding it down, wrenching the table loose from the floor. One of its hands shot out and caught Justine around the throat; the other reached for Steve, but he was already pivoting out of the way when he saw the first twitch of muscle, and he caught the arm at full extension and broke it across the edge of the table. The snap of the fracture was counterpointed by the crunch of the Chitauri crushing the life out of Justine Ichesco. Garza had fallen back and drawn his sidearm; out of the corner of his eye Steve saw the admiral stepping to the side to look for a better shot. In front of him the Chitauri sprang from the table. He saw it looking at him, and could have sworn—in the split second before it shifted its focus to Garza—that he saw recognition in its eyes.

THE ULTIMATES®

AGAINST ALL ENEMIES

A novel by
Alex Irvine

Based on the
Marvel Comic Book

POCKET **STAR** BOOKS
NEW YORK   LONDON   TORONTO   SYDNEY

Pocket Star Books
A Division of Simon & Schuster, Inc.
1230 Avenue of the Americas
New York, NY 10020

This book is a work of fiction. Names, characters, places and incidents either are products of the author's imagination or are used fictitiously. Any resemblance to actual events or locales or persons, living or dead, is entirely coincidental.

First Pocket Star Books paperback edition September 2007

POCKET STAR BOOKS and colophon are registered trademarks of Simon & Schuster, Inc.

For information regarding special discounts for bulk purchases, please contact Simon & Schuster Special Sales at 1-800-456-6798 or business@simonandschuster.com.

Cover design by John Vairo Jr.
Cover art by John Van Fleet

Manufactured in the United States of America

10 9 8 7 6 5 4 3 2 1

ISBN-13:   978-1-4165-1071-0
ISBN-10:   1-4165-1071-0

AGAINST ALL ENEMIES

ceeding per directive. Prospects for the imposition of order are improving both here and in other locations where our enemies have failed to dislodge us. Evacuation to the lower fourth dimension is no longer necessary or desirable. We can, and will, continue to perform our duties. As of now, operational directives will be issued from the Western Spiral Arm.

A breeding program is in place, concurrent with assimilations and technological development. Force increase is assisted by improved cloning technology. We are approaching a viable population. If events do not demand immediate action, we anticipate being able to initiate full-scale operations in approximately ten solar years.

One of the lessons of the <Arizona> setback is that we must avoid concentrating our forces where the humans can bring concentrated firepower to bear. Rather, we should recall that their impulse to act in large forces served us well in the <South Pacific>, and we should attempt a similar misdirection if the opportunity presents itself. Our actual deployments will be smaller and more widespread, and we will be exploring the assimilation of forms other than the human. Conservation of mass limits our options in this direction, but the benefits of deploying scouts in nonhuman form make it worthwhile for us to pursue all possibilities.

Currently we are maintaining low-profile deployments in a number of North American and European locations. Our primary goal with these deployments is surveillance of human security measures, with a secondary goal of influencing policy where deployment makes that possible. The addition of nonhuman scouts has complicated communication channels somewhat, since a shift in form is necessary prior to any communication; however, these challenges are being addressed.

The elimination of <Kleiser> created a temporary leadership vacuum that has since been filled. Current command structure is more efficient than what existed under <Kleiser>, and more flexible in its approach. <Kleiser>, due to an unfortunate indulgence of desire for revenge, placed too much emphasis on the miniscule but formidable portion of the human population which has undergone genetic or technological augmentation, specifically <Steve Rogers> and <Rogers'> colleagues known as the <Ultimates>. New leadership is refocusing on the ideal of order, without counterproductive individual grudges and predispositions.

We are no longer focused on human political centers in <New York> and <Washington>; the events leading up to the <Arizona> setback made clear that our surveillance must be diversified, encompassing human technological research and cultural production as well as the standard intelligence targets of military and political activity. The <National Socialist> host understood that the imposition of order requires domination and control of cultural production as well as military strength; we are redoubling our efforts on this front. Much of this effort consists of suborning existing structures, such as film production, to increase the dissemination of material that prepares the human mind for the idea of order. Consolidation of cultural production in fewer and fewer hands has made this endeavor much easier. To take one example, <Hollywood> filmmaking has absorbed the idea of order—translated, in human terms, as "traditional values"—far more easily than we might have expected given the chaotic and inconsistent history of that industry. The <American> political discourse, by and large, has followed this trend as well.

What remains is to take these existing political and cultural trends and systematize them. Developments in ordnance, asset strength, and facilities will parallel this exploration of human cultural production.

2

AT THE TABLE IN THE TRISKELION MEETING ROOM down the hall from Nick Fury's office sat six people and a video monitor. The monitor, situated between Clint Barton and Janet Pym, showed the hangdog face of Bruce Banner. On the other side of the table, Tony Stark sat between Steve Rogers and Nick.

Every time we walk into this room, thought Tony, something bad happens, or is set into motion. Usually he got juiced, almost high, when he was headed into a meeting. There were deals to be done, money to be made, angles to figure. Today, however, Tony's carefully cultivated cynicism was threatening to mutate into genuine misgivings, which was strange since the presentation he was about to give could only be considered good news.

In any case, it was time to get things started. He stood up and said, "Okay, so there's good news and there's bad news. First, the bad. I couldn't get security upstairs to let me bring martinis down from the heli-pad."

Nobody laughed. Perfect, Tony thought. They weren't supposed to. He started to feel better. A little self-deprecation, an intentionally unfunny joke, and before they knew it, the audience was liking him despite themselves. On the other hand, this was not a typical pitch audience, in that he knew them all already; also, here he wasn't Tony Stark, multibillionaire industrialist. Here he was Tony Stark, dissipated but necessary in-habitant of the Iron Man suit.

Steve looked annoyed. "Can we—"

"We can, and we will, Cap," Tony said. "The good news is that due to the enormous black-budget oppor-tunity given Stark Industries in the aftermath of the Hulk incident—thanks again, Bruce—I stand here be-fore you to announce that I've got a prototype imaging technology that will be of great interest to all of us."

Tony saw Steve and Nick exchange a glance. Mili-tary, he thought. No patience for the art of presentation. On the video monitor, Banner's face remained glum. I know what you're thinking, Brucie, Tony thought. We threw you out of a plane when we needed you, and now you're back in this cell until we might need you again. Well, it's true. But you brought it on yourself when you shot that needle into your arm and created Captain AmeriHulk.

Then again it wasn't like Banner was the only one whose character could be considered . . . murky. They all had secrets. Going clockwise around the table . . .

Who knew what sins Hawkeye would be atoning for when he finally met his maker? Years in SHIELD's black ops would have piled them up by the dozen. And Janet, ah, Janet. Darling, Tony thought, nobody likes a mutant. Yet here you are. Steve, Captain America, you brought your proto-fascist politics with you out of the iceberg, even though they have thus far stayed hidden behind those blue eyes and that charming naïvete. Nick, our fixer, which of us will you throw under the bus the next time you need a favor from Capitol Hill? Banner's already gone. How long before you need another sacrificial lamb?

It won't be me, Tony thought. I don't need these people. This is my world. I command resources that would be the envy of most of the world's nations. Also I am fairly damn sexy, and cynical enough to avoid the gee-whiz save-the-world complex that most of the rest of my Super Hero counterparts suffer from.

Before he let himself get further carried away with self-analysis, Tony returned to his meeting patter. "Imaging technology? Who needs it?" he asked, letting the obvious rhetorical question hang for just a moment. "Well, we do. SHIELD's got great satellite coverage, and the best street-level cameras around, but there are times when you need to look a little more deeply."

He'd lost Nick. "Sometimes I hope that God will one day decide that you can only shovel so much bullshit," Nick said, "and then he's going to strike you dead."

"He might," Tony said. "He just might. But before he does, let's go into another room where I've set up a little presentation. Sorry, Bruce. We'll have to tell you about this part later."

He opened the door and with a nod and a smile indicated that everyone should exit. They filed out without comment, but Tony caught a couple of looks that told him he'd gotten what he wanted. They were bored already, which would make the coming surprise that much better.

"Ta, Bruce," Tony said to the monitor. He led the party down the hall to another meeting room, selected for its north-facing windows and general congeniality. Stopping the party at the door, he said, "You won't see much at first, but don't worry. Like the Jamaicans say, patience make de day come quick."

As Nick walked past, Tony clapped him on the shoulder and said, "You know me, General. The play's the thing. God, would it be boring just to show you machines."

"I could stand a little boredom," Fury said, pausing for a moment to let Steve by. Then he shrugged Tony's hand off. They started forward together, and Tony angled himself to go through the doorway first, counting on Fury's ingrained military courtesy toward civilians.

This was the part where Tony had relied on the word of a staffer downstairs that Nick Fury hadn't been in this particular conference room since the Triskelion was built. Just inside the doorway, an extra framework was erected, shaped roughly like an airport screener but—in accordance with Stark Industries' design standards—much more attractive, utilizing mirror-polished metal alloys instead of utilitarian off-white plastics. As Fury entered the room, everyone else had already started to mill around inside, wondering where the presentation was.

The moment Fury's shaved skull passed below the screener's crossbar, a metal mesh deployed from both sides of the screener, snapping around his upper body. A split second later, automated clamps hooked around Fury's thighs and ankles, freezing him where he stood. Red lights flashed, and a Klaxon that wouldn't have been out of place in an old submarine movie started *ah-ooh-ga*-ing. Putting on a surprised face for the benefit of the other Ultimates, who looked like they were about to leap into action even though there was no visible opponent, Tony slowly turned around.

"What the—?" Fury's voice was nearly lost over the blaring of the Klaxon. He struggled in the clamps, but they were designed to restrain someone with the strength of Captain America. He didn't have a chance.

After letting the scene sink in for a few seconds,

Tony stepped up to the screener, paused to make sure that everyone in the room could see what he was doing, and plucked a small metal hemisphere off the back of Fury's uniform. Inside it was approximately one gram of Chitauri tissue.

He held the capsule up for all of them to see, keeping it within the screener's sensing field. "General Fury," he said. "I would never have imagined that you were a Chitauri in disguise."

It was perfect. He had the rest of the group looking back toward the screening walk-through, and immediately to their left was the panoramic view of Upper Bay, punctuated by the Statue of Liberty. Presentation, Tony thought. That's how you close a deal.

Of course, you also closed a deal by coming up with a product that worked, and demonstrating conclusively and dramatically that it worked. He studied the looks on his teammates' faces. Steve was suspicious in his typical knuckle-dragging way, and the others looked plain baffled as they worked out what Tony had just demonstrated for them. Fury, manacled and wincing at the Klaxons, was eyeing Tony with murder in his heart, but even he was obviously interested to see how Tony was going to explain himself. Perfect. "Now watch," Tony said, and with a flourish stepped away from the screener and dropped the capsule into his coat pocket.

As soon as he took the capsule out of the screener's range, the Klaxons cut out and the clamps relaxed. Now free, Fury stormed over to Tony and stabbed a finger into his chest. "Where the hell did you get that?"

"Ah, I do love that Klaxon," Tony said, deliberately misunderstanding the question.

"You will tell me where you got Chitauri tissue, or I will have you thrown into a goddamn cell with Banner," Fury growled. "Right now, Tony."

"General," Tony said, spreading his arms, and playing to the group, "I can't give away my sources like that. Stark Industries takes very seriously its security obligations under the contracts we signed with the federal government. What you just saw—what all of you saw— was a device that detects the presence of Chitauri DNA. It's a variation on your standard bomb sniffer, but a hell of a lot more sensitive, and with some extra goodies built in. Stark Industries can be building a thousand of them a day by next week." He removed the capsule from his pocket and handed it to Fury. "You can check the validity of the sample, just so you know I'm not trying to swindle you, General. I've got more." This last he accompanied with a wink to the others.

"This is kind of closing the barn door after the horse is gone, isn't it?" Clint said.

"Well, we would have thought that after World War II, wouldn't we?" Tony answered. "The Chitauri being what they are, I wouldn't discount the possibility that some of them are still out there. And if there are some of them, there will be more. The universe's immune system, isn't that how they described them—

selves? T-cells multiply in the area of an infection."

He aimed this last bit at Fury, who was the one who would have to get the go-ahead from Washington to put the screener into production. Here's your angle, Nick, he was thinking. They don't trust us, but they also know that they have to rely on us when it comes to invasions by shapeshifting aliens. Give 'em the old only-good-Chitauri-is-a-dead-Chitauri spiel, and let's get this moving.

Fury picked it up; Tony could see his mind working. So did Janet Pym. "So what," she said. "Are we supposed to all be on permanent standby to go and take care of any random Chitauri who gets caught in one of these at the mall?"

"Think of it as the Super Hero Employment Act of 2006," Tony said.

"I'm thinking of it more as the Tony Stark Self-Aggrandizement Act," Janet responded. "If I were Nick, I'd kick your ass."

Tony shrugged. "He still can if he wants to. But I think he can appreciate the value of presentation."

Which was when Fury cracked him with a hard right. One second Tony was grinning at Janet, the next he was on his ass. "Ah, Jesus, Nick," Tony said. His eye was watering, but he knew Fury hadn't put everything he had into the punch. "Where's your sense of humor?"

Blinking his eye clear, he looked up at Fury, who was standing there with a broad grin. "What are you talking about?" Fury said. "That was funny as hell."

He reached down to give Tony a hand up. "I like this, man," Fury went on. "I'll take it to Washington ASAP. Meantime, you get some ice on that eye. You know where to find some ice, right?"

"Sure," Tony said. "As long as it's floating in something alcoholic."

"Men," Janet said. "You really don't know what a bunch of idiots you look like."

Tony tipped an imaginary cap to her. "And with that we adjourn." Truly, he thought, we are a snakebit group.

3

NICK FURY'S OPTIMISM LASTED EXACTLY TWELVE hours, which was as long as it took for someone in Washington to get wind of Stark Industries' new toy. He didn't know how it happened, although he wasn't naïve enough to think that the Pentagon and White House didn't have their little spooks inside the Triskelion. To a politician, he mused the next morning while on a plane to D.C., all facts are things to be simultaneously known and denied. That goes for E Ring of the Pentagon as much as it does the West Wing. But before you could figure out whether you should deny something, you needed to know it, which meant that everyone who worked for the government—at least in Fury's experience—was constantly spying on everyone else while at the same time disseminating bad information to throw everyone else's spies off the trail. Probably not the best way to run a democracy, but it was the way this democracy was run. If he was honest about it, Fury knew that he had edged into politician territory himself when he assumed command of the new SHIELD. He'd done his share of covering up and manipulating. Hell, he'd had Bruce Banner thrown out of an airplane, not knowing whether Banner would change into the Hulk or a splat. On the other hand, he still got to go out and shoot bad guys once in a while, so at least he hadn't become as useless and parasitical as most of his political brethren.

The plane touched down at Andrews Air Force Base and Fury got into a waiting limo, figuring he'd have forty-five minutes or so to organize his thoughts before he had to start choking on the mendacity of appointed officials. He was wrong, though. The minute he turned on his phone, it started ringing, and he was in the hornet's nest before the limo had even left the base grounds. The generals he ignored for now, since he had a working rapport with uniformed brass. The undersecretaries he had to call back, because he knew that while they were raking him over the coals they would also be cluing him in to what he could expect in the meeting. He made six calls on the ride, and each conversation made it clearer that he was in for a bad time.

Some of the agency types he was going to meet today were gung-ho about Tony's gizmo; some weren't; some were just professing outrage at the lack of accountability demonstrated by the fact that an alcoholic libertine like Tony Stark had gotten hold of Chitauri tissue. Fury realized quickly that he was going to be the focus of their dissension, since tearing him a new one was the one thing they would all be able to agree on. He already knew what was going to happen. The political appointees would be so hung up on covering their asses that they would be willing to bury a piece of tech that could save millions of lives. He could already see it happening, could imagine the tortured logic of Washington rising up and strangling the good work that Tony had done. The uniforms would be his buffer there. They would know when he was being dog-piled, and they'd step in to help him out.

He got out of the limo, rubbing a spot on his head that he'd somehow missed when he'd shaved that morning. It'd be a hell of a lot easier if he could just go bald. The stubble annoyed him, as if it might indicate that he'd been careless in other ways too. Oh well, he thought. Time to dip my toes in the piranha tank and see which one of them goes after me first.

There were nine people in the room when Fury was ushered in. The first to greet him was a delegate from the Joint Chiefs, an admiral named Esteban Garza. "General Fury," Garza said, and shook Fury's hand. "Glad you could make the trip."

Already in interpretive overdrive, Fury read the subtext: the Joint Chiefs weren't going to take an active role here, but they wanted him—and everyone else—to know that they were going to be keeping an eye on things. "Beautiful morning for a plane ride, Admiral," Fury said, and made the rounds shaking hands until he reached an empty seat.

The White House delegate was a staffer named Maureen Fowler, whom Fury had never met before that morning. Once Fury was in his seat and gotten out a notepad, Fowler stood and said, "Thank you all for coming. I'm just here to try and keep the discussion moving. The President wants to know what the ramifications of this development are, and what should be done and not done, and he wants the discussion to stay in this room for now. There will be no minutes and no recording, and we'd prefer that you take no notes."

Several of the attendees put away legal pads and tablet PCs.

"Thank you," Fowler went on. "Now, to catch everyone up and make sure we're all leaving from the same station. We are informed that Stark Industries has done some extraordinary work in the area of detecting certain foreign substances. They are to be applauded for their initiative. We are also informed that members of the military and intelligence communities, as well as the executive branch, are concerned that this new technology may be something of a double-edged sword. I suggest that General Fury catch us all up, and then we'll go from there. General?"

Fury stood and nodded at Fowler. "I may not be able to tell you everything you're looking to learn. I just heard about this yesterday myself. But what I can tell you is that Tony Stark gave an impressive presentation yesterday in which he was able to detect a gram of Chitauri tissue, encased in metal and attached to a human body passing at normal walking speed through an airport-style screener. How it works exactly, I don't know. I'm not an engineer. But does it work? I can assure you that it does. We tested the tissue sample Tony used and verified that it was in fact Chitauri."

He sat and put on his best meeting smile. "There. Now you know as much as I do."

There was a brief pause while everyone waited to see if Maureen Fowler was going to pick up the reins again. Fury made a bet with himself: whoever spoke first, if it wasn't Fowler, was going to be the biggest pain in the ass at the meeting.

The bet was on when a functionary from the congressional Office of Management and Budget spoke up. "I've been reviewing my files, and I don't see any record of Stark Industries bidding on any contracts related to these, ah . . . materials," he said.

Poor kid, Fury thought. OMB knows they need to show up, but they also know that they don't have anything to say about this. So they sent you. He couldn't even remember the kid's name.

An undersecretary from the Defense Department named Ozzie Bright said, "Stark Industries is into shit that OMB has nightmares about. You're sure as hell not going to get details about it at this meeting." Bright looked over at Fowler. "Maureen, I want him out of this meeting. We can't talk about any of this with him here."

Fury watched the quick political calculus happen in Maureen Fowler's head. "Travis," she said, decision made. "Would you mind if I caught you up after we're finished here?"

The OMB staffer blanched. "I'm going to need to report to—"

"I know," Maureen said. "And I'll make sure I give you something to report." She looked at her watch, and reflexively Fury looked at his. It was ten forty-two. "We'll be done here in time for a cup of coffee at twelve-thirty. How does that sound?"

Travis might have been new to Washington, but he knew when to throw in the towel. He gave a resigned nod and left the room. When he was gone, Fowler said, "Okay, Ozzie. You made your point. Now can we get on with things?"

There goes my bet, Fury thought.

"I'll get on with things," said Vince Altobelli from Homeland Security.

Right away Ozzie flushed. Ah, the old DoD/DHS turf war, Fury thought. That's what I should have bet on. "Vince," Ozzie said, "you can wait your—"

Altobelli kept right on talking. "What I want to get

on with is the question of how in the hell did Stark Industries, which is run by a for-Chrissake dipsomaniac playboy, get hold of Chitauri tissue? General Fury, you're going to need to convince me of a couple of things here."

Midway through Altobelli's opening gambit, Ozzie Bright shut his mouth. He's thinking the same thing, Fury guessed. Probably hates agreeing with Altobelli about anything.

"Well, Mr. Secretary," Fury said, being extra polite, "Tony Stark's personal habits are not what I would consider ideal either. But the truth is, his black-budget access is mostly outside my purview. He works with your department, he works with Ozzie's department, he works with everyone. Now I know that both DHS and Defense have Chitauri samples because I made sure you got them after Arizona. And yes, there are samples at the Triskelion. I've checked our inventory, and it's intact. Have you surveyed yours?"

Might have been a little too aggressive there, Fury thought to himself. He glanced over at Garza, who leaned back in his chair, looking amused.

"You're trying to tell me, Fury, that Tony Stark got Chitauri samples from our labs when all he had to do was walk into your basement and waltz out with whatever he wanted?" Altobelli demanded. "I know how SHIELD works. You think you've got your own little island out there and you can do whatever the hell you want. Don't come in here and smear my department and this government, when we're the ones who have to step in and clean up the mess after one of your team goes berserk and wrecks Lower Manhattan."

"I hardly think that's relevant, Vince." Heads turned toward Admiral Garza.

"No? I do." Altobelli looked like he was just getting warmed up.

Garza leaned over the table. "Are we here to score points or figure out what to do with Tony Stark's new toy?" Nobody responded. Garza went on. "Really. I want to know. Because I could damn sure think of some uses for something that would detect Chitauri anyplace they might have cause to go through a doorway. How about we consider that for a minute?"

It took all of Fury's self-control not to smile. Uniforms, he thought. They always stick together.

"Then I'll ask a question having to do with the use and dissemination of this technology," said Ozzie Bright. "That is, if nobody minds."

"I think we can proceed without the sarcasm, Ozzy. If *you* don't mind," Maureen Fowler said.

Bright cracked a smile. "I surely don't, Maureen, and thank you for keeping us all in line. My dog died yesterday, and it's put me a little off my feed. Now, General Fury. I think we can all understand that we don't need to know the details about where Stark got the samples, or how he spends his leisure time. And I think we can all understand that Stark Industries is doing all kinds of things, working on all kinds of projects, that some of us in the room may not have the clearance to hear about. Am I right so far?"

"Yes, sir," Fury said. Not just right, he thought. Also grandstanding. Fury wondered if there were cameras in the room somewhere contrary to Maureen's order, or if Bright, as a former congressman, was just playing to an imagined audience because he'd never gotten out of the habit.

"Okay, then. The question uppermost in my mind is this. Can you offer this meeting—and *government*—any assurance that the Chitauri will not simply engineer their way around this problem if the technology becomes widely available?"

Fury had been expecting some variation of this question. He hadn't expected it to come from Defense, which usually wasn't quite as paranoid as Homeland Security. Even so, his canned answer came out smoothly. "Mr. Secretary," he said. "I don't know if I can assure you of that. But I can assure you that they will not have to engineer their way around anything if we sit on this tech because we're afraid of how they'll react when it starts working."

"That's a typical uniform attitude, if you don't mind me saying, General. Build it, get it out there, play with the new toy, the hell with the consequences."

"The Joint Chiefs will find that an interesting opinion," Garza said with exaggerated mildness.

"Hell with the Joint Chiefs, Admiral, and I don't mean that disrespectfully." Bright was redder in the face now, thrusting his finger at whomever he spoke to. "If we give this away now, before we've really thought through how to use it, we could be handing the Chitauri our best tool on a platter."

"If there are any Chitauri left," Altobelli said.

"Oh, there are Chitauri left," Fury said. "You can count on that. You ever heard of a subway tunnel without a rat somewhere in it? It's part of the territory. They came here, and we killed most of them. Then the rest of them multiplied. Then we killed them again. I don't have any reason to expect we've seen the last of them now."

"Which is exactly what you would say to keep your . . . what was it, General? Remind this meeting of your last appropriation."

"One hundred fifty billion dollars," Fury said without missing a beat.

"And you're going back this year for the same, is that correct?"

"It is."

"So you have a real interest in making sure that the threats SHIELD is chartered to counter are taken seriously."

Fury felt his temper rising, and told himself not to open his mouth, but somehow he already had. "I don't think Homeland Security is in any position to throw that particular stone, Mr. Secretary."

That did it, he thought. Now the knives are out. Garza wasn't looking amused anymore.

"You mind if I pick this up again for a minute, Vince?" asked Ozzie Bright. Altobelli nodded.

Bright stood and put both of his hands flat on the table. "It's my opinion, ladies and gentlemen, that security reasons compel us to limit the dispersal of this technology to venues and situations that are strictly controlled and monitored. Its loss to the Chitauri would be a devastating blow."

Not nearly as devastating as never having had it in the first place, Fury thought.

"I'll ask you to indulge me in a little historical parallel," Bright went on. "During World War II, hard decisions were made about utilizing certain technologies and acting on the information gained thereby. Had the Allies saved every life and thwarted every minor movement they learned about by cracking the Enigma code, the Nazis would quickly have abandoned Enigma; by sacrificing those necessary lives, the Allies maintained their intelligence superiority over the Nazis long enough for that advantage to prove decisive. Do you understand the analogy, General Fury?"

Fury made his tone as level as he could. "I understand the analogy, Mr. Secretary, but I think circumstances here are different enough to render it invalid."

"Well," Bright said. "With all due respect for your understandable difference in opinion, I suggest that the facts speak for themselves."

And Fury knew he had lost. Maybe not just because of his lapse in temper, but he had lost all the same.

4

STEVE WAS WATCHING *SOME LIKE IT HOT* ON
cable when his cell phone rang. He had to resist the
urge to walk over to the phone on the wall in the
kitchen. He'd spent twenty-seven years talking on
phones tethered to walls, and he was having a hard
time getting used to the change. He checked the cell
phone's caller ID, saw that it was Nick Fury calling.
"General," he said.

"Cap," came Fury's voice. "You home?"

This was another thing Steve couldn't get used to.
Of course he was home. That's where you were when
you talked on the phone.

Only now that wasn't true anymore.

"Yeah," he said.

"Good," Fury said. "I'm downstairs. Let me buy you a beer."

On his way out, Steve walked over to the TV and turned it off. Then he remembered that he'd been sitting next to the remote. Now that's even stranger than the phone, he thought. I never even saw a television before I left for the war; every time I've ever used a TV, it's had a remote. And yet I still go to turn them off manually. Walking downstairs, he wondered if the problem was that he just assumed all electronic things had switches. Then he decided that the whole thing wasn't worth worrying about. There were more important problems.

Such as why Nick Fury had come looking for him at ten o'clock on a Tuesday night.

"I'm kind of a morning person, General," Steve said when he came out the front door of his building. "If you're looking for a drinking buddy, I might not measure up."

"I don't even care if you drink," Fury said. They got into Fury's car—his personal car, Steve noticed, not one of the service limos that usually took them around the city. General Nick Fury, director of SHIELD, was driving a green Toyota Corolla. "I saw that look," Fury said. "This is my incognito car."

"So we're incognito?"

"Just don't feel like drawing attention."

"Okay," Steve said. "Where are we going?"

"Bar I picked because it has the same name as a

restaurant I like in San Francisco. It's called the Boulevard, up in Greenpoint."

Greenpoint, Steve thought. The name brought to
mind Polish butchers. "I used to get pierogies in Greenpoint sometimes."

"You still can. Don't walk around thinking New
York's completely different. In some neighborhoods,
fifty-eight years isn't that long." They were driving
under the Brooklyn-Queens Expressway. Fury turned
left and doubled back, parking right in front of a bar set
in the middle of a block of four-story walkups.

Inside, the Boulevard was a woody, comfortable
spot. Bar on one side, booths on the other, with a space
in the back for a pool table. The back door was open,
and Steve could see out into what looked like a small
courtyard. Two TVs played the Yankees game. There
were six or eight people sitting around, all wearing the
costume of a breed Steve had learned was called the
hipster. The bartender was a big longhair with tattoos,
wearing a black shirt that caught Steve's eye because
of the German lettering on it. He gave the shirt a closer
look, and realized it was a soccer jersey. Deutsche
Fussball-Bund.

"For Pete's sake," he said to General Fury. "We go
and fight a war so this yahoo can be a soccer fan."

Fury shrugged. "Past is past, Cap."

Not to me, Steve thought.

Fury bought a beer and a ginger ale and the two of
them sat in a booth beneath one of the television sets.

"So, General," Steve said. "You must have brought me out here for a reason."

"I did," Fury said. "I brought you out here because I spent the morning getting my ass chewed by politicians and I wanted to talk to a rational human being."

"Tony's new toy?" Steve asked.

Fury nodded. "Washington's afraid that if we use it too soon, the bad guys will figure out a way around it. Plus I got in the middle of a pissing contest between two Cabinet departments." He shook his head and drank. "Should have known better. Anyway, long story short, they quashed it. Gave me this long rigmarole about how Tony shouldn't be trusted with certain materials, how I couldn't be trusted because I was running SHIELD like some kind of shadow junta, blah blah blah."

"Let me get this straight," Steve said. "They know we have a tool that would work against the enemy, and they're telling us not to use it because if we use it, the enemy might find out about it?"

"That's the upshot. And you'll appreciate this. One of them actually gave me a high and mighty speech about Enigma, how the Allies didn't always act on the information they got after they broke the code because they didn't want to let on that they'd cracked it."

"Is that true?" Steve asked.

Fury just looked at him.

"And good men died because of it," Steve said.

"Yes, they did," Fury said. "But it wasn't necessarily

the wrong call. Would more of those good men have died if the Nazis switched to a new code and the war lasted six more months?"

"Wrong question," Steve said vehemently. "You have information, you act on it. You have the enemy in front of you, you take him out."

"I don't disagree," Fury said. "But you and I aren't always the ones who make the call."

Politicians, Steve thought with disgust. "They're out there, though. We didn't get them all. Washington must know that."

"Washington," Fury said, "knows what it wants to know. And it doesn't want to know this. Well, some of them do. And I had this thought as I was walking out of the meeting, Cap. I thought, you know, SHIELD could do whatever it wants. But we decide to go through these channels because that's the way things are done in this country, or should be. And then I had another thought, which was that ninety-nine times out of a hundred that might be the best way to do things . . . but this might be the hundredth time."

He killed his beer and tipped the glass at Steve. "And that, soldier, is what is known as a privileged communication."

"Understood, sir." Steve sat and nursed his ginger ale while Fury went to the bar and came back. The jukebox started blaring, and Steve's mood soured further. A year after he'd been thawed, he still didn't get the music.

"So I thought to myself," Fury said when he'd settled

in the booth again, "uniforms stick together. And it occurred to me that maybe you needed to have a beer. Or a ginger ale. Whatever." Fury raised his glass. "The uniform."

"Damn right," Steve said, returning the toast. "The uniform."

A cheer went up from a group of three people at the bar. Steve saw that they were looking at the TV over his head. He turned to see the other TV, and watched a Yankee trotting around the bases.

"You look like you just bit into something rotten," Fury said. "Let me guess. Dodgers fan?"

The depth of his anger surprised Steve. "Hell yes. That's one of the worst things about coming back. Los Angeles? How could they move to Los Angeles? And the Giants moving, too? And who are these Mets? That's not baseball."

"Now it is," Fury said with a shrug.

"And this designated hitter rule," Steve went on.

Fury winked his good eye. "Un-American, right?"

"It is," Steve insisted. "You play the game the way the game is supposed to be played . . ." He trailed off, and realized that he was really thinking about something else. "Sometimes I think the uniform's all I have," he said. "I turn on the TV . . . you know, I was just thinking tonight. Before I got thawed out, I'd never seen a television in my life. Now it's on all the time, everywhere. You can see anything."

"Except what's really going on."

"Well. You don't need to see everything. I mean, the average person doesn't."

"You don't think so?"

Steve set down his glass. "No, I don't. That's what we're here for. We're here to keep the boogeymen out from under the bed. It doesn't do any good if we get rid of the boogeyman and then put his picture on the six o'clock news for everyone to get scared of all over again."

Fury was looking at him, and Steve suddenly realized that the general hadn't responded because he was waiting for Steve to figure out the implications of what he'd just said. "No," Steve said. "I don't believe that. I don't believe in all of this mumbo-jumbo about keeping people scared. This is America. We don't do things like that."

"Well," General Fury said, "we try not to, anyway."

That's not an America I recognize, Steve thought. And it's not an America I want to live in. The America I believe in doesn't let political squabbling compromise its security.

And if that's how things really are, then I'm going to do something about it. I've done dirty jobs for this country before, and I'll do it again.

He felt like he was in dangerous territory. You're coming close to going off the reservation, son, he told himself. But if what General Fury was telling him was true, America had fallen a long way since Roosevelt had told the country that the only thing it had to fear was fear itself.

Fury was looking at him. "I can see the wheels spinning, Captain Rogers."

"Just thinking all of this over, sir. What do we do?"

"What do we do? We play the game the way the game is supposed to be played." Fury drained the rest of his beer and stood. "Back to running SHIELD. Shadow military governments don't run themselves. Thanks for coming out."

"Any time," Steve said.

Outside, Fury offered him a ride home, but Steve decided he'd rather walk.

"You sure?" Fury was jingling his keys, obviously in a hurry to get somewhere else.

"Yeah," Steve said. The only company he wanted right then was his own thoughts, and his own misgivings, and his own sense that something had to be done.

Fury unlocked the Toyota, but paused before getting in. "Cap," he said. "This country needs people like you, but the people who run it aren't like you."

Steve nodded.

"You need to understand that or else you're going to go off and do something we'll all regret."

"Yes, sir," Steve said. He lifted a hand in a half-hearted wave, and walked off. Maybe it's *because* I understand that, that I might do something we'll all regret, he thought. That night he didn't sleep at all.

5

Status Report

Intelligence gathering suggests a possible technological advance that necessitates an accelerated mission plan. We proceed accordingly.

The impulse to individuality simultaneously retards
the progress of *Homo sapiens* (to borrow their
unwieldy classification system) as a species and
enables startling acts of innovation on the part of individual members of the species. This is one reason why
Homo sapiens was targeted for ordering. The parallel
influences of chaos and reason, however, make
humans a particularly difficult case to manage. Under
no circumstances should we mistake the actions and

rationales of one member of the species for a general tendency on the part of the species as a whole.

A further complication is the observed phenomenon of a member of the species reasoning through a set of circumstances and then acting in a way entirely opposed to the logical conclusion of this reasoning process. Again, this observed phenomenon was one factor in the initiation of the human ordering project; it bears repeating in the current context, especially in view of the influx of new forces unfamiliar with the nature of the human.

The human team known as the <Ultimates> suffers from all of the defects in reason that afflict *Homo sapiens* as a species; yet they have proved a difficult obstacle. We are intensifying our surveillance of all current and former members of this organization, and have reason to believe that this surveillance will enable us to penetrate the organization and remove it as an obstacle.

Progress in nonhuman form assimilation has been particularly successful in furthering this goal.

Increased surveillance, and increased density of assimilated assets in place, is ordered in the following locations:

<Manhattan, New York>. Location of team member <Tony Stark> as well as his corporate endeavor, <Stark Industries>. Location of team member <Nicholas Fury>. Location of team member <Janet Pym>. Location of <Ultimates> headquarters, <Triskelion>, previously infiltrated. Full schematics of <Triskelion> are available and will be utilized as part of the human ordering project.

<Brooklyn, New York>. Location of team member <Steven Rogers>.

<New Rochelle, New York>. Location of team member <Clinton Barton>.

<Wilmette, Illinois>. Location of former team member <Henry Pym>, believed to be engaged in research directly related to our endeavors.

<Washington, District of Columbia>. Frequent destination of team member <Nicholas Fury>, for political consultation and guidance. Also seat of government of the nation <United States of America>, which provides the <Ultimates> with financial and infrastructure support.

<Uppsala, Sweden>. Frequent location of team member known as <Thor>. Notes regarding symbolic significance of this identity to one iteration of human mythology attached.

Deployment orders pursuant to intensification of surveillance efforts in these locations attached.

Assimilation and infiltration activities in other areas of the planet are to remain unchanged. We consider the <Ultimates> a primary threat, and we redirect our resources to reflect this conclusion.

Previous efforts to eliminate the <Ultimates> focused on direct attacks on members of the group as well as the <Triskelion> headquarters. At this time that strategy is no longer considered viable. Current strategy prioritizes more indirect methods. Results indicate that this approach is successful at this time, and it will be pursued. The timetable for execution of this phase of the human ordering project accelerates due to security questions noted in appendix. Time before missing humans provoke police investigation not known, but estimated to be less than .01916 solar year.

Appendix: Field Report

Priority human asset assimilated in <Falls Church, Virginia>. Mission security compromised by presence of human asset's mate and offspring, contrary to advance reports. Human asset's mate and offspring eliminated.

Priority nonhuman asset assimilated in <District Heights, Maryland>.

Priority human asset assimilated in <Evanston, Illinois>.

Priority human asset assimilated in <Manhattan, New York>.

6

ANOTHER DAY, ANOTHER FRUITLESS HOUR SPENT
trying to reason with people whose minds were dead-
ened and senses numbed by the onslaughts of multime-
dia consumer capitalism. Today Thor was in Nick Fury's
office trying to convince Nick to throw SHIELD's
weight behind an effort to release the Stark screener
technology. Normally this wouldn't be the kind of action
he could endorse—what the world needed was less surveillance, not more—but Thor knew what was coming.
He hoped to be able to impress the importance of this on
Fury, but he wasn't optimistic. For all of Nick Fury's
virtues, he was still a man of his times.

And this, Thor thought, is the difference. I am neither a man nor of any time. In this way it becomes impossible for us to understand each other.

Perhaps I understand Steve Rogers a little better than most, because he is lost in time as well. But he is also a creature of duty and obedience, and I understand only the first of those. In obedience I have not the slightest interest.

"So, Loki said something to me the other day," he began, just to get Fury in the right frame of mind.

"Oh, did he?" Fury said, not bothering to hide his skepticism. He was at his desk comparing two sets of figures.

"He said that of all the Ultimates, Steve Rogers was his favorite. I think your conversation the other night really made him a fan."

Fury put down his pen and squeezed the bridge of his nose. "Okay," he said with his eyes closed. "I get it. If I have to raise my right hand and swear that I believe you're the Norse god of thunder just to get you to leave, I'll do it." He raised his right hand, looking down at his desk. Ten seconds or so later, he looked up. "You're not gone."

"You're not very convincing," Thor said.

"Neither are you, Mister Son of Odin, or Wotan, or whatever we're supposed to call him. I don't believe in gods—any of them—and until you bring Jesus Christ himself in to walk across the Upper Bay from Battery Park to here, that isn't going to change. Far as I'm concerned, you're a garden-variety anti-globalization wacko who got hold of some tech that nobody can reverse-engineer. Doesn't make you anything special."

Thor had started smiling at "Wotan," and couldn't stop. "Quite a speech, General Fury."

"You provoke me," Fury said.

"Well. Let me provoke you to pay attention."

"Right now I'm paying attention to a question. Where's the belt and hammer?"

"Safe," Thor said.

"If you had to get them right now, could you?"

"Do I have to?"

Fury shook his head and laughed. "Here I go, getting sucked into a conversation about possibilities with a crazy man. Okay, never mind, crazy man. What did you come in here and screw up my day for?"

"You need to get Tony Stark's new technology into the—as much as I hate to say it—marketplace, General," Thor said. "Believe me or don't, but it's more important than anything else you can do right now."

"Okay," Fury said. "Let's say I believe you. How do you suggest I explain to the congressional inquiry that I knew I had to do it because of the word of the Norse thunder god?"

Thor put away his smile. "Is that the worst problem you can think of?"

Fury was about to answer when his office door opened at the same time as a knock came from the hall. "Excuse me, General, but I just need—"

The uniformed man in the doorway was dark-haired, lithe, mischievous. Loki.

Perfect, Thor thought as he looked back at Fury and saw on the general's face only the beleaguered annoyance of the desk officer who in his mind is never far from the field. "Please," he said. "Come in."

"We were just discussing how to circumvent a political roadblock to the production of an extremely important technology developed under a black-budget contract by Stark Industries," Thor said. "I believe General Fury has political concerns, with which I sympathize, but I can't agree with his decision."

Loki winked at him. "General Fury, all I need is just this one signature," he said, approaching Fury's desk with a manila folder opened to expose a document.

"I don't think I have to tell either of you how important it is to be able to recognize Chitauri infiltration wherever it may occur," Thor said. "And Tony's innovation—"

"Goddammit," Fury said. "You keep talking, and I'm going to have to kill one of my only competent secretaries. Have you ever heard of a goddamn security clearance?"

Thor put the smile back on. "Oh, but General. He already knows."

In a double take that would have done Jim Carrey proud, Fury's head snapped back and forth between Thor and Loki. Then he caught himself and said, slowly and angrily, "Are you telling me you think this man is Loki?"

"I don't have to think it, General. Should I make introductions?"

Fury stood behind his desk and pointed at his secretary. "You. Get the hell out and forget whatever you heard here."

"Yes, sir," Loki said, and closed the door behind him.

"And you," Fury went on, now pointing at Thor, "are one crazy son of a bitch."

Thor spread his hands. "General. After all we've seen in this past year, you still think it's crazy to believe in shapeshifters?"

Fury glared daggers at him.

"And the truth is, I don't care about what you think where my mental stability is concerned. I know what I know. However you want to rationalize it to yourself is fine."

"Oh," Fury said. "You're going to lecture me about rationalizing? Let me get out my tape recorder."

"General Fury," Thor said. "That was Loki. Last night he was telling me that after your conversation with Steve Rogers, Steve was angry about the suppression of Tony's tech. Is that true?" Fury didn't answer. "Is it also true that you talked about baseball, and that Steve drank only ginger ale?"

Still only silence from Fury.

"If you need to think I'm crazy because that's the way your world makes sense to you, be my guest," Thor said. "But this happened. And what needs to happen now is you need to get control of the Stark Industries technology before someone else does it for you." Thor stood. "That's what I came to tell you. I'll leave now, but remember: if you don't act, someone else is going to. I know that, too. You can figure out how."

On his way to the helipad, Loki fell in alongside him. "Not everyone finds your righteousness charming," Loki said.

"It isn't meant to charm," Thor said. "It's meant to be right."

"You know it's not going to work," Loki said.

Thor looked down at him. "What's the name of Fury's secretary?"

"Who cares?" Loki shrugged. "He's downstairs filling out a report on something ridiculous like equipment depreciation."

"I don't care," Thor said. "What's his name?"

Loki sighed. "Arthur Kostelanetz. Why?"

"So I can know who I'm going to be accused of assaulting," Thor said, and leveled his half brother with a roundhouse right.

When he got outside and into the helicopter, Thor opened his cell phone and called Steve Rogers. The phone rang only once before Steve's recorded message clicked on. Thor shut the phone, opened it again, and redialed. Again the message. One more try, Thor thought. He called Nick Fury.

"I've had enough of you today," Fury said when he answered the phone.

"Do you know where Steve Rogers is, General?" Thor asked.

"No. And if I did, I wouldn't tell you. I'll see you next time we convene as a team, and I hope not before." Fury hung up on him.

Mortals, Thor thought. It's too much for them. Everything is too much for them.

He called Fury again.

"Did you not hear me?" Fury said.

"No, I did. But I wanted to find out if your secretary Kostelanetz is all right."

"Is that—" Thor could almost hear Fury doing another double take over the phone. "You son of a bitch," Fury growled, and hung up again.

Thor laughed. What could you do?

He leaned forward and tapped the pilot on the shoulder. The pilot leaned his head back, still keeping his eyes front. "Where can you put me down in Brooklyn?" Thor shouted into his ear.

The pilot leaned forward to consult some gauge or other, then leaned back again. "What part of Brooklyn?"

"I believe it's called Flatbush?"

"What?"

Thor sighed. "Flatbush!" he shouted. "Flatbush Avenue!"

Again the pilot consulted a display. "I can't get you down any closer than the Brooklyn Navy Yard," he yelled. "Unless you want to set down in an empty lot."

"Fine, yes," Thor shouted, nodding, "let's do that."

"You going to explain it to General Fury?"

"He'll know why. Just do it."

Ten minutes later Thor was stooping as the helicopter angled up and away to the southwest. He was in the middle of an acre or so of cracked and weedy asphalt, once a truck yard and now just one more place where the commerce of New York had come and gone. When he got to the fence, he jumped up and caught the razor wire, bracing his feet on the top of a fencepost before vaulting over. As his feet hit the ground, he saw three passing teenagers gaping at him. "Pretty good trick, isn't it?" he said with a grin, spreading his hands so they could see that he hadn't cut himself.

"Damn," one of them said. "Homey's a ninja."

They watched him walk down Flatbush Avenue back toward Rogers's apartment, which was in the as-yet-ungentrified hinterlands of Brooklyn. The block Rogers lived on looked like nobody had put a coat of paint on anything since he'd left for the war. At times like these, Thor thought, I would just as soon fly, and to hell with this pretense for mortals and their small fears. He felt the absence of Mjolnir in his hands. Then he cracked a smile again, thinking of the teenagers and their wonder and what must have seemed an impossible thing to them. Being immortal had its privileges . . . and its drawbacks, Thor thought, remembering the dark and shining malice on the face of his half brother.

Steve Rogers is my favorite, Loki had said. That much Thor had told Fury. What he had not mentioned was that Loki had said something else. *Rogers I love,* Loki had said, *because he will squeeze so hard with his fists of order that chaos will inevitably squirt out.* And laughed, Loki had, long and loud.

Thor picked up his pace, spurred on by a sense he couldn't shake that something was about to happen, some trick about to be played on a man whose goodness would be the lever that evil would use against him. To be a god was to know things; the joke of fate was that too often, what even the gods knew was not quite enough.

Rogers wasn't home. Thor stood on the street, watching the mortals pass. What would he have told Rogers? That Loki had taken a special interest in him? Rogers believed in flag and country, nothing else. His was a pure belief, not ignorant of nuance but dismissive of it, deeply invested in a black-and-white view of the world. There was an innocence about it that gave Rogers much of his strength, but that innocence was also part of what made him a useful tool for those who operated by deceit. Strength of belief, Thor thought, was admirable, but it was a lever that when used against you always tipped you long before you knew it was being used.

And so, Thor thought. I have come looking for him to call him a naïf and tell him that my half brother, another god he doesn't believe in, has a plan for him. Hardly an errand with good prospects of success.

To know, and not be believed. This was the lot of the gods. All the same, Thor was glad he wasn't a mortal. Fate would do what Fate did, to Steve Rogers and to them all.

the funeral, and I'll see her there, and then maybe we'll talk a few more times, but she will be a widow in her seventies and I'll be a super-soldier figurehead for SHIELD, and he knew how that would go. Someone would call him when she died.

Snap out of it, he told himself. Quit wallowing.

The door to Bucky's room was open, which meant he was probably awake. Knowing he was a friend of Captain America's, the nursing staff—all of whom had kids who were Captain America fans—took outrageously good care of him. They did everything but cure his cancer.

Steve tapped on the door. "Hey, Buck," he said.

No answer.

Two steps into the room, Steve was certain Bucky was dead. He lay on his back, mouth open, tubes and needles everywhere . . . but the monitor next to the bed ticked off a steady heartbeat. Steve took a deep breath, let it out slowly, and settled in the chair next to Bucky's bed. He wondered where Gail was. Usually when Bucky had to go into the hospital, she spent most of her time there with him.

"Ah, Buck," he said softly. He didn't want to wake Bucky but he couldn't stop himself from talking. He had to talk, even if it was just to hear himself thinking things through.

"I need you on your game, pal," he said. "You want tactics and strategy, bad guys taken out and objectives accomplished, I'm the guy. But what do you do, Buck?

What do you do when you might be walking past the bad guy on the street, and there's a way to find out but they won't let you use it?"

Bucky snorted and shifted a little in the bed. Steve waited to see if he would wake up, but then Bucky's breathing settled back to normal. He hasn't got much left, Steve thought, listening to the shallow, wheezing breath of his oldest friend, and his eyes started to sting.

"They're not with us, Buck," he said. "Everyone wants shades of gray, but that's what it boils down to. We're fighting the bad guys, and they're not with us."

The monitor chirped, and Steve heard a whir and click as one of Bucky's machines dispensed meds. For a while Steve couldn't think of what else to say. Then it came to him.

"All enemies foreign and domestic, right?" he said.

"Right," came a voice from the doorway behind him.

He turned, and there was Gail. "All enemies," she said again. "Foreign and domestic. You do what you know is right, Steve."

"Yeah," Steve said. He looked down. "But the thing that I know is right . . . it's against the law. It's wrong."

She stepped over to him and put a hand on his shoulder. "We have to trust someone to know when to make that decision. We have to trust you, Steve."

His cell phone rang. Gail whacked him half-seriously on the shoulder, where her hand had just been resting. "You get out of this ward with your phone. They're not supposed to be on in here."

Steve muted the phone without looking at the call. A passing nurse stuck her head in the door and said, "Turn your phone off in here."

"Already did, miss," Steve said. "Sorry."

"No, you didn't," she said. "I can still see the display. Either turn it off or you're going to have to leave the ward."

"Okay, I'm turning it off." He flipped the phone open and as he was hitting the power button, he saw that the call had come from Admiral Esteban Garza, one of the top members on the Joint Chiefs.

He stood up. "I have to take this one, Gail."

"Go," she said, and he was struck by how strong and dignified she was in her old age. Would she have become the same if he'd never hitched a ride on that rocket?

Wrong question, he thought. All the questions he came up with were wrong.

"Take the call," Gail said, shooing him out the door. "Then turn your phone off and come back, and we'll talk until he wakes up."

The cell phone prohibition extended out into the main corridor, and Steve kept on walking until he was outside. Why was Admiral Garza calling him instead of Nick Fury? The soldier in Steve didn't like circumventions of the chain of command. He called Garza back, though, as soon as he'd gotten away from the crowded sidewalks around the hospital.

Garza picked up on the first ring. "Captain Rogers," he said without preamble.

"Admiral," Steve said. "I was visiting a friend in the hospital."

"Is he dying?" Garza asked.

"Not right now."

"Then get to the Triskelion. I'll have a chopper there. I need you at Andrews pronto."

Three hours later, Steve was walking alongside Garza down an underground hallway that could be entered only through a triple-keycarded steel door in the basement of an anonymous Quonset hut set all the way out at the western perimeter of the base. "This was brought in to us last night," Garza said, "and the first time I saw it was this morning. I believe you'll be able to offer an expert opinion."

They came to a dead end, with another featureless steel door in front of them. It had been a long time since Steve saw a sign. We're off the map, he thought. This place doesn't exist. Remembering his conversation with Fury the night before, he thought: this is where the boogeymen live.

Admiral Garza slid his keycard through a slot. A panel opened in the wall, exposing a keyboard, and he entered a long alphanumeric code. The door opened to reveal a small room, and Steve followed Garza into it. Garza's keycard was waiting in a tray on the other side. The room was a white cube with a single workstation and another door on the wall opposite the one they'd come in. At the workstation sat a pale woman with gray-shot blond hair and haunted eyes. She stood when they entered.

"Admiral Garza," she said, then looked Steve up and down. "And you must be Captain America."

"Steve Rogers," he said, and extended his hand.

She didn't take it. "I assume you're here to observe the specimen?" she asked Admiral Garza.

"No, Justine, we thought we'd take you to lunch. Cap, meet Justine Ichesco." Garza walked over to the other door.

This time access involved a complicated series of key-card readings, code entries, and simultaneous turnings of physical keys. Everything but a secret handshake, Steve thought. The door opened and they went into a larger room, one wall of which was obviously one-way glass. So we're being observed, Steve thought . . . and then his attention was riveted to the thing on the steel laboratory table in the middle of the room.

It had the rough shape of a man: bipedal, bilaterally symmetric, and so forth. But it was more than seven feet tall, and its limbs were deformed, each a different length than the other and each jointed in a slightly different way. But it was the face that Steve couldn't look away from. Scrambled somehow, as if a late Picasso had been given flesh, the face brought to mind another malformed humanoid, in the Arizona desert, with fire and falling steel all around . . .

"They do that when they've been badly injured," he said, keeping his voice level. "Lose their cohesion."

"So you're sure it's Chitauri?" Garza asked.

"I'm sure," Steve said.

"Sampling matches existing specimens of recovered Chitauri tissue," Justine said.

Garza stepped closer to the strapped-down body. "Well, this one's a ways past injured," he said. "We killed it on the base perimeter last night."

"Then you can expect its shape to scramble even more," Steve said.

Justine walked around to the other side of it. "How many of these have you seen?"

Steve remembered starships falling from the desert sky.

The Chitauri opened its eyes.

Steve felt the adrenaline shock like a punch in the chest, his super-soldier overdrive kicking in. The Chitauri snapped the straps holding it down, wrenching the table loose from the floor. One of its hands shot out and caught Justine around the throat; the other reached for Steve, but he was already pivoting out of the way when he saw the first twitch of muscle, and he caught the arm at full extension and broke it across the edge of the table. The snap of the fracture was counterpointed by the crunch of the Chitauri crushing the life out of Justine Ichesco. Garza had fallen back and drawn his sidearm; out of the corner of his eye Steve saw the admiral stepping to the side to look for a better shot. In front of him the Chitauri sprang from the table. He saw it looking at him, and could have sworn—in the split second before it shifted its focus to Garza—that he saw recognition in its eyes.

A bell went off in his head as the Chitauri caught him with a roundhouse kick, using the momentum to get a running start at Garza. The admiral began firing, emptying the nine-shot magazine of his old Browning. Each of the shots hit the Chitauri and froze it in place for an eye blink before it drove forward once more.

Until Steve tackled it, crushing its head into the floor. Already he could tell that its shape was decomposing. Where the human flesh was peeling back, some recognizable Chitauri features shone through, and in other places the only thing visible was an anatomical mishmash. Between the bullets and its weakening hold on its human shape, the Chitauri looked like some of the bodies Steve had seen in the aftermath of an artillery barrage in Europe. But it could still fight; it threw him off into the one-way glass, which rang with the impact but didn't crack. Back on his feet, Steve saw it closing on Garza again, and reflexively he drew his arm back to throw his shield.

He had no shield.

The lab table would do just as well.

Tearing the twisted steel tabletop loose from the frame, Steve flung it Frisbee-style. It hit the back of the Chitauri's head with a wet crunch.

The creature's arms shot straight out and its back arched. Momentum carried it forward to slam into Admiral Garza and bear him down to the floor, but Steve could tell it was dead before the thud of their impact reached him.

On the other hand, that's what Garza had thought last night.

"Admiral," Steve said, pulling the limp body off Garza. "You injured?"

The door burst open and a response team fanned out, weapons trained on Steve and the admiral. Garza put out a hand, palm down, and the team lowered the muzzles of their rifles. With his sleeve, Garza swiped at the Chitauri blood on his face. "We'll need a medic for Justine," he said. "But I don't think there's any hurry." One of the response team was already kneeling over her where she lay, the table frame tipped over onto her body. I did that, Steve thought. He felt as if he'd defiled her somehow, even though he could hardly have been concerned with where the frame fell. He'd had a Chitauri to kill.

This is where they keep the boogeymen, he thought. I was right.

"Captain Rogers," Garza said. "Follow me."

Five minutes later they'd returned through the three security-keyed doors and were in a ground-level office framed off from the rest of the Quonset hut by naked two-by-fours and drywall. "We're under construction here," Admiral Garza said. He was still rubbing at streaks of blood on his hands.

"Admiral," Steve said. "Is this the first time you've caught a Chitauri on base grounds?"

"Caught? Yes," Garza said. "I suspect there might be others." He paused, picking at one thumbnail. "Captain?" he said.

"Yes, sir."

"Can I count on you to get Tony Stark's toy to the right person?"

"With all due respect, sir, I think Tony's the right person."

Garza looked him in the eye. "Noted. Now can you get Tony's toy to the person I am about to tell you to get it to?"

In other words, Steve thought, are you willing to commit industrial espionage against an American company for the benefit of Americans? Is this what it's come to? Once he'd had an argument with Thor about the point at which it became necessary to contravene your ideals so that other people could believe that those same ideals still existed. In other words, at what point do you grant yourself the privilege of knowing better than other people what's best for them?

Now, I guess, Steve thought. I guess that time is now.

"Yes, sir," he said. "I can."

"Good answer," Garza said. He handed Steve a business card. "Memorize it."

Steve did, and handed it back.

"You know why Stark can't have it, right?"

"I'm guessing it has something to do with politics," Steve said. All at once he couldn't look Garza in the eye.

"Politics," Garza repeated. "Damn right. If Tony Stark built these things, the next day Nick Fury would be walking sentry duty in Barrow, Alaska. That's how things work down here."

There was a long pause. Steve looked at his hands, heard again the sound of the table crushing the Chitauri's skull, hunted around in his mind for words that weren't there.

"You know, Cap, there are people in this government who think like you do. And like I do," Garza said. "But there aren't enough of them, and they aren't always in the right places."

"Someone has to stand up," Steve said.

"Right. But that someone can't always stand up in front of everyone. Not right away. It's not the way we'd like to do this, but it's the way we can make it work. Know what I mean?"

Steve didn't like it. No. That wasn't true. Part of him did like it, the part that wanted to act, to be done with rules and procedures. You saw the enemy, you hit the enemy.

But then there was the part that knew the consequences of acting before you knew what you were doing. Last year's Hulk incident was all the proof anyone would need of that.

"I know what you mean, sir," he said.

"Good," Garza said. "And the name I gave you? I can't give this to Fury, for the same reasons I just outlined. He's too vulnerable. The Hill doesn't like him anyway. They think he's too much of a loose cannon. But you—you're untouchable politically. Anyone who goes up against Captain America better be planning to retire."

"I understand, Admiral," Steve said.

"And what the hell, we need a loose cannon here and there. Can't all be desk jockeys like me." Garza grinned and chucked Steve on the shoulder. "Time for me to move along. Good work in there today, Captain Rogers. Make this happen."

"Yes, sir," Steve said. "I will."

8

TONY SPENT MOST OF HIS MORNING RUNNING through quarterly reports, and then he went downstairs to see what the R&D boys had come up with for the new Iron Man prototype. And lo and behold, when he got there, who should he find but Nick Fury?

"General?" Tony said. "To what do I owe this unexpected pleasure?"

"Well, let's see." Fury started ticking off points on his fingers. "SHIELD is curious about how Stark is spending all of that money we got for you; I'm curious to see what this new toy can do; and I want to make sure that you understand the ramifications of what Washington told me yesterday."

"Ah." Turning to the assembled tech team, Tony said, "Ladies and gentlemen, would you excuse us?"

When they'd filed out, Tony sat on the stairs that led up to the prototype staging area. The new suit loomed over them. He'd had it redone in darker colors as a whim, but on the inside there were real innovations to be excited about. The new battery could deliver 15 percent better acceleration, a full eight g's, and (luckily for Tony's brain) the team had come up with better acceleration-damping gel. His turning capacity was improved, the servos and condensate hydraulics had finally caught up with the tensile strength of the armor plates . . . "It's a doozy," Tony said when he'd finished listing all of the new gadgetry. "Oh, and the force field and force beams, I'm getting 30 percent more repulsion per square centimeter."

"Do tell," Fury said.

"I'll be happy to outfit all of SHIELD's shock troops with a slightly less gaudy version, General," Tony said with a mock toast. Then, as if he'd reminded himself, he added, "Listen, if we're going to have to talk much more, I'll need a little refreshment. Especially if you're going to break my heart again about my marvelous screener."

"Are you of the opinion that martinis are going to cure your cancer, Tony? Or are you just a garden-variety boozehound?"

"In no way," Tony said as he stood, "am I a garden-variety anything. Let's go upstairs."

Tony maintained a modest—for him—suite of apartments on the top floor of Stark Industries' headquarters. At times he imported Jarvis to work there, when he knew he wasn't going to get home for long stretches, and Jarvis had a tray of martinis waiting for Tony and Fury when they came out of the elevator into Tony's study. "General Fury," Jarvis purred. "Your company is far too rare a pleasure, sir."

Swiping his glass from the tray, Tony rolled his eyes. "For God's sake, Jarvis. What are you trying to do here? General Fury has closed-minded and brutish superiors. Haven't you heard of don't ask, don't tell?"

"Don't ask," Jarvis shot back. "And General, you're under no obligation to tell." With that, he left through the kitchen door.

"You didn't take your drink, Nick," Tony observed.

"Spare me," Fury said.

Now it was Tony's turn to roll his eyes. As he did it, he thought, *my God, sometimes I come across just like Jarvis.*

As if he'd read Tony's mind, Fury quirked a smile and said, "Not that there's anything wrong with that."

"Go to hell, General Fury," Tony said with a grin. "Now, what was it you wanted to talk about again? Ah; wait. I remember. We talked about the toy, so now you must be waiting to hear about Stark Industries' fiscal responsibility, as well as my reaction to the news from Washington. Which, since you haven't given it to me, I assume must be bad."

"Bad for you, yeah," Fury said.

"I'll be honest with you, Nick," Tony said. "I'm trying to be a good citizen and do the right thing for my company at the same time. Do you see my conflict?"

The phone rang. "It can wait," Fury said.

"Not when this line rings, it can't." Tony picked up.

"Tony, it's Hank Pym."

"Well, Doctor. How can I help you?"

"I need to ask you a favor."

"A favor," Tony repeated.

"Nick won't take my calls, and I need to get a message to him. This is crucial, Tony. What if I told you there were still Chitauri around?"

"Oh, for God's sake," Tony said. "Call back when you're taking your meds again."

Listen to me, Tony thought. If Hank Pym wasn't a wife-beating sycophant, I might actually feel badly about the way I'm lying to him. He hung up.

"That wasn't Hank Pym, was it?" Fury asked.

"Nope," Tony said. "Business. This line's too important for troglodytes like Pym."

"Pretty short for such an important call," Fury observed mildly.

"I know how to get to the point."

"Okay, then I will, too. I hear you talking about conflict, and I get a little worried about what I'm not hearing you say." Fury sat in one of the chairs Tony had turned toward the window. "Believe me, Tony. I know how you feel."

"No, you don't," Tony said. "I might have made six hundred million dollars this year on those screeners."

For a long moment Fury was silent. Then he stood back up and said, "That's one of those comments that makes it hard for me to spend time around you."

"Oh, General Fury," Tony said. "You're not still mad about my little demonstration the other day, are you? Come on. You were the one I needed to convince."

"That's got nothing to do with it. What worries me is that there was a leak, and I don't think it came from SHIELD."

Tony noticed his drink was already gone. He called for another, mostly to give himself time to cool off. Banter was one thing, the kind of bullshitting you did with people you worked with. It was something entirely different when someone who ought to know better—a friend, no less—accused you of being the source of a serious security breach. Jarvis brought the drinks and, sensing the tension in the room, left without comment. "Okay, Nick," Tony said. "Apart from a desire to cover your own ass after you got chewed out in Washington, what makes you think the leak is here? Are you somehow under the impression that I would let Washington know about a program so they could get cold feet and step on it?"

Nick didn't turn around. Over his shoulder and out the window, Tony watched a helicopter landing at the Triskelion, far away to the south. He could see the entire spread of the Upper Bay, except Liberty Island, which was blocked by Fury's shining head.

"I have to tell you, Tony," Fury began. The tone of his voice, more measured and softer than was usual, hinted to Tony that something unpleasant was coming. "There's quite a few people in Washington who are still fighting the last battle when it comes to you, you know? They want your contracts reviewed, they want your security clearances revoked on lifestyle-risk grounds . . . the whole works."

Now Fury did look back at Tony. "I'm not a hundred percent sure they're wrong," he finished.

"Oh, aren't you," Tony said.

"No, I'm not. I believe SHIELD needs Iron Man; I'm not sure I believe that the defense business needs Stark Industries."

"This is because I have a drink in the morning and I'm not a picket-fence family man?" Tony said. He was getting angrier by the second here, and found himself not caring whether he alienated Nick, or the government, or anyone else. He was Tony Stark, he was Stark Industries, the economies of nations rose and fell with the check marks he made in the margins of *The Wall Street Journal* every morning. "You want to apply those same standards to the people professing their worries about me, Nick? Or is what we have here another version of just plain old jealousy? How many congressmen wish they had my money and my women and my looks?" Tony laughed. "Tony Stark!—not just a billionaire playboy, but a billionaire playboy egotist! Keep our homeland safe from this monstrosity!"

He got quiet, realizing that of all the people in the world, Nick Fury was perhaps least likely to be affected by a rant. "Nick, I've got enough juice in Washington that if I put my mind to it, I can get this project cleared. But now you're telling me that there's going to be opposition that has nothing to do with the project. So do you want me to see what I can do, or will it be easier on your office if I just stay out of the way and keep coming up with great ideas that nobody will use? I can go either way. Just let me know."

"Okay, Tony. Then the truth is, you almost punked out in Arizona; we have multiple reports to that effect. You drink like a rock star, you go through women like a rock star . . . there are legitimate security concerns that come with this kind of lifestyle. I'm sure I don't have to tell you what a honey trap is."

"No. And I'm sure I don't have to tell you what a brain tumor is."

Nick was silent for a moment. "No."

"Well, then. I'm sure that you understand why I could not possibly care less about what the defense bureaucracy in Washington thinks about my girlfriends or the olives in my martinis."

"Yes, I do," Nick said. "And I understand something else, too."

"What's that, O swami of SHIELD?"

Now Nick turned around to look Tony in the eye. "I

understand fear. You don't think of yourself this way, but you're listening to the clock tick, and you're worried that when that tumor finally gets you, people are going to stand around your coffin and say what a waste it was that you never did anything but make money and play with fancy gizmos. So now that—"

Tony looked away from Nick, his attention caught by a flash outside the window. "Uh oh. Gotta go, country needs me," he said, and shrugged out of his suit coat as he headed for the elevator.

"What . . . ?" Nick glanced back at the window. Wish I could see the look on his face, Tony thought. The elevator door opened, and Tony held it for Nick, who was barreling across the room with his Grim Reaper face on. A big fireball like that coming out of the Triskelion, Tony thought. Yes sir, that'll take the steam out of your armchair psychoanalysis any day.

"Move this goddamn thing," Fury growled. The elevator door shut, and the bottom dropped out of Tony's stomach. Express train to hell, he thought. As the door closed, he heard the phone ring, but Hank Pym could wait. After seeing Nick Fury caught speechless, Tony had the idea that this was going to be a pretty good day. He couldn't wait to put on his suit.

9

Status Report

The tension between order and chaos that constitutes much of what humans call personality is proving to be a useful if delicate tool. It is observed that in intra-human conflicts, the side operating at a material and technological deficit prioritizes the sowing of chaos, while the side with a surplus of materiel and personnel prioritizes direct assault and the imposition of order. Thus the imbalance between plenitude and insufficiency becomes a determinant in tactical and strategic choice. Lessons are available from this observation, and are being processed and incorporated into short-term planning. A new emphasis on the sowing of chaos is instituted, and assets redeployed accordingly.

In the longer term, open conflict is unavoidable and desirable, once resources are more fully developed. Sensitivity to human political activity will offer cues as to the correct time to abandon small-scale operations designed to compromise key individual targets in favor of a standard battlefield configuration. Assimilation efforts accelerate, and prognosis for the human ordering project is rated good.

Diversionary tactics, although of limited long-term value, have previously proved useful in managing the enemy's movements and priorities. Activities in this vein continue. Reports are imminent on the success of the most recent diversionary mission, location <Triskelion, New York>. Although complete ramifications will not be known immediately, early signs should indicate whether the mission was successful on its terms and should be repeated. The strategic truism that surprise and morale erosion are force multipliers need not be retested; what remains to be seen is the specific realization of this truism in the actions of <SHIELD>, especially with respect to the political treatment of current <SHIELD> initiatives.

Political reaction to <Andrews> mission unfolds as expected. <Garza> has contacted <Steven Rogers>. Details of the conversation are not available due to minimal assets and difficult communication channels. It however appears as if both <Garza> and <Rogers> have acted according to mission plan. This situation will be monitored intensively.

Intelligence gathering and resource placement in

<Wilmette, Illinois> improves. Assets are in final placement anticipating orders to execute planned mission.

Mission Timeline and Preliminary Report: Triskelion

-.090349 solar year: Assessment of security procedures in and around Triskelion. Identification of possible weak point in shipping and receiving of cargo due to involvement of several different groups.

-.078222 solar year: Identification and surveillance of contracted non-military personnel involved in logistics.

-.038874 solar year: Targeting of <Roger Boudreau> and <Antonio Puyol> due to length of service, with presumed increase in institutional trust, and absence of family and social networks.

-.030582 solar year: Assimilation of <Roger Boudreau> and <Antonio Puyol>. Preparation of ordnance.

-.022916 solar year: Elimination of two employees of contracted logistical service, causing reassignment of their duties to assets in place, <Boudreau> and <Puyol>.

-.000342 solar year: Deployment of assets in place on mission.

-.000171 solar year: Assets in place destroy portions of Triskelion. Assets lost as a planned consequence of mission.

Appendix

Priority nonhuman asset assimilated in <Ronkonkoma, New York>.

Priority human asset assimilated in <Buenos Aires, Argentina>.

10

STEVE ROGERS COULD NOT REMEMBER EVER
being so angry.

Thirteen SHIELD contractors were dead, and three
soldiers. The Triskelion had an irregular hole in its side
sixty feet wide and extending up through the third floor
over the loading dock where the explosion had occurred.

The fires were almost out, and already the grim
work of recovering remains had begun. Choppers circled overhead. New York City fire department boats
had come and gone, their offers of help rebuffed for security reasons. Now came cleanup, and the painstaking
reconstruction of how this had happened. Except Steve

already knew the important thing: two Chitauri suicide bombers had left a smoking hole in the Triskelion, sixteen families grieving, and SHIELD with a black eye whose consequences none of them would know until the media vultures had finished picking over the corpses.

And if Tony Stark's screeners had been installed at the loading dock, none of it would have happened in the first place.

Before coming down here to work with the fire and cleanup crews, Steve had replayed the security tapes. Frame: the boat eases into the dock. Frame: a forklift comes out to start offloading pallets. Frame: one of the boat's crew says something to the forklift operator. Frame: the crewman hops on the forklift and picks up a pallet. As he turns it around, another member of the boat's crew hoists a stack of three large totes.

Right there, Steve thought. No man can lift three of those when they're loaded, especially not a skinny fifty-year-old, which was what the man had been. Correction: what the man had looked like.

Frame: the two crewmen stop for a brief conversation with Master Sergeant Antonio Cullen, who grins and waves them through.

I can reconstruct that one, Steve thought. *Hey, this isn't on the manifest. Yeah, I know, it wasn't scheduled until tomorrow, but common carriers, who knows when anything's going to get anywhere . . .* and now Sergeant Cullen was dead.

Then a different camera. Frame: the forklift stops about ten feet inside the intake door. The man with the totes—the *Chitauri* with the totes, Steve corrected himself—drops them and rips the top off one. The forklift driver loosens a cable from inside the shrink-wrap holding the boxes together on the pallet. The two of them bend over a small black box.

The view dissolves into static.

From the outside camera: Sergeant Cullen and four of the contractors hired to move freight around inside the Triskelion are annihilated in a stop-motion bloom of fire threaded with black smoke. The camera washes out. When its light meters stabilize, the dock area is in ruins. Small fires burn on the boat, one slowly catching on the clothing of an unconscious or dead crew member. The hole blown in the side of the Triskelion has cross-sectioned three floors. Papers from upstairs offices flutter out over the Upper Bay, wafted by the scorching updraft from the fire burning in the intake warehouse. A woman lies dead near her desk, one of her arms dangling over the edge of the exposed floor. Major Christina Akinbiye. Steve had poured her a cup of coffee three weeks before in the Triskelion cafeteria.

After that he couldn't look at it anymore. When he'd gotten downstairs, response teams were already reporting nonhuman remains.

Some of which he was still cleaning up. Steve gritted his teeth and let slip a curse that Gail would have slapped his face for.

Since nobody knew what the hell would happen if a seagull happened to fly by and pick up a snack of Chitauri tissue, every cell needed to be collected and accounted for. They were still, almost a year later, doing final cleanup on the Arizona site. Getting the Triskelion shipshape wouldn't be nearly as big a job, which wasn't much consolation since it sure wasn't the kind of job for which Steve was suited. But he was here and General Fury wasn't, and Banner was still locked up downstairs until they put him in front of a firing squad. So instead of hunting down the aliens, Steve was picking up pieces of them. It wasn't his job. He was wasted here.

"It's like a Willie and Joe cartoon," he said to the tech closest to him.

The tech looked up from bagging a bloody piece of acoustic tile. "A what?"

"Never mind," Steve said. He should have known better. Might as well have made a joke about a political cartoon from the Civil War.

Resentment was so thick in the back of his throat that he could practically spit it out. God, he hated them. Hated them worse than he'd ever hated the Nazis or the Japs. He would have killed them all himself, shot them in the back as they fled. If God Himself came down and gave Steve Rogers the gift of prophecy, and he knew that the Chitauri would leave tomorrow and never come back, he would still have killed them as they filed onto their ships. *And they could have done something about it.*

From the circling cluster of choppers, one detached itself and came down to land on the sea-level helipad. The blast of prop wash blew away some of the smoke that still hung over the dock. When General Fury got out, Steve looked to the skies, searching for some resolve that would help him stop himself from saying something he shouldn't . . . and there was Tony Stark, showing off in his suit, blasting back and forth long after it might have done any good.

Steve knew at that moment that he couldn't hide from it any more. Admiral Garza had been right.

Fury strode through the wreckage to Steve. "Tell me," he said.

"Chitauri in human form. Suicide bombers," Steve said. He bent over and picked up a stringy gobbet of flesh, now sparkling with scales. Holding it up for General Fury's inspection, he snapped, "They lose their cohesion when they're dead. Only when they're dead."

"Hold on there, soldier," General Fury said. "Aim that anger where it counts."

Steve dropped the bit of flesh into a collection bag, sealed it, and put the bag in a plastic tote not unlike the one that had carried the detonator. Then he stood up, looked General Fury in the eye, and said, "With all due respect, sir, that's the problem here. It might have counted."

"I don't follow you," General Fury said.

Pointing up into the sky, Steve said, "If Tony's tech had been installed, they would have been tagged. I

could have done something." Whatever resolve he'd
been looking for failed Steve, and he kept talking. "But
instead Washington wanted to be careful. Well, this is
what careful gets you when you're fighting an enemy
who isn't afraid to die. We've got sixteen in the morgue,
and who knows how many others burned. People died,
Nick. Excuse me. General."

Fury didn't answer right away. Eventually, after Steve
had bagged and tagged two more pieces of Chitauri tissue, he said, "You're relieved. We can find someone else
to do that."

"I'm not doing anything else," Steve said.

"I am relieving you of this duty, soldier," General
Fury said, and let it hang.

Not hurrying, Steve bagged one more piece of tissue
and then stood. "Yes, sir," he said.

"That's more like it," Fury said.

He was about to say something else when Tony
came in for a landing on the ruined dock. "Perimeter's
clear out to a mile," Tony said. "Can someone give me a
hand with the helmet here?"

"I'll do it," Steve said. He worked the helmet's seals
and clamps loose and lifted the faceplate away, releasing
a flood of greenish gel.

"Hell of an upgrade," Tony said. "Although I guess
we can talk about that later."

Steve leaned in close to him. "One thing," he said
quietly, not wanting Fury to hear. "Your screener would
have stopped this."

Caught up short, Tony looked at him, a puzzled expression on his face. He wiped some of the gel away from his eyes. "You're not blaming me for this?"

"Not a bit," Steve said, still keeping his voice down. "I don't blame you. But I wanted you to face what happened here because I might need your help."

"My help?"

But Steve had already turned away. "General," he said. "I was here. I'll take media point on this. What we have is two Chitauri suicide bombers. I don't have to tell you that this is a new tactic for them, and it tells us quite a bit about where they think they are strength-wise."

"Well, that's not going to help the reporters," General Fury said.

"No?"

"No. Because we're not going to tell them that," General Fury said. "People do not need to hear that alien suicide bombers got into the Triskelion. They are more than willing to laugh at what incompetent idiots we are, accidentally blowing ourselves up, but they'll forget all about that the next time we save their asses. They will not forget the idea of infiltration, and that is what needs to be managed here."

"Managed," Steve said disbelievingly. "You're worried about how to manage this."

"Would you rather see our funding gutted because we come across as a bunch of amateurs? Would you rather go back to working out of whatever space the

Army can spare at Fort Drum? Remember what we talked about the other night, Cap."

Steve looked around and spread his hands. "Isn't this part of what we talked about the other night?"

"What did you two talk about the other night?" Tony wanted to know.

"Nothing," Steve and General Fury said in unison.

A silence fell, broken by the thud of circling helicopters and the scrape and shuffle of the tissue-recovery detail. "Fine," Steve said. "Okay. My offer to take media point stands. You let me know how we're going to handle it."

"Well," Tony said. "That's a little disappointing from our straight arrow."

Steve spun and jabbed a finger in Tony's direction. "You get that one free," he said quietly. "But don't ever say anything like that again. Is that clear?"

He could tell Tony was trying not to smile, but right then Steve didn't care. Tony Stark could have his bravado. That, and money, was all he had.

"Clear, *mon capitaine,*" Tony said.

"French," Steve said with disgust. "On top of it, he speaks French."

He stripped off his gloves and threw them on the dock. "General. Permission to stand down until a briefing whenever you decide to schedule it."

"Okay," General Fury said. "Where are you headed?"

"I have a date. If Washington can screw around while we get infiltrated by aliens . . ." Steve let the thought trail off. "You always know where to find me."

"A date," Tony said as Steve walked away. "He's learning."

And later that night, after steaks at Peter Luger's—which made Janet laugh about how old-fashioned he was, but somehow she was the only one of the team who could make that joke without it making him angry or maudlin—Steve took a piece of paper out of his pocket. He was walking down Broadway in Brooklyn, under the elevated BMT tracks. No, not the BMT anymore, now everyone just called it the JMZ line. There was no more BMT, no more IRT, everything was just the MTA. Janet was on a cab back over the Williamsburg Bridge. He found a pay phone on Havemeyer and made a call. On the way back to his apartment, he dropped the paper down a storm drain.

11

NICK HAD MAYBE FIVE MINUTES' NOTICE THAT
Tony Stark was about to appear in his office and was,
in the words of the desk sergeant, "loaded for bear."
Fury put away a report he'd been about to sign off on
and started to straighten his desk, a pre-meeting reflex he had ingrained in himself when he'd made the
transition from commando to command. It was useful in that it cleared the mind as well as the desk.

Two minutes after he'd been served notice of Stark's
approach, there was a knock at the door. "Come on in,"
Fury said, and in walked not Tony but Steve Rogers.

"Don't tell me," Fury said.

Rogers looked like hell, at least for him. Physically

he wasn't any different, but there was a look in his eye that Fury didn't like at all. He remembered thinking, the day before yesterday after Tony had said *He's learning,* that he didn't want Captain America to learn. He wanted Captain America to act when he was told to act.

Now it looked like Steve had both learned and acted, and hadn't done either one the way he was supposed to. "What else was I supposed to do?" Steve asked.

"I said don't tell me," Fury said, "and I meant it."

The one thing Fury had left on his desktop was a copy of the business section of that day's *New York Times,* the front page of which featured a story about a breakthrough Chitauri screening technology. Accompanying the article was an illustration of Tony's screener, run through Photoshop just enough to avoid being identical. A single line midway through the piece noted the breakthrough had been "partially derived from a canceled defense project," which Nick read as a wink from someone in Washington who had authorized the leak. Limiting himself to people who had attended the meeting where Tony's project was discussed, Nick had done some initial handicapping of likely sources. His early favorite for the leak was Garza, although it might have been any of them. Even Altobelli or Bright, who had made such a big deal out of the security risks. The way Washington worked, that might have been nothing but a charade to polish up their collective deniability.

Nick quashed an impulse to find out whether either

Altobelli or Bright held directorships or stock in Stark Industries or in the company that had miraculously invented a tech that did exactly what Tony's would have. What bothered Nick more than identifying the source of the leak from Washington was that the leaker had used Steve Rogers to pipeline the project specs to this, who was it . . . SKR TechEnt. Ten minutes on Google had taught Nick that SKR was a development clearinghouse, basically four walls and a roof where control-freak venture capitalists funneled projects they wanted to keep an eye on. But Nick had been around the block long enough to figure out that more was going on there than met the eye. The whole setup screamed shell company. Who had decided an outfit like SKR could possibly be the best company for the job?

"Tony's going to be here any minute," Fury said. "Keep your mouth shut until I tell you to open it. That's an order."

Steve didn't like it, but he was a soldier. "Yes, sir, General," he said.

As if on cue, Tony Stark barged in without knocking. "Nick, goddammit," he began, then caught himself up short when he saw Steve standing off to the side of Nick's desk. "Ah," he said. "This goes higher than I'd thought."

"How do you mean that?" Nick asked.

"Him," Tony said, pointing at Steve. "If you were just going to do this yourself, you wouldn't need to wave the Human Flag over there."

"Permission to speak, General," Steve said.

Fury didn't take his eyes off Tony. "Granted."

"I did it, Tony," Steve said. "General Fury didn't know."

"He—" Tony took this in for a long moment. "Well. What a coincidence. And am I to assume that when you were picking up little bits of fricasseed Chitauri, and you said to General Fury something about how *we* could have done something, it had nothing to do with today's newspaper article?"

"Saw this, did you?" Fury said. He picked up the paper. "Figured you might have. I was as surprised as you until Captain Rogers here showed up and let me in on what happened."

Fury didn't look at Steve as he said this. They could get their stories straight later. Right now the important thing was keeping Tony on board, and if Tony could blame Steve for the whole thing, he might just be able to get over it and remain a member of the team. Apart from the fact that Steve *had* done it, so Nick had told the truth, mostly. Steve hadn't let him in on what happened yet, but he was damn sure going to the minute Tony left.

"I hope, at least, that some kind of insubordination or espionage charge is going to keep me from losing sleep over all the money this just cost me," Tony said. He shoved his hands in his pockets. "I wasn't that pissed about this when it was just me not making as much money as I might have. This is different. Now someone else is making money that should have been mine. And the PR, Jesus. This is killing me."

"No, the tumor's killing you," Steve said. "Also I'm hoping it's the tumor making you complain about money when we've got a new Chitauri conspiracy on our hands, because if it isn't, then you're pretty much the shallowest son of a bitch I ever laid eyes on."

Tony turned to Fury. "So my medical history is public now, Nick? This is how they tell you to build team unity?"

"What I came to say is this," Steve said. Fury held up a hand to stop him, but Steve pointedly didn't look at him. "I was going to say it to General Fury, but since you're here, Tony, I'll say it to both of you. The people need this. And I'm going to make sure they get what they need."

"Soldier, I don't have to tell you that's not your job."

"Maybe not," Steve said. "But I'll do the jobs that need doing, whether they're supposed to be mine or not."

In the silence that followed, Fury thought: so this is how it begins.

Eventually someone had to say something, and as might have been expected, it was Tony. "There's going to be a review of Stark Industries' defense contracting policies," he said. "Even with all the skimming and no-bid lard, I can make more money doing other things. Headaches like this are the last thing I need."

"Your financial decisions aren't really what we're talking about here," Fury said.

"Well, I don't appear to have much to say about national security or the typical courtesy that one might hope would be extended when one's proprietary tech is going to be stolen and farmed out to a glorified machine shop," Tony said. "So it looks like my finances are the only thing I can talk about. General, I don't suppose you have a bottle in your desk."

As a matter of fact, Fury did, but he wasn't about to break out the bourbon at ten in the morning. Not even for Tony Stark. "Afraid not," he said.

"And I don't guess that Captain America here is about to go up on espionage charges?"

"I don't see how that's in the national interest," Fury said.

"Ah. National interest. There was a time when intellectual property was part of national interest. I guess that isn't the case now."

"Oh, for Pete's sake," Steve said. "Are you really going to get self-righteous about this?"

"No, Steve, I'm going to stay angry. You might be able to bamboozle the general here with your line about the people, and dirty jobs, and whatever else, but I'm going to tell you what that is. You've always been a latent fascist wrapped in a flag that we all happen to love, and we've cut you too much slack for it. Not anymore."

Steve took a step toward Tony. "Knock it off," he said.

"Go to hell," Tony said. "You want to take a swing at me, go right ahead. Who are you serving? Whoever fed you SKR TechEnt, why do you think they did it? Do you think they care about the people? Who are 'the people,' anyway?"

"They're the ones I rode a Nazi rocket for," Steve said, moving even closer to Tony. "They're the ones I got shot up with experimental chemicals for. They're the ones I pledged my life to, and if you're about to say that they don't know who I am and don't care what I've done, I'm here to tell you that doesn't matter. I believe in them. You don't believe in a damn thing except your bank balance."

"The people, huh?" Tony said. "Shouldn't you say *der Volk*?"

Faster than Fury could see, Steve leveled Tony with a pile-driver right hand. Tony went over backward, banged his head against the wall, and sprawled next to the ficus tree Fury had brought with him from the last SHIELD headquarters. Then something happened that Fury never would have figured: Tony shook his head and got to his feet. Blood streamed from a cut under his left eye, and he couldn't quite focus his eyes, but he got up. Fury's opinion of Tony Stark changed in that moment. Before then, he'd always thought that Tony without his suit was just an unusually smart rich guy . . . but anyone who could take a shot from Captain America and get to his feet was more than your ordinary CEO.

"Don't ever say that about me again," Steve said. He was breathing hard, from anger rather than exertion. "Ever."

"You wouldn't be so pissed about it if you didn't

think it was true," Tony said. He leaned against the wall and hawked an enormous gob of blood into a handkerchief. Blood had started coming from his nose, a slow trickle compared to the flow on his cheek.

"Next time I'm not holding back," Steve said.

Tony grinned. "Next time I won't stand there and wait for you to do it."

"All right," Fury said. "I've seen enough. What's done is done. Now it's up to us to make sure that the consequences work for us. You two want to kill each other, do it some other time. Right now what we need to do is find out who we get in touch with at SKR."

"Can't beat them, join them," Tony said. "You're a better politician than you give yourself credit for, Nick. And I hope that now you're not so worried that the original leak came from Stark Industries." He pressed the handkerchief to the cut on his face and added, "Now if you'll excuse me, there's a plastic surgeon whose golf game I need to interrupt."

After Tony was gone, Fury said to Steve, "Sit." He indicated a chair.

"Sir," Steve began, but Fury cut him off.

"No. I did not say talk. I said sit."

Steve sat.

"Thank you, Captain. Now. I am going to ask questions and you are going to provide answers."

"Yes, sir."

"The first question is who asked you to leak the screener."

After a pause, Steve said, "Admiral Garza."

Sometimes, Nick thought, the obvious answer is the correct answer. "And I assume that Admiral Garza suggested SKR?"

"Yes, sir," Steve said again.

Fury caught himself pacing the room. Pacing annoyed him, in himself more than in others. He went back around behind his desk and sat. "I'm going to repeat one of Tony's questions to you. Why do you think Admiral Garza suggested SKR?"

Steve shifted in the chair. "I didn't give it that much thought, General. Something needed to be done, and Admiral Garza found a way. That's as far as I took it."

"Did Admiral Garza suggest to you that SKR was ready to take the screener into production?"

"No, sir. He suggested them, and I made the call."

Something about the newspaper article was bothering Fury, but he couldn't figure out what it was. "See, Cap, my problem here is that I'm not necessarily opposed to this, but at the same time I can't have SHIELD team members doing end runs around Congress whenever they don't like the political winds."

"This isn't just any circumstance, sir."

"Agreed, Captain. The point still holds. I took a lot of heat about Tony Stark at the meeting in Washington, because people there think he's a loose cannon. Now I get home, and I have an actual loose cannon to deal with, who also happens to be the public face of SHIELD. This is one more headache than I need."

Steve stood. Fury eyed him but didn't comment on the small insubordination. Mostly he'd put the conversation on a chain-of-command footing because he wanted to calm Steve down. Now it didn't seem necessary. "General, I stand by what I said to you earlier and to Tony. This needed to be done. I did it. I'll take whatever heat is coming my way. Admiral Garza showed me the corpse of a Chitauri caught on the grounds of Andrews. Then we have the bombing downstairs. I'm not the most politically savvy guy in the world, but even I can tell something's coming. Do you want to look back and know that you didn't do everything you could?"

Now Fury stood to look Steve eye to eye. "I don't know, Cap. Do you want to be the guy who stands up later and says he had to destroy the village in order to save it?"

"I don't get the reference," Steve said.

"You don't need to. Do you want to be the guy who uses the flag as an excuse to burn the flag? And what if Garza's got some other plan? You know as well as I do that you can't trust a single person in Washington. You should have brought this to me."

For the first time since he'd come into the room, Steve's gaze wavered. "Admiral Garza suggested I not do that, sir."

"Which is exactly why you should have done it, Captain Rogers. You're dismissed."

12

FOR HANK PYM, REGRET WAS SOMETHING TO BE suffocated by work. Also booze, but he was doing his best to keep the two separate. This morning he'd woken up with his eyeballs throbbing and a railroad spike in his head, but here he was at the lab at seven a.m., coffee slowly working its way through his system and his tech, Greg, already in place at a microscope.

"Do you ever sleep?" Hank grumbled. First things first; he went to the lab coffee pot and got it going. Then he glanced at the morning's news feed. "Hey, would you look at this," he said.

"What's that?" Greg said, eye still glued to the microscope. "Oh, and as far as sleep, the answer is no. Not when there are eggs to count. You tell me to get fertility data on *Myrmecia pilosula,* that's what I'm doing, boss."

Lab techs, Hank thought. Either they're humorless drones or merry pranksters. Why couldn't any of them be normal? Not that he was complaining. Greg was like Super Lab Tech. He worked hard, made few mistakes, and didn't ask too many questions about things like how Hank had invented a wireless method of controlling ants. In a way, Hank felt badly about keeping Greg so completely in the dark. It would have been nice, not to mention more efficient, if Greg understood a little more about the goals of Hank's various projects. *So, Greg,* Hank imagined saying. *There's these aliens, and they can take the appearance of human beings, and I think I can figure out a way to get ants to detect them so we can stop them from taking over the world. You on board?*

Ay yi yi, Hank thought. Time for some normal conversation.

He pushed back his chair. "You see the news today? All of a sudden everyone's in love with screening technology again. SKR TechEnt. Hmm. Wonder if I should send them a proposal."

"Might not be a bad idea," Greg said. "But I thought they were a consortium kind of thing. A bunch of venture types creating a collective in-house lab or something."

"Whatever," Hank said. "There must be someone there who can read a proposal." He sat back and thought about it.

It occurred to him to wonder if anyone at SHIELD was involved. Wouldn't have been the first time that Fury and the gang had put the media to work for them . . . although that thought led down a memory path that Hank didn't want to travel again. He couldn't help it, though. He dreamed, when he wasn't too drunk to remember his dreams, of two things: Janet and the Hulk.

The Janet dreams were usually short, overwhelming spikes of sensation. He could feel the headset, and through it came the mechanical buzz of predatory satisfaction felt by the tetramorium ants he'd turned loose on her. In the dream, that feedback always crested as the darkest of pleasures, which was the curdled pleasure of revenge—and he woke up with a pain in his chest and guilt like a second skin. Hank knew he couldn't undo what he had done, but he had resolved to atone for it. He would make them understand that sins could be expiated, failures forgiven, if he had to spend the rest of his life in the lab to do it.

When he dreamed of the Hulk, too, it was typically the same moment over and over again: the tearing at the corners of his mouth as that homicidal freak tried to rip off his jaw. Never in his life had Hank felt so vulnerable, and never had he expected his size advantage to be so completely and easily overcome. He hated himself when he woke from that dream, even more than after the Janet dreams, because the Hulk had made him look weak. Flat on his back, mouth wide open, unable to get loose . . . he couldn't think about it. Even Steve Rogers hadn't shamed him that way.

"Huh," Greg said, startling Hank out of his self-loathing. He looked up and saw that Greg was reading about the screening tech over his shoulder. "Lot of R&D goes into something like that," Greg went on. "Wonder who's keeping his name off it."

"Me, too," Hank said. The fact that Greg's thoughts were moving along the same lines as his made him feel a little less paranoid. Maybe he could call Tony again, although he couldn't go to that well very often. The next time he'd have to have something concrete. Tony Stark was the only real human being in the whole damn Triskelion; he'd done Hank a huge favor giving him the Chitauri sample, and Hank would pay him back for it. Starting today, with any luck.

"If it was me, I'd just train dogs," Greg said. "Nothing beats Fido when it comes to sniffing."

"Except what we've got here," Hank said. "These little guys put dogs to shame. Nothing against dogs, but they work one at a time. What I've got here is the equivalent of a million dogs who can communicate almost instantly by chemical signals, and don't need to be housebroken."

Greg laughed and went back to his microscope. "There's your proposal, Hank. Write it up and send it out."

Hank got up and started running the checklist on the new headset he'd designed to test a little screening process of his own. It all seemed to be in order, so he went to the farm closet, where he kept something like fifty million ants of twenty-seven species that he'd found best suited to the kind of work he wanted them to do. Once he'd had them move boxes and make coffee; now he was going to put his little myrmidons to work protecting the people who crushed them on sidewalks and fried them with magnifying glasses. Good thing they weren't sentient enough to bear a grudge or note the irony, he thought.

"*Paraponera clavata,* come on down," he said, rolling one of the farm boxes out of the closet. He didn't have too many of these, maybe ten thousand, but it was plenty for a test run. The inside of *P. clavata*'s farm mimicked a system of tree roots, reflecting their preferred habitat on the South American Atlantic coast. They were big, about an inch long, and mean as hell.

"What have you got there?" Greg said, coming over from his workstation.

"Bullet ants. Most toxic insect in the world except for my soon-to-be-ex wife."

Greg chuckled. "Scientific objectivity."

Hank grinned along with Greg, but he hated himself for making the joke. "You know why they're called bullet ants? People who are lucky enough to have been both shot by a bullet and stung by one of these ants say that the experiences hurt about the same. Fierce little bastards, aren't they?"

"Keep 'em in the box. Jesus," Greg said.

Back at his terminal, Hank ran through the broadcast sequence he'd written. With any luck, it would provoke *P. clavata* to swarm and bite the Chitauri tissue sample he'd hidden in one of the lab wastebaskets. Then Hank would switch off that signal, send them back to the farm, and call Nick Fury with the test results. Presto! New reputation, big welcome back into the great stew of mutual exploitation that was SHIELD. If Fury could keep using Banner as a researcher after what happened in Manhattan, there was no reason for him not to take Hank back.

Also, maybe Janet would start returning his calls.

He finished the pretest check and went back to the farm. "Okay, fellas," he said. "Showtime." Hank leaned a four-foot two-by-four against the edge of the farm's top, and then slid back part of the lid.

"Putting them through their paces?" Greg asked from his workstation.

"Yeah. If any of them look like they're coming after you, go ahead and step on them. There's plenty."

Greg looked nervous. "Are you saying they might come after me?"

Only if you're a shape-shifting alien, Hank thought. "No," he said. "They have a very specific assignment. I want them to find something in the trash. So stay clear of your trash can and you shouldn't have any problem." Greg didn't look any happier, so Hank decided to cut him a break. "Look, if you want to leave until this is over, go ahead."

"No, I guess I'm okay. It's just that what you said about their stings, man, that shook me a little."

"Don't blame you," Hank said with a smile. "But like I said, they're looking for something else. If I've got this tuned right, none of them will even give you a second thought." Insofar as ants could be said to think, he added to himself.

The way it was supposed to work, he rehearsed to himself as he slid a thin stick down into the farm, was simple. The signal went out saying that the ants should detect and go after Chitauri tissue; the ants sent out scouts; they found the tissue; they swarmed the tissue; he cut the signal and sent them home. Hank's previous experiments in this vein had him predicting that the whole thing would be over in three minutes or so. He had the cut-and-return-home commands polished perfectly, to the point where the last couple of times he'd run them he hadn't found a single straggler. The search command was a little tougher to nail down absolutely, since ants were sensitive enough to find minuscule traces of whatever they were assigned to look for, but in this case Hank had been careful enough with the Chitauri tissue sample that he didn't believe there was any contamination. So, unless there was some odd chemical in the air that to an ant would mimic the characteristics of Chitauri tissue, everything was good to go.

The more adventurous members of the *P. clavata* colony were already exploring the stick when Hank got back to his terminal, put on the headset, and sent the search command. As soon as he did, the colony erupted like a bomb had gone off. Ants swarmed over the tree roots and boiled around the base of the stick that led out of the farm. "Everybody out of the pool," Hank said. "That's right."

From behind him he heard Greg say, "Wow. What are they looking for again?"

"Lunch," Hank said. "It's the best way to get them to do anything."

"Me, too," Greg said. Hank was preoccupied with the computer, watching the microtransmitters he'd attached to some of the bullet ants to see if they would fan out in a mathematically expressible way. Some species were pretty random, but others—usually the more aggressive ones—operated almost as if they had the equations worked out ahead of time. The bullet ants, he decided after watching them move for less than a minute, were about as decisive a species as he'd ever seen. They came out of the farm, went down the two-by-four, and spent only a few seconds sniffing around before making a beeline . . . wait. Two beelines.

Hank turned around, tapping on the headset as if it were a balky old television. It was a dumb reflex, but he'd gotten into the habit back when he was still using wires. A thin stream of the ants were marching in the direction of the trash can, which was good; but a much heavier stream were headed toward the workstations, which was not good. Greg's eyes got wider as the ants got closer. "Hey, Hank?" he said.

"Sit tight," Hank said. "There must be some contamination from their target sample over there somewhere."

He turned back to the monitor and fired off a new command refining the search to prioritize the most intense source of Chitauri tissue particles. "Okay," he said, swiveling around in his chair again.

Now *both* streams of ants were headed for Greg.

"No, Hank, not okay. Jeez, look at this. They're all over me . . . ow!" Greg leaped out of his chair and started slapping at the ants crawling up his legs. "Ow, ahh, Jesus!"

Hank turned to stab a cutoff command into the keyboard—for this experiment, he hadn't got all of it programmed into the headset's subvocalizer—and then he froze under the weight of a horrifying realization. *Oh, no,* he thought, and spun around again.

The ants were all over Greg now, stinging him by the dozen. His yelps of pain had progressed to full-throated screaming, and then into a sound that no human being could make. As Hank locked eyes with him, he saw that Greg's face was starting to contort. The muscles jumped, sank, began to reform themselves as Greg's skin began to blister and peel. One of his eyes burst and from the socket glittered a reptilian vertical pupil.

"Did you think we would not find you?" the Chitauri said, and sprang.

13

Status Report

Prospects for the success of the human ordering project are immensely improved. The integration of operational goals with the mechanisms of the human form of government known as representative democracy presented a number of challenges due to that government's differences from the totalitarian institutions previously subverted and redeployed. The primary difference lies in the timetable, and the delay between initiation of programs and fruition as expressed in direct action. Lessons in this area have been learned at nontrivial cost in assets and time.

Current forecasts call for completion of asset placement in .084873 solar year. Enaction of final phase of human ordering project to commence immediately after completion of asset placement in <United States>, and to progress beyond <United States> according to existing post-assimilation plans. Pre-<Arizona> project components including chemical and hormonal treatments of water supplies are still envisioned as part of the current project; however, differences in asset structure call for variations from former versions of the project. In addition, human awareness of the ordering project necessitates increased sophistication in assimilation and subversion. Previous iterations of the project have yielded important knowledge regarding human political institutions and cultural trends. This knowledge is being exploited as events and assets allow.

The issue of human surveillance and detection technology has recently become more prominent. Efforts are under way to retard the progress of this technology, but outcomes are unclear. In this instance, the lack of a truly authoritative central government in the <United States> complicates efforts to control the dissemination of new technologies. Market imperatives are such that humans are often willing to ignore the dictates of their elected officials if their crude risk-benefit analysis indicates such action to be worthwhile in financial terms. Possibly this process is underway with the <Stark> technology; intelligence efforts continue.

Alert

Resources in <Wilmette, Illinois>, indicate that secrecy has been inadvertently breached. Loss of

of Greg's skin away from the Chitauri's face; in return, the Chitauri squeezed Hank's throat until he could feel his larynx pressing into his airway. Trying to fight it off, Hank found that it was much stronger than he was; he couldn't loosen its grip. Its tongue flicked out and stung the flesh of his cheek.

"Very interesting, what you have done with these ants," the Chitauri said. "Their stings are quite painful." Hank tried to answer, but even with both hands locked around its wrist, he couldn't get out of its chokehold. The Chitauri plucked a bullet ant from behind its ear and pressed it into the back of one of Hank's hands. The pain that exploded up his arm when it stung was like nothing he'd ever felt before, and he gargled a scream through his constricted windpipe. All of the strength went out of his arm.

"Yes. Quite painful. We are very interested to explore your knowledge and abilities, Dr. Pym," the Chitauri said, showing its fangs. Its voice had transformed from Greg's cheery baritone to a gravelly chirp. "Your assimilation will be experiment as much as repast." It flicked its tongue across Hank's face again and made a wordless sound of hunger, as its free hand searched for and found a bullet ant stinging its forehead.

All at once, before he could make a conscious decision, Hank grew. And he grew fast; the headset cracked into pieces that bounced off his shoulders as he expanded, feeling his limbs lengthen and hearing the crackle in his ears that came as his anvil bones grew to the size of, well, anvils. The Chitauri's grip became a tearing pinch, and the alien fell free, taking with it a divot of skin from Hank's neck. Hank grabbed the Chitauri before it could hit the floor—then his head and shoulders crashed into the lab ceiling, starting a cascade of acoustic tiles and light covers, along with an explosion of dust. With a growl, Hank heaved against the ceiling and grew through it, feeling the steel roof beams bend and pop loose from their welds as the roof collapsed with a rumble. Standing thigh-deep in the sudden wreckage of his lab, his feet and legs on fire with the stings of *P. clavata* loosed from the headset's influence, Hank saw and heard people pointing and shouting in the parking lot his lab shared with a call center and two nondescript offices. As the debris from the lab's collapse settled, he could hear more normal tones of voice as well.

"Holy smokes, it's that giant guy," someone said from the smoker's refuge outside the call center, maybe a hundred yards from where Hank stood.

"What, the Hulk? I thought they got him."

"No, idiot. The Hulk is green. This guy look green to you?"

"Nope. Just big and naked."

They weren't even scared of him. He was fifty feet tall and had just destroyed a building with the back of his head, and *they weren't even scared of him.* Hank lost his temper. Raising the Chitauri up to eye level, he said, "Did you think I wouldn't have a way out of your kung-fu grip, asshole?"

"The ants, I'm afraid," the Chitauri said. Hank had it gripped around the torso and one arm. Its other arm, damaged in its ascent through the lab's roof, dangled over Hank's thumb. "Pain causes confusion, which compromises the ability to think."

"You're goddamn right about that," Hank said, and crushed the Chitauri in his hand.

Gasps came from the parking lot. "He just killed that guy!" someone shouted, and then people were running. Hank looked after them, mouth open, his fury beginning to recede. No, he wanted to say. Not a guy. You don't understand.

But they'd seen the gout of blood that came from its mouth and trickled between Hank's fingers, and that was all they were going to understand. Screwed up again, Hank thought. Even when I do the right thing, it doesn't work. He could already hear Fury saying that he should have kept the Chitauri alive so they could interrogate it. Like the rest of them, Fury wouldn't understand.

Hank looked around at the sound of sirens. Think, he told himself. Worry about Fury later. The thing to do right then was get out of there.

He took a deep breath and laid the mangled Chitauri down between his feet. Then, exhaling so his lungs wouldn't rupture, he slowly let himself back down to normal size, accompanied by a spattering on the floor as his unclenched hand shrank away from the blood that coated it. Two things to do, he thought. Hide the body, find the sample in the trash can. Then I'm out of here.

Wait. Three. Better get dressed, too.

Two hours later, he called Tony's private number. It rang for nearly ninety seconds before Tony finally picked it up. "Hank," Tony said.

"You watching the news, Tony?" Hank asked.

He was in the basement of the house he'd grown up in. His old bedroom had been redone as a TV hideaway for his father, and Tony was there now, watching helicopter footage of his destroyed lab with a reporter on voiceover speculating about terrorism.

"As a matter of fact," Tony said, "I was just having lunch with Nick. The topic of your lab accident had come up, but we're definitely curious about what you might add to our discussion."

"I'm going to tell you again, Tony. There were survivors."

"Of course there were. We know that."

"You . . . then why did you cut me off last time? Is Nick there?"

"Why don't we put this conversation on the speakerphone?" There was a pop, and then Tony's voice came over the line again. "How's that?"

"Fine," Hank said. "Nick? You there?"

"I'm here, Doctor Pym." Fury sounded farther away, but Hank didn't know how the room where they were was laid out. It frustrated him not to be able to get a mental picture of the arrangement.

"There were survivors, Nick."

"I believe Tony just told you that we knew that."

"Yeah," Hank said. "He did, but he still hasn't explained to me why he cut me off when I told him that before."

Tony started to say something, but Fury got there first. "I'll take this one, Tony. Doctor Pym, Tony cut you off because you are no longer a member of this team. That was true when you talked to Tony a couple of days ago, and it's true now. I asked him to take your call today so we could get that clear."

On TV, a reporter was interviewing one of the people Hank remembered from the parking lot. She was saying that the giant guy had killed someone. The interview cut to a police lieutenant saying that no bodies had been recovered from the site, and from there the report went to a fire department team tearing into the wreckage of the lab. The reporter noted that several members of the police and fire departments had been bitten by extremely venomous ants, which led to a short interview with a Northwestern University political science professor on whether poisonous insects might be used in a terrorist attack.

Hank knew he didn't have much time. He needed SHIELD to swoop down and trump the local investigation with black-ops credentials. "Remember what they said to Janet about being the universe's immune system, Nick?"

Fury said, "How exactly do you know about that, Doctor Pym?"

Are you going to step in here, Tony? Hank wondered. How's Nick going to feel about you feeding me tissue samples? "It's important for me to keep up on certain things," Hank said. "For research purposes."

"You will immediately cut out whatever the hell it is you're doing that involves access to classified discussions among the team, Doctor Pym. Do not cross me on this."

"Nick, I'm watching TV right now. The fire department is snooping through my lab, and the police are there too because someone told them they saw me kill somebody. There's a dead Chitauri in the lab freezer, Nick. When they find it, what's going to happen to me? It's long past time when you could feed me any bullshit. Is SKR an accident, and now I've got a spy in my lab? You tell me what the hell is going on!"

"What's going on is that you were working in an area you shouldn't have been working in, and now you've got a problem," Fury said coldly.

"And I have to say you're sounding a little bit paranoid, Hank," Tony added.

"Oh, am I? Okay, I'll put it to you this way. If the police show up at my door with an arrest warrant, I'm going to sing like a canary, and SHIELD can go to hell. If, on the other hand, SHIELD wants to step in and get the cops out of my lab, I might be able to tell you something interesting about the results of the last experiment I got done before a goddamn Chitauri spy made me wreck my lab. If that's paranoid, then I plead guilty."

Silence on the other end of the line.

"You've got a little time to think about it," Hank said. "Call me back."

He hung up and watched the report loop back to aerial footage of his lab. The ants worked, he thought. And they'd work a hell of a lot better than whatever sensor SKR TechEnt had come up with. Hank watched the television and worked himself up into a cold fury over how Tony Stark was treating him. He resolved that Tony wouldn't get away with it forever. You couldn't just treat someone like that, especially not Hank Pym. No, sir. When Nick decided to cover his ass and come in to get the Chitauri out of the lab, Hank would have a chance to talk to him without Tony around, and General Nicholas Fury was going to get an earful. That was for sure.

15

THE CALL FROM GENERAL FURY CAME WHILE
Steve was in the middle of a cheeseburger and a TCM
showing of *The Thin Man.* "Need you at the Triskelion
pronto, Cap," Fury said. So Steve got there pronto, and
found his way to a helipad where General Fury was
waiting for him with Tony Stark and, of all people, Thor.

"What's he doing here?" Steve said, pointing at the
self-professed god of thunder.

"You'll find out when we get there," General Fury
said.

"Get where?"

"Illinois," Tony said with a wink. "Try not to start any
fights this time, okay?"

Two hours later they were standing inside a police cordon that extended in a hundred-yard radius from a partially collapsed single-story building in a business park in Wilmette, Illinois. Hazmat-suited SHIELD personnel picked through the wreckage, while under the blades of the turbocopter that had brought the SHIELD team, General Fury was making an emphatic point to a local police detective. "I've got reports of a murder taking place here, General," the detective said. "You can say national security this and terrorism that, but what am I supposed to tell people? We're not investigating a murder?"

"You will tell them to talk to me," General Fury said. "If we determine that a murder has been committed, that part of the investigation goes back to you once we get it untangled from some other things that, I promise you, you don't want to know anything about."

Steve could tell from the detective's face that he did in fact want very much to know, but that he knew he never would. "I have your word on this?" he said eventually. "This isn't Chicago. If somebody was killed in there, we've got to know who it is."

Fury handed him a card. "You call me at this number tomorrow morning. By then I'll know what I can tell you and what I can't. Fair enough?"

The detective took the card, but he didn't like the deal. "As fair as I'm going to get, is what I'm hearing."

"You're hearing right, Detective. Now I'm going to ask you a favor."

"Oh, well, we're getting along so well already. Sure. Whatever I can do."

"I know you're going to go right home and find out who was actually the tenant of this building," General Fury said. "So I'm going to save you that trouble. His name is Doctor Henry Pym. I am going to ask you, as a professional courtesy, to not contact Doctor Pym until you hear from me. Can we agree on that?"

"Is he the giant guy?" the detective asked.

"Detective," General Fury said. "You have all kinds of witness reports saying all kinds of different things, I'm sure. If you let me get to what I need to do here, I can save you a lot of work putting them all together."

A silence hung between them, broken after thirty seconds or so when the detective lit a cigarette and said, "Okay. Fine. I'm calling you at eight a.m., General. Hope you keep early hours."

"Eight a.m.," Fury said, rolling his eyes. "I'll be lucky if I get to sleep by then."

"Boo hoo," the detective said, and walked away trailing cigarette smoke.

Fury walked back over to where Steve was waiting with Tony and Thor. "Nick," Tony said. "I'm supposed to be at an art opening with Scarlett Johansson. Please explain to me why this is more important."

Steve kept his mouth shut, but he was just about fed up with Tony's posturing. General Fury had briefed them during the flight, as a result of which Steve knew that Tony had taken the call from Hank Pym that had brought them all here. What Steve couldn't figure out was why Thor was along. He couldn't imagine that General Fury had decided to trust an obviously crazy pinko with something as serious as the details of a new Chitauri incursion. Regardless of what Thor had done with the Chitauri bomb in Arizona, Steve didn't for a minute believe in a thunder god. Either the bomb hadn't done what the Chitauri said it would, or the tech in Thor's hammer had some secret function that he hadn't told any of them about. Whichever it was, Thor was a loose cannon and a security risk. If it was up to Steve, Thor wouldn't have been let within a mile of the Triskelion.

But that wasn't his call. It was General Fury's.

That thought led Steve in an uncomfortable direction, recalling the Chitauri at Andrews and the phone call he'd made after dinner at Peter Luger's. From any angle, Steve knew, he was going off the reservation. Good soldiers didn't do that.

Or did they? It had been a long time since he'd been just a soldier. When he'd ridden a Nazi rocket into the troposphere, he'd earned the right to think for himself. General Fury still wanted him to be the super-soldier chess piece, moved here and there without question, but General Fury—there Steve was going off the reservation again—too often had to make decisions polluted by political considerations. Maybe it was up to the soldiers to simply do what was right.

General Fury didn't answer Tony in any case. He

turned to an approaching member of the response team and said, "What have you got?"

Pulling off her suit's hood, the tech said, "Well, he was right about the Chitauri in the freezer. We're pulling the whole appliance as soon as we get it sealed. Looks like Pym squished it pretty good, but you can never tell. I've got guys in there sterilizing the blood on the floors. Also he mentioned a test sample, right? That we haven't found."

Looking away from her to Tony, General Fury said, "You have any idea about that?"

Aha, Steve thought. That's why he's here.

"None," Tony said. "Is that what you brought me nine hundred miles to ask? If it is, then I've got a jet warmed up and waiting over at Palwaukee."

"Not until I get an answer. Did you give Chitauri tissue to Hank Pym?"

"Nick, how much do you really want to know about how I spend black-budget money?"

General Fury walked over to Tony and stood a little too close to him. "I want to know," he said quietly, "whether you hired Hank Pym or diverted resources, including Chitauri tissue, to him. That's what I want to know."

"Okay," Tony said. "Yes, I did. He really has done some interesting work. Hard to tell from this," he waved a hand at the wreckage of Pym's lab, "whether any of it worked, but if you want my opinion, SHIELD's shooting itself in the foot by turning him into a pariah. I mean, my God, the things some of us have done and you cut him loose for spousal abuse?"

"Cut it out," Steve said.

Tony flipped a hand in Steve's direction without looking at him. "Okay, Romeo. I know you and Janet have a thing going now," he said before continuing his spiel to General Fury. "We've all got our hands dirty, Nick. I happen to think Hank Pym is a coward and I wouldn't piss on him if he was on fire; but if he can help us, that's more important." Then he looked over his shoulder at Steve and said, "Of course you'd never do anything that wasn't perfectly aboveboard. That's why all of us regular people who compromise their morals seem so filthy to you."

"I told you the other day," Steve said. "Next time you and I go at it, I'm not holding back."

"Then do it," Tony said.

"Stand down, Captain," General Fury said. "Last thing in the world I need is TV cameras catching the two of you in a fight. Tony, get the hell out of here. Cap, you and Thor meet me back in the copter."

He walked away toward the lab, where the techs were clearing some of the rubble to make way for the sealed freezer. Halfway there he stopped, turned around, and called, "Tony. I meant it. Out. Now."

Tony winked at Steve and said, "*Au revoir, mon ami.* Next time let's fight some bad guys, how does that sound?"

Steve didn't answer. He watched Tony walk to the cordon and duck under it. A car pulled up out of nowhere, and the door was open before Tony could reach for the handle. A guy like that, Steve thought, everything done for him, everyone bends over backward for him, and what is he? An amoral boozehound with a brain tumor. That's not the kind of person we need running things around here.

"So that's why Nick brought Tony," Thor said. Steve had forgotten he was there. "What do you think the two of us are doing here?"

Steve shrugged. "I'm following orders. You, who knows?"

"Not me," Thor said. "Although it's crossed my mind that the general thinks the two of us might correct each other's worst tendencies."

"Give me a break," Steve said, and started to walk away.

"Steve," Thor said, and for some reason Steve stopped. He waited for Thor to go on and deliver whatever loony speech he'd cooked up this time.

But Thor surprised him. "Steve, you need to stop thinking all the time that you're different from the rest of us."

Steve turned around. "I'm different from you, that's for sure."

"Fair enough," Thor said. "If that's the distinction that makes you feel better, go with it. But I'm going to give you some advice. When someone wants something from you, ask yourself why they want it, and who wanted them to ask you."

"Okay, Ann Landers," Steve said.

Thor chuckled. "Funny. Anyway, that's Loki's advice, not mine. He asked me to pass it along."

"Oh, for Pete's sake," Steve said, and walked over to the lab building's doorway. On the way, he spotted a chalk circle with a spatter of Chitauri blood in it. The team hadn't yet gotten around to sterilizing it.

We're chasing them, Steve thought. Always a step behind.

He went inside. "Watch out for the ants, sir," a suited tech said. "Some of them bite like hell."

"Thanks," Steve said. The inside of the lab, although partially cleared out, was a complete wreck. He could see from the shape of the bent beams where Hank had gone through the roof, and how on his way through he'd snapped the main support beam, causing most of the rest of the roof to come down. The collapse had crushed most of the ant farms, and the response team was getting ready to fire off a series of insecticide bombs because nobody knew for sure whether Pym had created some kind of mutant ant that might get out and wreck the local ecosystem.

Fury was observing the removal of the freezer. He saw Steve picking his way through the wreckage and said, "What brings you in here, Captain?"

"Well, General," Steve said, and finally let go of the

question he'd been asking himself all night. "I've got another version of the same question for you. Why did you bring Thor and me?"

General Fury looked surprised. "You serious, Captain? Muscle. We didn't know what was out here. Didn't know whether we might have to take Pym down, for that matter. Turned out we didn't need you, but better safe than sorry." He winked his good eye. "Sun Tzu says that somewhere, right?"

The next morning, which made it the third day after he'd made the call from the pay phone on Havemeyer Street, Steve was eating breakfast at his kitchen table when he heard a knock at the door. Probably the kids down the hall selling candy bars again, he thought, fishing in his pockets. He still couldn't believe that anyone could keep a straight face while asking two dollars for a candy bar, but that was the world now . . . and what the heck, if any of that money really did go to whatever cause they said it did, the rip-off would be worth it.

Opening the door, Steve was all ready to give the kid his two bucks and complain about it, but instead of the kid, he found himself looking at Admiral Esteban Garza. "I—oh," Steve said. "Admiral. I was expecting someone else."

"Captain. May we come in?"

Steve stepped aside and let Garza pass. A second man, who had *spook* written all over him, followed.

Garza stood in the middle of Steve's living room, not speaking or touching anything while the spook took out some kind of sensor apparatus and scanned every surface. It took ten minutes or so, at the end of which he said, "Looks clear, Admiral."

"Okay, Larry. Fire me up a baffler and then Captain Rogers and I will have a talk."

Larry pocketed his first apparatus, came up with another one, and put it on the coffee table between Steve's couch and the TV. He flipped a little toggle switch on its face, and it began emitting a low hum.

"All set?" Garza asked.

"Yes, sir."

"See you in the car, then." Larry left without another word and Admiral Garza sat on the couch.

"Go ahead and finish your breakfast, Captain," he said.

Steve found that he wasn't hungry anymore. "If it's all the same to you, sir, I'd just as soon talk first," he said. "What's with the spook stuff?"

"I don't really have to tell you that, do I?" Garza said. "You know what we're doing here."

I do, Steve wanted to say. And even though I think it's the right thing to do, something about it makes me sick to my stomach.

"Anyway," Admiral Garza said. "What I'm here about is the next step."

"The next step," Steve repeated.

"We've got the screeners in production, Steve. That's

an important step. But already there's pushback from Altobelli; he's twisting all kinds of arms on the Hill to try and limit SKR's ability to sell and install the screeners. What needs to happen now is a concerted push on our part. We need to tell the American people that this can help protect them, and tell them that they need to get behind us so we can make this argument—their argument—in Congress and over the airwaves." Garza leaned forward and tapped Steve on the shoulder. "You're going to be critical to this effort. Americans feel like they know you, Steve. They admire you. The women have crushes on you and the men want to be like you."

Steve's bullshit detector went off. "Admiral," he said. "With all due respect, you're laying it on a little thick."

"This is a pitch, Steve," Admiral Garza said. "You don't have to do a single thing I'm asking you to do. I can't order you around. All I can do is trust that you and I have similar ideas about what this country needs. Can I trust in that idea, Captain Rogers?"

The real question here, Steve thought, was whether Garza could trust Steve to do as he was told. Which was exactly the question he had been chewing over himself the night before. It was decision time. Could he commit to this, not knowing what exactly might come of that commitment later?

On the other hand, could he stop now?

Garza stood. "I can see you need some time to think," he said. "You know how to find me, right?"

He started to walk toward the door, but stopped when Steve, too, stood. Admiral Garza turned to face him, and Steve said, "Admiral, I wouldn't have come this far if I didn't think we were doing the right thing."

Garza nodded as if he'd heard what he needed to hear. "Good, Captain. You're going to be needed as we move forward. I might ask you to come to Washington soon. Will you be able to navigate that with your commitments to SHIELD?"

"Yes, sir. I will."

Admiral Garza opened the door. "And we'd like you to meet some people in Los Angeles, too," he said before leaving. "You won't mind a little fun in the sun while we save the world, right?"

Sun Tzu probably said that somewhere, too, Steve thought, as the door swung closed.

nation of naïvete and chivalry wash over her and cleanse her of the trauma she'd suffered at Hank's hands. Or (more accurately and flippantly) the mandibles of Hank's minions.

Since the night they'd had dinner at Peter Luger's, though, he'd been different. Since a short time before then, really. Something had happened to him, and he'd been acting distant, even bitter. Some bitterness wasn't particularly strange for someone who had been through the upheavals Steve had, but she'd watched him get over it in the aftermath of the confrontation with the Chitauri; for a while after Arizona, he'd been positively basking in the adulation of twenty-first-century America, while still somehow retaining the boy-next-door quality that had attracted her to him in the first place. At Luger's, he hadn't been like that at all. Something had been on his mind, distracting him in the middle of sentences. He hadn't even commented on her dress, which she'd chosen specifically to provoke him because he was still such a fuddy-duddy about women's clothing. After dinner, he'd disappeared, saying he had something important to do, and she hadn't seen him since.

Janet sat back on her couch, TV on at low volume, glass of wine in her right hand and the fingers of her left drumming on her knee. It was almost time for the phone to ring. Every night at about eleven, Hank called her from wherever he was in Illinois. Every night she let the phone ring. He only called once each night, but he never gave her a night off, either, and he left the same message, practically verbatim, each night. *Janet. Forgive me. I'm not asking you to forget, but please, I love you. Forgive me.* For the last week or so, Janet had begun to consider either taking out a restraining order or just picking up the phone. The first option would be great if successful, but might also provoke him into another rage. She shivered a little at the thought. The second might work out better in the long term, but talking to him . . .

The phone rang.

Janet let it ring, and waited for the message. The machine clicked, and Hank said, "Janet. We need to talk. It involves . . . let's just say it involves Kleiser, and I need your help." Dead air stretched out. "Janet," Hank said again.

She picked up the phone, but did not speak.

For a third time, Hank said her name. "What?" she asked softly.

"You picked up the phone," he said, amazed.

"What do you want, Hank?"

"I—there isn't time to tell you everything," he said. "God, Janet. So good to hear your voice."

No, she thought. We are not going down that conversational road. "Hank. What do you want? Why did you mention Kleiser?"

"Because two days ago a Chitauri tried to kill me in my lab." Hank paused. "Is this line secure?"

"Hell of a time to ask that question," Janet observed.

"You're right, never mind. The 'terrorist attack' in Illinois? Heard about it?"

"I read the papers, Hank."

"Then you'll notice that they didn't mention me. Or the Chitauri. They're back, Janet. There were survivors after Arizona, and now they're back. Fury knows about it. He was at my lab right after it happened doing the old scrub-and-shrug. Thor was there, too, God knows why. And your boyfriend. Uh, Steve."

Janet didn't know what to say. There was too much to respond to. Typical Hank. Throw out a jumble of conversation containing three or four things that needed to be addressed separately, and then pick the one you didn't address to get pissed about. "Are you okay?" Janet asked.

"Yeah," he said, and added, with real feeling, "I'm glad you asked."

"What happened to the Chitauri?"

"I killed it. Fury's probably got it in a tank by now. Janet, they must have told you something. Nobody will talk to me. What's going on?"

She sat back on the couch. "Come on, Hank. You know I can't—"

"Fine," he said. "Maybe next time they'll kill me and you won't have to worry about it anymore."

"Oh, for God's sake. Do you . . . no. I am not doing this."

"Do you love him?" Hank asked.

"I'm not doing this," Janet said again.

"I wonder if I'm the only one it's happened to," Hank mused, his tone of voice suddenly different. She wondered if he was taking his meds, and appreciated once again how glad she was to have someone stable in her life now.

As she looked out her living-room window, she could see across the Williamsburg Bridge, and just about pinpoint the rough location of Steve's apartment farther away; not that she could see it directly, but a wasp always knows the way back to its nest, and she'd inherited some of that trait in the form of a nearly unshakable sense of bearings and distance. Right there, she thought . . . and then she heard Steve's voice on TV.

"I have to go," she said to Hank, and hung up the phone.

Staring at the TV, Janet fumbled around on the coffee table for the remote. When she found it, she accidentally changed the channel, then started a DVD, then finally got back to where she was and got the volume up to where she could hear it without straining. Steve was speaking into a cluster of microphones against a banner backdrop she couldn't quite read from the angle of this network's feed: ". . . here today to lend my support to efforts to keep Americans safe through the immediate and widespread distribution of SKR TechEnt's screening technologies. After the terrorist attack in Wilmette, Illinois, two days ago—as well as other incidents and intelligence not publicly available—it's time to present a united front. Civil libertarians and ACLU types are going to raise hell and file their lawsuits, but the average American knows that now more than ever, it's critically important to maximize the protection of the public through surveillance and screening of public spaces. This is not Big Brother; the government isn't putting a dime or a single man-hour into it. This is the free market with a conscience, doing its job. If you're not doing anything wrong, you don't have anything to worry about."

Steve's voice was swept under a tide of questions from the assembled reporters. A splash across the bottom of the screen announced the location as Los Angeles. "My God, Steve," Janet whispered.

He was answering a question about why the Department of Homeland Security wasn't getting behind the screener tech. "Governments work slowly," was Steve's answer. "And sometimes events call for speed. Governments work through consensus, and sometimes events call for decisive leadership. I believe in America, and I believe in our government. In that order."

The phone rang. Janet let it. "Janet," Hank said on the machine. "Pick up. Janet. We've got to talk." The machine beeped.

She watched Steve take another six or eight questions, and with each answer she felt herself falling away from what she thought she'd known about him. "All enemies, foreign and domestic," he said. "We will protect this nation."

The phone rang again, and again Janet didn't pick it up. "My God," came Hank's voice. "You must be watching what I'm watching." There was a pause, and then he added, "That's some man you got there."

Janet picked up the phone. "You go to hell," she said, and hung it up again. Then she unplugged it from the jack. She'd gotten a new cell, and so far he hadn't called her there, but she knew he'd find it if he really wanted to.

In the meantime, she needed to think. And she needed another glass of wine.

She ended up doing both thinking and drinking at the lab, where by approximately four in the morning she was in that exhausted interim space that lay at the end of too much work, too little sleep, and a bottle of red wine. She'd come down to finish the monthly update on the next-generation super-soldier project, which Fury was going to want tomorrow, and which meant Janet had to deal with Banner. Knowing all that, she'd decided to get it out of the way, file the report, and then sleep all day and let her dreaming brain figure out what to do about Steve.

Banner didn't sleep much; he was too depressed, and his physical cycles were too disrupted by all of the drugs keeping him from going green again. Janet had known this, but had counted on his morose self-pity to keep him from talking too much . . . but things didn't turn out exactly like she'd planned. Bruce was talkative and relatively unself-pitying, which was rare for him but made it hard for her to keep her own confused wallow going. Instead she found herself confiding in him from the other side of the transparent wall at one end of his cell, especially when they were opposite each other on either side of the exchange tray through which they passed various drafts and documents.

"You know Steve and I have been dating, right?" she asked while they were both running over the version of the report they planned to submit to Fury.

"Who doesn't?" Bruce said. "I'm the only one on the team without a girlfriend, so whenever anyone else gets maudlin, they come dump it on me."

"As if you're not maudlin enough," she said.

Bruce cracked a rueful smile, which was the only kind he seemed to be capable of. "Careful there, Miss Wasp," he said. "That almost sounded like backhanded sympathy."

The truth was that Janet did have a sort of backhanded sympathy for Bruce, even though he'd done one of the dumbest things she'd ever heard of when he shot himself up with Hulk juice mixed with super-soldier serum and destroyed much of lower Manhattan . . . because, he'd said at the time, he wanted to give the Ultimates a public enemy as a way of letting them show the American public what they could do. But weren't there enough real enemies? And was that Bruce's real reason? Janet had a feeling the real reason had a bit more to do with Betty Ross than Bruce had ever let on. God, she wanted to ask him about it; in his current mood, he might even tell her, which would sure liven up the report editing process . . . Janet bit her tongue. It wouldn't do any good to start talking to Bruce about that now.

He'd be lucky if he ever saw the outside of the cell again.

"So what about Mr. Captain America, anyway?" Bruce wanted to know.

Janet put down her pen. "He's different lately," she said. "He's had this harder edge the past few weeks, and then tonight I saw him on TV giving a press conference about this new—" She caught herself, wondering how much Bruce knew about the suppression of Tony's screener tech and its subsequent leak to SKR. No way was she going to be the first to tell him. In some ways the Ultimates as a group were like a bunch of third-graders where gossip was concerned, but this was one of the times, Janet thought, when you needed to know when to keep your mouth shut.

She shrugged. "Sometimes it seems like his whole patriotic thing is an excuse," she said, and wanted to go on, but wasn't sure what she might think it was an excuse for.

"Last refuge of a scoundrel," Bruce said.

"What?"

"Samuel Johnson said that," Bruce explained. "Patriotism is the last refuge of a scoundrel." He must have seen her expression change, because immediately he started to backpedal. "Not that I think Steve is, you know—"

Janet stood and slid her copy of the report in the exchange tray, half-edited. "Why don't you finish these," she said, and walked out.

Status Report

Operations involving <Steve Rogers> continue to progress. Assets in place around <New York> and <Washington> signal readiness to commence the next phase of the human ordering project. Observations of human cultural production including television broadcasts indicate that <Rogers> is behaving according to projections. These observations increase confidence in further projections, which are to be acted on beginning immediately.

<New York> assimilation of nonhuman targets should commence immediately as preparation for the next wave of diversionary missions.

In addition, redirection of assets away from infiltration and control of human cultural production will commence. The institutions in question behave according to rules that defy systematization, and the institutions are thus useless for our purposes. Assets previously dedicated to this portion of the human ordering project will receive orders attached to this directive.

Further misdirection and subversion operations to commence in <New York> at the earliest opportunity. Assets in place are given initiative to assess and execute as rules of engagement indicate.

Impact of research of <Henry Pym> involving manipulation and control of arthropods, order <Hymenoptera>, uncertain. Consideration of possible consequences for success and timeline of human ordering project continues. Laboratory at which <Henry Pym> conducted research was destroyed during combat with assimilated asset in place; however, <SHIELD> appears to be constructing a new laboratory with similar facilities in close proximity to current residence of <Henry Pym>. Placement of new assets and adjustment in placement of existing assets to commence immediately per previously issued directives.

Further, it is directed that construction be restarted on facility abandoned after events in <Arizona> 1.10453 solar year ago. Financing and rearrangement of asset deployments is under way, and will be refined as events dictate. This directive should in no way be considered an expression of doubt in the human ordering project; rather, infrastructure penetration should—as <Kleiser> articulated—be one of the primary long-term goals of

fense of Pym to Fury the other day had been mostly motivated by annoyance at Fury's high-handedness. The truth was, if Tony never had to lay eyes on Hank Pym again, it would be too soon.

Another thing that galled him was that he'd had to fly into the Podunk Palwaukee airport again, also because of Fury, since Commandante Eyepatch had decreed that the team should come out to observe a demonstration of Pym's ant wizardry in Illinois. Why not just bring him to the Triskelion, Tony had asked, instead of dragging everyone off to the Chicago suburbs . . . but Fury had been his usual stubborn self.

So here they were. Tony, Fury, Clint, and Thor. Just like last time, except that Clint was along this time and Steve had flatly refused to come (once again getting away with it when the rest of the team wouldn't have been able to, Tony thought sourly). Janet had begged off for reasons that, Tony assumed, were more reasonable than whatever Steve had come up with. If he'd bothered to come up with anything at all.

A SHIELD tech team had built Hank a new lab not too far from his old one, where Hank could show off his repertoire of tricks with all of the new ants Tony had flown in from all over the world. Probably he'd just gone out on the sidewalk and kidnapped a bunch more since then; Hank Pym in his headset was a kind of ant Pied Piper. Tony imagined mother ants telling their babies to never, ever get close to the human with the metal hat on. The anthills around the lab were probably ghost towns by now. Sidewalk ants, leaf-cutter ants, regular old harvester ants, Hank had them all. One of these days he was going to invent a technology to turn himself into an ant, and then Hank Pym's human problems would be solved. Tony had half a mind to start the research himself, just to spare the world more of Hank's paranoid, self-pitying neediness.

All in all, Tony was in the perfect frame of mind to watch a scientific demonstration.

The new lab was about the same size as the old one, but without the thrown-together quality that had been obvious in the old one even when Tony had observed the ruins from out in the parking lot. Whatever their deficiencies in creative thinking, SHIELD teams had a good eye for organization. This space was arranged around a slightly raised central control desk, with all kinds of terminals and headgear piled on it. No organizational impulse could survive the prolonged presence of Hank Pym. Ringing the outer wall of the lab were small doors, behind each of which was an ant farm designed along the environmental lines of each species' favored habitat. Compartmentalized areas in front of each door provided space for observations of the ants and experimentation with various headgear and control broadcasts.

"Ants and wasps have a common ancestor. They're really very similar," Hank said, in response to a question Tony hadn't heard. Tony immediately found his attention wandering to the question of whether Hank's headset would have any power to control Janet Pym, and what one might do with that control in the event one had it . . . oh my.

He snapped out of it in time to see Hank putting on one of his helmets. Something about the sight took all the steam out of his Janet fantasia, which was just as well, since Tony had better things to do than joust with a jealous Steve Rogers. The world was full of women. He could find one who wasn't an emotionally scarred mutant.

"Okay, people," Fury said. "Everyone up on the island."

The four Ultimates, plus Hank and two SHIELD techs, clustered in the middle of the lab. Hank touched a terminal screen, and walls slid across the gaps through which they'd entered, sealing the command platform off from the rest of the lab. "The walls have a mild electrical current running through them, too," Hank said. "They won't come near us."

"They're just ants," Clint said.

Hank laughed. "Say that again after you've been stung by a bullet ant."

"Where's the target?" Fury asked.

"There are three," Hank said. "I have a couple of things to show you."

"Okay. Where are the targets?" Fury asked, less politely this time, and with sharp emphasis on the plural verb and final *s* in *targets*.

Hank shot Fury a wink. "You'll see soon enough.

Just wait. In ten minutes, you're going to wonder why you ever worried about screeners in the first place."

A veiled shot at me, wondered Tony? Or not so veiled? It didn't matter. Years had passed since Tony's ego had been vulnerable to people like Hank Pym. Genius or not, Pym was a pathetic bundle of inferiority and worry. If you were going to worry about what people like him said about you, you might as well carry grudges against bugs that hit your windshield.

Various chirps and audio dingbats started percolating out of Hank's terminals as he powered up the main control routines. It fit exactly with Tony's perceptions of Hank that the good doctor was one of those geeks who had a different sound effect for every keystroke. "Okay," Hank said. "When I was designing and rehearsing this experiment, it occurred to me that you might not be impressed enough if I only had the ants find a sample. So what I've done here is run three parallel routines, involving different groups of ants. Each one is instructed to look for a particular mass of Chitauri tissue, as expressed by the density of particles in the air. They can tell the three samples apart on this basis alone, but what I want to call your attention to is the way that each species will come out, reconnoiter, and then focus in on the sample they're directed to find."

"I can't wait," Tony said.

"Actually, neither can I," Hank shot back. "This is the first time I'll ever have kept these three plates spinning live. Oh, and I went for one final little flourish. Each of these three species typically attacks one of the others on sight. So if you see an ant massacre out there, you'll know I dropped the ball. If not . . ." He shrugged and grinned to himself at how smart he was. "Everybody ready?"

"We have the Orkin men in place?" Fury called out.

"Yes, sir," said a white-suited SHIELD tech waiting near the front door.

Hank spun on Fury. "Are you kidding me? These—"

"We bought these ants, Doctor Pym. We will dispose of them as we see fit, when we see fit." Fury's expression and tone of voice suggested that he wanted to say much more. "Now. Kindly proceed."

"You people are sick," Hank said. He put on the headset. "Exploitative, manipulative, soulless . . . sick." As if to emphasize the last point, he checked the time and then popped a pill from a prescription bottle before tapping in a final touchscreen sequence. "All of you go to hell. On five, four . . ."

Hank counted off the last three seconds on his fingers like a TV stage manager. At zero, he clenched his fist, and three of the ant farm doors rose smoothly until the inhabitants of each cell had a twelve-by-eighteen-inch portal to the world. Ants in tidy columns filed out of each, and then spread across the floor. When members of one species encountered another, they touched feelers briefly before continuing on their assigned errands. When all three species had intermingled on the floor, Tony gave up trying to follow what was going on and went over to a series of ant's-eye-view monitors installed along the back wall of the control island. Thor was already there.

"What's your take, O namesake of my favorite weekday?" Tony asked him.

"Really?" Thor said. "I would have figured a party boy like you would be partial to Friday."

"Where I went to college, Friday was retroactively extended to include Thursday. Made us all look forward to it a little more. How about you, Clint?"

"Agreed. Plus who had classes on Fridays, anyway?"

Thor shook his head, and Tony could see him thinking: Americans. Both of them watched the screens and saw mortal enemies passing each other by without more than a passing exchange of pheromone . . . which was also kind of like some of the undergrad weekends Tony remembered, but that was another story. "It really is pretty impressive," he said.

Thor shrugged. "It hasn't worked yet. If we could get them to detect my brother, now, that would be a science project I could get behind."

"Oh my God," Tony groaned. "Is anyone on this team sane?"

He returned his attention to the ants, which on the monitors he could sort of distinguish by species. Not that he knew which of them were which, but he could see that one of them was smaller and browner than another, which was thicker through the thorax than the third, which was an odd reddish color with black legs.

Or at least, so it looked through the monitors. Each of the three species seemed to be forming a kind of scouts' perimeter, with more resources following right behind. Tony wished he had a way to tell which of them was looking for which sample, and said so.

"There's a real-time graphic on one of the monitors somewhere," Hank said. "Not sure where. But sure, you can see which of them is going where."

Tony looked around and found the graphic display. Sure enough, on it you could follow what was happening in terms of closing distance to each sample. From the looks of it, all three teams were closing on their samples, and there didn't appear to be much deviation or overlap. If that was the truth of the situation, then Hank had done some very good work indeed. "You feel like explaining this to me?" Thor asked over his shoulder. "I avoid these machines when I can."

Tony compiled, and about the time he'd finished with the explanation as he understood it, the first team of ants found its pot of Chitauri gold. So all Tony had to say was, "See? Where the glowing spot is, that's the target they found."

"Just like I planned it," Hank was crowing. "You just wait. Give it forty-five seconds. God, look at those deployment patterns. I'm too good."

That, Tony thought, was up for debate, but it was beyond question that within about forty-five seconds, just like Hank had said, both of the other species had tracked and located their targets as well.

"Whoo!" Hank shouted. "That's your ant for you, ladies and gentlemen! SKR TechEnt can . . ."

"Excellent result," Nick Fury cut in.

"Hell yes, it's an excellent result," Hank said. "Better than any machine. Life will find life."

Well, Tony thought. I don't know if we need to turn this into an ant versus human machine ingenuity kind of grudge. The tech Steve Rogers had leaked to SKR was good. Very good. The only thing Tony had trouble swallowing, since he'd been on the wrong side of backroom political decisions before, was the question of where SKR was getting their Chitauri samples for calibration purposes. He surely hoped that SHIELD wasn't involved in it.

"And here, look at this," Hank went on, unfolding a piece of paper from the pocket of his lab coat. "I predicted the order."

"How many other pieces of paper do you have in there, Doctor Pym?" Clint asked politely. Thor suppressed a grin; of any of them, Tony thought, he was the one used to having his motives questioned.

Hank just rolled his eyes. It looked like he was on the manic side of one of his typical swings.

Time to ensure that the whole thing stays civil, Tony thought. He was the last person who wanted to make nice with Hank Pym, but if Washington was going to step on his innovations and then farm them out to a bunch of yokels, the situation demanded a little extra effort. "It's good work, Hank," he said.

"It sure is, Doctor Pym," Fury agreed, and Tony saw a shift in his torso, as if Fury had almost shaken Hank's hand, which might have caused Tony to faint dead away from surprise. But Fury's discipline held. "SHIELD extends both congratulations and thanks," he went on. "We'll gladly accept records of your experiments so we can continue on our own."

There was a moment of stunned silence.

Whoa, Tony thought. So much for civility.

Hank's jaw literally dropped. "Nick," he said. "I thought . . . I mean . . ."

"And we'll be dismantling this lab," Fury said. He dipped into his pocket and came up with a check. "I think you'll find this is a generous consulting fee. Good luck in your work, Doctor Pym."

As they filed off the command platform and out the front door, the tech team was already bringing in boxes and tools. Tony glanced back at Hank, just once, and wished he hadn't when he saw the devastating expression of betrayal and dashed hope on Hank's face.

19

"THEY DID WHAT?" STEVE SAID. HE COULDN'T believe it.

"Wrote him a check and then took his lab apart." Clint was tearing off pieces of a pencil eraser and idly flipping them across the room, where they stuck in a bulletin board, finding creases even Steve couldn't see. "I've seen some dirty shit in my time, Cap, but that was about the coldest thing I'd ever seen someone do face to face. At least people who were supposedly on the same side."

The pieces of eraser embedded in the bulletin board formed a pink connect-the-dots outline of an ant. Clint had gone through five erasers.

"Dirty stuff, huh?" Steve said.

"You don't even want to know."

Except Steve did. He was no babe in the woods, despite what all of these turn-of-the-millennium types seemed to think. He'd been in Europe during World War II, for Pete's sake.

Still, there was a whole world of black-ops stuff that he didn't know much about, and something about his recent Washington experience made him want to know more. A good soldier learned everything he could about his enemy. Clint Barton would know about this kind of enemy: not the Chitauri, but the kind of enemy who worked through apathy and betrayal and perversion of the ideals that Steve held dear.

"What made you get out of it?" he asked Clint.

After a pause, Clint said, "Truth? I wanted to have a kid. And I wanted to be able to get up in the morning and feed my kid his Cheerios and know that I wasn't going to go off and spend the next two days doing things that would disgust him if he knew about them."

"You didn't get out of black ops before you had kids, though."

"No," Clint said. "No, I didn't. But I wanted to even then, and I wish I had. Not all of us have super-soldier serum in our consciences, Cap. Sometimes it takes a while for the doing to catch up with the wishing." He flicked his wrist and stuck his latest pencil in the ant's head. "Listen, why don't we have this conversation over pizza instead of in the office, you know?"

The next thing Steve said was one of the hardest things to say he'd ever encountered. "Truth?" He looked at Clint to see if Clint had picked up on the copying, but couldn't tell. "I think someone's listening at my apartment."

"Whoa," Clint said, and sat up straight. "You don't think they're listening here? Or are we talking about a different someone?"

"You know what? I think you're right about the pizza. Let's get out of here," Steve said.

An hour later, they were munching on slices in Tompkins Square Park, surrounded by remnant freaks and moms with strollers. "You know what happened with the screener Tony invented," Steve said.

"I know he didn't get to make it," Clint mumbled around a mouthful of crust. "I try not to pay attention to political stuff. It's never paid off for me."

Wish I'd learned that lesson, Steve thought, and then realized that for a long time, he hadn't had to learn that lesson. He'd never been interested. But then came the long freeze, and the reawakening into this time when he was Captain America instead of the freak who was the butt of paratroopers' jokes . . . until they saw him in action. "Yeah," he said. "I don't know if it's paying off for me, either, but when that happened, I thought I had to do something."

Clint very carefully wiped his mouth and set his napkin on the paper plate he'd carried all the way from the place he'd suggested up on Avenue A and 14th. "Cap, I have the feeling you're about to tell me something I don't want to know," he said.

"Maybe," Steve said, and waited.

Clint leaned back on the bench and closed his eyes. "Oh, well," he said.

"I hate this," Steve said. "I hate that it happened, and I hate that I did it, but you know what? I try and I try, but I can't figure out a way to think that it was the wrong thing to do."

"You leaked it," Clint said.

"I leaked it," Steve said, and told him the rest of the story. When he was done, Clint cracked his knuckles and sailed the paper plate twenty-five feet into a trash can. Steve watched the long, sweeping arc, and thought: we all have roles to play. Then he remembered Fury, last week, saying that there were some things people didn't want to know.

"Why'd you tell me that?" Clint asked.

"Because you've seen people at their dirtiest," Steve said. "I—I need to know that I'm not one of those people. I did what was right, Clint. The Chitauri are out there. I killed one at Andrews. Andrews Air Force Base. And nobody wants to do what needs to be done."

"Oh, man," Clint said.

"What?"

"Nothing. Keep going," Clint said. "Tell me."

"When the people who should be trusted with these problems can't be trusted," Steve said, biting hard on every word, "what do you do? What does a soldier do?"

Clint shrugged. "I don't know. It's been a long time since I was any kind of soldier, really. Are you asking me about chain of command and manuals and that kind of crap?"

"No. Well, maybe. What I'm asking you," Steve said, "is what do you do when you know you have to do something wrong to do something right?"

Standing and stretching, Clint said, "Steve. I've heard this argument before. Usually when someone makes it, bad things happen not too long after."

"Sometimes they're right, though," Steve said. "The people who make those arguments."

Clint shrugged and started walking back toward Avenue A. "Sometimes. I guess you'll find out."

Steve sat there, thinking. Ten minutes later, he got a call from Admiral Garza.

Ten minutes after that, he was in a limousine heading up the FDR while Garza briefed him on a new threat.

"The Chitauri have gone after the Triskelion, Pym's lab, and they've infiltrated Andrews," Garza was saying. He leaned forward and tapped on the window that partitioned off the driver's seat. The window whirred open, and Garza said, "Go ahead and hop on the Harlem River Drive, Kyle. We'll just do a circle while Captain Rogers and I talk."

"Yes, sir," the driver said, and the window whirred shut again.

"Anyway," Garza went on, "we've deployed surveillance teams on individual Ultimates, as well as some other SHIELD assets, and we've seen a couple of things that we wanted to pass along. I don't guess I have to tell you, Steve, that you're the one we trust right now."

"Yes, sir," Steve said.

"So we're going to take a little ride. Oh, and before we get there, I should tell you that the first screeners are coming out of the factory tomorrow. SKR's done a hell of a job." Garza clapped Steve on the shoulder. "I hope you're not having conscience troubles, Captain. What you did was difficult, but the right thing often is."

Exactly what I was just telling Clint, Steve thought.

The limo cruised along the Harlem River and looped around onto the West Side Highway. "Who's buying the screeners, sir?" Steve asked.

"Well, there's a couple of markets. There's some interest from airports, of course, and the primary market for this tech will be existing places that have screeners and think of these as an upgrade. But I'm sure you've already figured that there's a more hush-hush angle on the enterprise as well. We've got CIA and NSA networks arranging for installations at various targets we think the Chitauri might be interested in. Military facilities, government offices, and so forth."

"What about the Triskelion?" Steve asked. "After what happened . . ."

"Already in process," Admiral Garza said. "In fact, I'd

be surprised if there wasn't a heap of those screeners already sitting around in the Triskelion's basement."

Steve nodded. "Good." Remembering the carnage on the loading dock, he felt a flush of the fury he'd experienced then. However Tony's tech got out into the world, if it choked off the Chitauri until every last one of them had been hunted down and killed and preserved in a jar, the methods were justified.

The limo turned off the West Side Highway and rolled through side streets before coming to a stop in front of a turn-of-the-century apartment building on 81st Street. Looking out through the windshield, Steve could see straight down to the bulk of the American Museum of Natural History, and beyond that into the cool green of Central Park. "We're here," Garza said. "What I'm about to show you is . . . well, you're going to have to use your best judgment."

Garza opened a small drawer set under the front seats and took out a rectangular case of polished metal. It looked like the kind of box used to ship handguns on airplanes. Opening it, Garza removed a small machine that bore a resemblance to a gun. It had a handle and a trigger, but where the muzzle of a gun would have been was what looked like a microphone head.

"We've had our own geniuses working over the Stark tech," Garza said. "This is a handheld version. It's only a prototype, but lab results are promising. Let's go see how it performs in the field."

They got out of the car, Admiral Garza stowing the

handheld sensor in his coat pocket. All at once Steve realized where they were: in the next block, around the corner, was the apartment Janet had moved into after Hank Pym's last assault. Steve had only been there twice; Janet was still clearing things out of the old place, and the two of them were busy enough that they usually met up for dinner or a night out. Thinking of Janet reminded Steve that he hadn't spoken to her in a while. He'd been distracted, the good soldier leaving his girl behind when he went off to fight a battle. But he needed to keep in mind that Janet was a soldier in this battle, too. Not an easy trick when you'd grown up in the nineteen-thirties.

Layered over his swirl of emotions about his relationship with Janet was a rising unease about why Admiral Garza had brought him here to show him how the new sensor worked. Reflexively Steve began scanning the surroundings for things that could be used as weapons. Most trash can lids nowadays were plastic.

Garza stopped at the corner and leaned in close to Steve. "How this works is, the lab boys have isolated a protein they think is the catalyst for the Chitauri ability to change shape. There's nothing like it in any human species, and this little toy is specifically designed to recognize and discard results that match up with terrestrial species that can mutate or regenerate. So it's not going to freak out if it runs across frog DNA, or a sign that a skink somewhere is regrowing its tail. Watch." He took the sensor out of his pocket and swept it in a semicircle on the corner. Passersby glanced over and then kept walking; this was New York, after all.

"Nothing," Garza said. "Right?"

Steve looked at the sensor. "I don't know, sir. What does it do when it gets a hit?"

"We've designed it for a quiet response, so a possible subject won't immediately know he's been tagged," Garza said. He started walking toward Janet's building, and Steve felt a rush of adrenaline start to flow through him. "When you see a little green light go on, right here, that's a hit." He pointed to a small LED display about where the hammer on a gun would be.

"Admiral Garza," Steve said. "It's not an accident that we're walking toward Janet's building, is it?"

Garza looked grim. "I'm afraid not, Captain. We've tagged one bogey around here. It's been disposed of, but I'm guessing it wasn't working alone." They had reached the building's front steps. "Look at this," Garza said. He pointed the sensor at the front door, near the knob. The little green light glowed.

Dear God, Steve thought. Had they gotten in?

"That's the one we took out," Admiral Garza said. "We swept the area afterward, and traced it back to a bus stop over on Central Park West. We're still running down the bus."

Steve had his phone out to call Janet, but Admiral Garza stopped him. "We're keeping a close eye on her, son. Right now she's at the Triskelion lab. I just wanted to bring you into the loop on this."

Realizing he'd been holding his breath, Steve sighed. "I appreciate it, Admiral. Can we get more of those made? SHIELD sure could put them to good use."

"I'll see what we can do," Admiral Garza said. They turned away from the door and went back down the steps, Garza a step ahead of Steve. Right as Garza put a foot on the sidewalk, he said, "Captain."

The light on the sensor was on. Steve looked up and down the street. There were no pedestrians on the block. Every nerve in his body on high alert, he watched Garza sweep the sensor out toward the street; the light went off. When Garza turned the sensor back toward the building, it came on again, well before it was pointed near the doorknob.

Around the south side of the building was a narrow breezeway that ended in an eight-foot concrete wall. New York City was notoriously without alleyways, but here and there quirks of gas-main placement or lot shape had left these kinds of gaps. Steve and Admiral Garza moved slowly down the breezeway, Garza moving the sensor in a slow arc. "Right there," Garza said softly, as the sensor's light went on. He pointed at a metal grille covering a basement window, and went to the next grille. "Here, too."

As the words left Admiral Garza's mouth, another sound almost drowned them out. From the courtyard behind the building, Steve heard the unmistakable rusty groan of a fire-escape ladder being dragged down to vertical. Before Garza could say another word, Steve had cleared the wall with a running jump, using his hands to pivot on the top of the wall so he landed beyond a row of flower pots against the inside. The world slowed and dilated into combat time, and on the second-floor landing of the fire escape he saw a human form just taking its first step up toward the third floor.

Janet's floor.

20

STEVE CAUGHT THE CHITAURI BEFORE IT HAD gotten to the third-floor landing by vaulting up from the second floor and driving the alien down under his weight. "Ah, Jesus, man! Okay!" the Chitauri said. Its voice was muffled from Steve's forearm mashing its face into the iron stairs.

"They must send you to acting school," Steve said. He turned the Chitauri over and pinned it on its back. It looked like a kid, maybe nineteen years old, Puerto Rican if the T-shirt of the Virgin Mary was anything to go by. Leaning in close and putting his full weight on the Chitauri's collarbones, Steve growled, "Who'd you kill to take this form? What was his name? Did he have a family?"

"I don't know what you're talking about, man," the Chitauri said. "You want my name? It's Eddie Guzman. You a cop? Arrest me, then, fine, okay, but let me get up." Some of the tension went out of its body.

"One chance," Steve said, not because he was uncertain but because he wanted to learn something about this adversary. When you could look your enemy in the eye before you killed him, you could learn something about the next time you would have to fight.

"One chance what?" the Chitauri said.

"Live or die," Steve said. "Which floor were you headed for?"

Something changed around its eyes. "Third floor," it said, and spat in Steve's face.

He blinked reflexively—not even the super-soldier serum could eliminate that response—but the Chitauri's saliva was already in his eyes, and they burned like they were going to melt out of his head. The Chitauri twisted out from under him. Steve took a blind swing at it, and connected, but he could barely see, and he felt the fire escape tremble as the Chitauri jumped. Swiping at his eyes, he saw as if through a hundred feet of water. The alien was on the ground and running.

Steve was about to jump after it, but with its head start . . . wait. He looked up, at the cat's cradle of phone and cable lines strung from a line of telephone poles to the buildings on both sides. Good thing they haven't gotten around to putting all of them underground yet, he thought, as the geometry did itself in his head. Steve jumped up and caught the cable-TV line going into the fourth-floor apartment, jerking it out of the wall box and swinging down and across the courtyard like Tarzan. The pain in his eyes wasn't going away, but through their watering he could see the Chitauri had already gotten to a high brick wall that divided the courtyard from a basketball court on the other side. In the three or four seconds it took Steve to cover the length of the courtyard, the Chitauri had already gotten its hands on top of the wall.

Steve hit the Chitauri square in the back with both feet, feeling its spine crack in the split second before his momentum crushed it into the brick wall. Letting go of the cable, Steve got the Chitauri in a chokehold and broke its neck as they fell together into a tangle of morning glory and some kind of bamboo that lined most of the courtyard's interior. The Chitauri was dead before they hit the ground, but Steve made sure, holding its face pressed into the soft earth while his vision slowly cleared and the pain in his eye sockets lessened to a minor irritation. When the Chitauri hadn't moved for a full minute, Steve picked it up in a fireman's carry and walked back across the courtyard. He threw it over the wall into the breezeway and vaulted over after it.

"Dammit, Captain Rogers," Admiral Garza said, "you almost hit me with that thing."

"Sorry, Admiral," Steve said. He pinched his eyes shut for a second, then blinked away the last of the Chitauri's saliva. He was starting to feel normal again. "I didn't want to say too much out loud in case that little fracas drew some attention."

He looked around as he said it, and noticed Kyle, Garza's driver, standing sentinel at the head of the breezeway. On the concrete between them, the Chitauri was already starting to lose the cohesion of its human shape. "God Almighty, but they're hideous," Admiral Garza said. "What the hell happened to your eyes?"

Steve looked up from the body of the dead Chitauri. Ignoring Garza's question, he said, "Admiral Garza. Let me take this to General Fury. He'll do the right thing, sir, once he can really see what's happening."

"Are you sure of that, Captain?" Garza responded. "Seems to me that General Fury's had more than enough chances."

"Sir. You've said it, I've said it, General Fury has said it. Uniforms have to stick together. Request permission to inform General Fury and mobilize a SHIELD team to perform recovery."

Admiral Garza stowed the sensor and scratched at the back of his neck. "Reluctantly granted. But under no circumstances will you tell Fury about this sensor, and only if it is unavoidable will you inform him that I was present when this happened. Understood?"

"Understood, sir."

"I'll be in touch, Captain. I've got a feeling this whole

situation's about to come to a head." With that, Admiral Garza walked back down the breezeway, Kyle falling in step with him as they turned the corner out of sight.

When Nick Fury heard that Steve had killed a disguised Chitauri in Janet Pym's backyard, his first thought was *God, I hope it wasn't just a burglar.* The way Steve had been acting lately, it wasn't impossible that he could have gone off half-cocked. Between his worry about that and Thor's tendency to see Loki everywhere, Nick was starting to get jumpy himself. Pretty soon he'd be seeing Viet Cong lying in wait for him at the grocery store.

But he got his ass to the Upper West Side so he could manage the recovery team, and he let Janet know that she probably shouldn't go home until all the loose ends related to this particular incident had been cleared up.

"Fine," she said archly. "The way you want reports every five minutes, I'll never be able to go home again anyway."

"You're welcome to return to the private sector, Miz Pym," Fury said, and hung up. He was going to have to do something about her and Cap, who shouldn't have had to be told about why you didn't fraternize with comrades. That was a conversation he wasn't looking forward to having. *I would be a much happier man,* Fury reflected, *if the members of my team did not have emotions. Maybe Janet and Bruce can build that into the next generation of super-soldiers.*

Janet called him back thirty seconds later. "Don't ever call me Pym again," she said, and hung up on him.

Fury chuckled to himself about that all the way to the scene. By the time he got there, NYPD had showed up to see why a big van and a bunch of people in bio-hazard suits were cluttering up the sidewalk. Fury gave them the old national-security spiel, and they took it with their usual lack of grace, and then he found Steve down at the end of a narrow walkway between two apartment buildings. The recovery team had already bagged and removed the body, and was now sterilizing the area. A SHIELD field medic was washing Steve's eyes out with saline solution.

"You okay there, soldier?" Fury asked.

Steve wiped away the solution that had run down his cheeks. "Just about, sir. The Chitauri spat in my eyes. Stung some for a while."

"Doc, take Captain Rogers and run a full workup on him," Fury said. "Head to toe. We need to make sure all he's got is red eyes."

"I'm fine, General," Steve protested.

"You look fine and you sound fine," Fury agreed. "But we're both going to leave it up to the docs to decide whether you are fine. Can we agree on that?"

Steve didn't look happy about it, but he started to walk back toward the street with the medic. "And call your girlfriend," Fury said as he passed.

"She's not my girlfriend," Steve said.

"Oh no?"

Steve turned to face Nick. "General," he said. "With all due respect, I would like to keep my private life private."

Nick looked him in the eye for a long moment, and then said, "I think the doctors can wait a minute. Let's you and I have a talk."

He walked Steve to the van, then stuck his head in and told the two techs prepping the dead Chitauri for the drive to walk around the block. When they were gone, Fury climbed into the back of the van and motioned for Steve to shut the doors behind them.

"All right," he said. "I hate pep talks, so this isn't going to be one. You want to say something to me about Tony's inventions, or Beltway bullshit, or anything else, now's the time. I'm sick and goddamn tired of having to wonder what's going on in your head all the time. You're not suited to keeping secrets, Cap. Don't ever play poker for money."

Steve was looking down at the floor while Nick delivered his short speech, and he kept looking at the floor long enough that Nick almost started talking again. But then Steve said, "General, I don't like feeling as if we're not doing everything we could."

"You don't think we are?"

"No, sir. I don't."

"You think we should have gone ahead and developed Tony's tech, and just used it ourselves?"

Another long pause, during which Nick could actually see Steve wrestling with something that he wanted to say but couldn't quite bring himself to. Then Captain America looked Nick in the eye and said, "I'm having a hard time with that, yeah."

"Remember last week, when you told me there were some things people didn't want to know? Boogeymen under the bed, I think you said. Well, this is what you were talking about. Then you told me that in America, we don't keep people scared. And so what do you do? You go on TV and stand there while people talk about terrorist attacks." Fury paused to consider exactly what he was going to say next. "I've given you a lot of rope, Cap, but the last thing in the world—literally—we need right now is dissent inside the team."

Steve nodded. "Yes, sir," he said, but he wasn't looking Nick in the eye anymore, and Nick could see him trying not to say something again.

"And we don't need secrets, either," Nick said. "So why don't you just tell me whatever it is that's on your mind, and we'll get it all out in the open and see where we stand?"

Red-eyed and obviously miserable, Steve looked up at Nick again and said, "I can't do that, sir."

Nick held the look for a long time. Then he stood up, or at least as much as he could inside the van, and put a hand on the door latch. "Then you and I are going to have a problem down the road, Captain." Pushing the door open, he said, "I think it's time for you to go to the doctor."

21

Status Report

Assimilated assets in place report that publicized screening technology manufactured by <SKR TechEnt> is being installed at the following locations:

Military facilities
<White House> and other national political offices in <Washington, D.C.>
Federal, state, and county government buildings
Airports served by commercial passenger carriers

In the majority of cases, new screeners replace existing screeners, lessening added inconvenience to human populations. <Steve Rogers> appears less willing to provide a popular face as political cover for a possibly unpopular security initiative; reconsideration of asset investment in cultural production has produced the conclusion that such investment is unwise and unlikely to yield desired rewards. Assets will monitor progress of security installations and continue to provide information regarding future installations. Progress of the human ordering project is partially keyed to locations at which this technology is in place. Comprehensive intelligence in this regard, driven by assimilated assets in place, is deemed critical to mission success.

Concern exists over scientific advances made by <Henry Pym> involving control and management of large numbers of arthropods, order <Hymenoptera>. Proposals to retard development of Pym's project are under consideration.

Mission Report

Operation located at and near residence of <Janet Pym> achieved planned goals. Sequential loss of assets in place is deemed likely to yield desired results with respect to actions of <Steve Rogers> and other members of the <Ultimates>. Mission timeline:

-.001944 solar year: Assessment of security and surveillance obstacles surrounding <Janet Pym>.

-.010837 solar year: Formulation of mission parameters and selection of necessary assets.

-.004107 solar year: Intentional loss of first asset due to interception by <Esteban Garza>.

22

THAT NIGHT, AFTER THE MEDICOS FINALLY DE-
termined he wasn't a threat to the survival of the
human race, Steve called Bucky. He hadn't seen his
old buddy since Bucky had gotten out of the hospital,
and even though Bucky was home, he clearly didn't
have much time left on this Earth. There were no
friends like old friends, and Steve wasn't going to let
his friendship with Bucky lapse now. It turned out
that Bucky was having a nephew of his over for dinner, but he was anxious to see Steve. "Hey, if there's
enough for four, there's enough for five," he said.
"Come on over."

So Steve did, and found when he got there that in addition to Bucky's nephew Grant and his wife Sharon, there was a fifth guest: an immense Newfoundland dog named Hobbes. Steve had never been much of a dog person, growing up in a small apartment and then shipping off into the Army, and he'd never even seen a Newfoundland before. Hobbes was some dog. Clumsy, overbearing, but so friendly at the same time that you had a hard time holding it against him when he knocked over your drink or drooled on your pants. Something about having a dog around also cleared away the hovering sense of doom about Bucky's cancer. Bucky looked awful; he'd never been a big man, and now he looked so wispy that Steve could have done wrist curls with him even before the super-soldier program came along. Dinner was simple but hearty, just like Bucky had always liked it: meat loaf, mashed potatoes, green beans. Sitting there with his best friend, ex-girlfriend, and a young married couple with a happily rambunctious dog, Steve longed for a life he was never going to have. And on the heels of that longing, he renewed his commitment to protecting those people who could have hearth and home and family. And dog, he added as Hobbes thumped his muzzle against Steve's elbow.

"Hobbes," Grant admonished. "Go lie down."

Hobbes did, but he didn't stay lying down for long. Bouncing to his feet again, he came over and sat next to Steve, tail swishing like a dust mop across the wood floor at the edge of the dining room rug. His head was a foot higher than the dinner table.

"He's decided you're the weak link, Steve," Grant said. "Don't feed him, or you're going to have to take him home."

"I don't think he'd like it," Steve said. "He'd hardly be able to turn around in my living room."

Bucky coughed, and everyone fell silent. When someone as sick as Bucky sounded sick, even for a moment, it seemed that everyone else stopped existing until they figured out whether Bucky was going to keel over dead. This time he didn't, though. When he was done coughing, he said, "What I was going to say is, how come you don't get a bigger place, Steve? God knows you could afford it."

"What, so I can have a giant dog? Nah. I like living where I grew up. Reminds me of where I came from and where I am now, both at the same time. Everything's kind of . . ." Steve trailed off, then shrugged. "I like it where I am."

Hobbes woofed, as politely as a dog of his size and ebullience was able. "Go lie down," Grant ordered him again, and again Hobbes did. This time he left them alone long enough that they got back into conversation, mostly about Grant's work—he was a midlevel executive with a mutual fund specializing in sustainable industries—and Bucky's recent hospital spell. Bucky was in surprisingly good humor for a man measuring his life expectancy in weeks; he was one of those people who refuse to let knowledge of their coming death interfere with their enjoyment of what life they have remaining. "Hell," he said a few times during the course of the meal, "I'm gonna die, but that's no excuse to get everyone else all depressed."

He'd just said it for the third time when Hobbes jumped up and turned quickly around twice, snuffling at the floor, before sitting down and gnawing at one of his hind legs. "I told you he needs a bath, Grant," Sharon said.

Hobbes yelped and stood up again. Steve looked back over at him.

"What the hell's gotten into your dog?" Bucky wanted to know. He was peering at Hobbes from his seat all the way at the other end of the table.

Grant got up and went over to Hobbes, who was now chewing on one of his front paws. "Hey, buddy," he said. "What the matter, fella?" He put his hand on Hobbes's head . . . and Hobbes growled.

"Whoa," Grant said, pulling his hand back. "What's that all about?"

He squatted down next to Hobbes and reached for Hobbes's paw. At that moment Steve saw, coming out from the heating vent in the corner where Hobbes had been curled up, a line of big black ants. "Grant," he said, standing up and pushing his chair back, "take a step back, there, okay?"

Grant looked up. "What are you talking about? Something's really bugging him."

"Grant," Steve said again. Hobbes growled.

"Easy, buddy," Grant said, and Hobbes looked up at

Steve. Should have known, Steve thought. If they can take the form of a person, why not a dog?

At that moment, Hobbes lunged and seized Grant's throat in his jaws. Sharon screamed and jumped out of her chair, knocking over her wine glass. Grant got both of his hands into the ruff around Hobbes's neck and tried to push him off. Steve was already reaching for the dog—no, the Chitauri masquerading as a dog—and Hobbes gave Grant a single hard shake. A warning. Grant gurgled and stopped trying to push Hobbes away.

Steve stood where he was. "You got bigger problems than me, bucko," he said. "How many more ants are going to come through that grate? I hear those bullet ants have a sting like a gunshot wound. How many can you take?"

Hobbes growled, and kept its eyes locked on Steve. He hadn't been lying about the ants. A thick column of them flowed up through the vent and disappeared into the dog's thick fur. Won't be long, Steve thought.

"Ants?" Bucky said. "Steve, what did you say about ants?"

"Long story, Bucky," Steve said. Hobbes let out a long moan and started to tremble. He was drooling on Grant's neck, thick saliva running down into the collar of Grant's shirt. One of his eyes twitched shut, and when it opened again, Steve was looking into the slit pupil of a Chitauri. Grant gasped, and blood threaded the saliva on his neck. Then the Chitauri began to transform in earnest. Hobbes threw himself up onto his hind legs, with a crack of rearranging joints, and great swathes of his skin and fur peeled away to reveal scales. Grant scrabbled backward on the floor away from this sudden monster, and Steve threw himself at it. There was pandemonium in the dining room as Sharon ran to help Grant get up off the floor and Gail pulled Bucky's wheelchair away from the table and backed up with it into the kitchen.

The Chitauri, which in mid-transformation looked kind of like a grizzly bear given an infusion of dinosaur DNA, roared as it grappled with Steve, and its jaws snapped near his ear. "Not a spitter like your friend was yesterday," Steve said, then grunted as it raked claws down his left side. They wrestled into the corner, slamming hard into the wainscoted wall. The impact knocked pictures to the floor all over the room. Steve was landing good hard shots on it, but the Chitauri was giving as good as it got—and as an added complication, dots of intense agony started to appear up and down Steve's arms and legs as the bullet ants, overwhelmed by being thrown around and crushed in the fight, started stinging everything they could get a stinger on. Most of those stings hit the Chitauri, which was losing progressively more of the dog shape, but enough of them got Steve for him to feel like he was skinny-dipping in a pool of acid. "You brought some unwanted guests," Steve grunted as the two combatants crashed through the side table holding the serving dishes with the rest of the night's dinner. Now he was covered in gravy and mashed potatoes as well as cuts, bruises and ant bites. "Enough already," he said. "Nobody starts a food fight and brings bugs to Bucky's house. You're going to have to go."

Jaws agape, the Chitauri slipped out of Steve's hold and bit down on his shoulder. The pain made Steve forget all about the ants. When the alien reared back for another bite, Steve caught one of its jaws in each hand. "Didn't you ever see *King Kong*?" he said. "That big mouth is what gets you lizards in trouble."

He pulled hard. Something cracked. He pulled again, and felt the flesh in his bitten shoulder tear, which made him angrier. The Chitauri's tail, suddenly regrown, snapped out of nowhere and pounded him on the side of the head, but Steve kept his grip. One, two, *heave* . . . and he felt something give in the alien's skull, its lower jaw breaking loose and twisting as Steve shoved it back into the Chitauri's throat. Its tail lashed furiously, and its claws left deep bloody furrows in Steve's forearms, but it was already getting weaker, and when he gave the broken jawbone another shove into its neck he felt something give way again and it went limp in his hands.

"Jesus, Steve," Grant said after a long silence. "That was my dog."

"That hasn't been your dog for a long time, Grant," Steve said. He let the dead Chitauri fall to the floor. "I'm sorry."

"But what is it?" Sharon asked.

Steve looked at her. "An enemy. That's all I can tell you. It's not the only one out there. They must have used Hobbes as a way to get close to me." He looked back down at the dead Chitauri, which was swarming with ants. Doctor Pym, he thought, we're going to need to have a talk.

"It has ants all over it," Grant said in the oddly child-like voice of someone slipping into shock.

"I know it does. They'll go away in a minute," Steve said. "Do you two mind going in the other room? I need to make a phone call."

"Okay," Sharon said. She helped Grant to his feet and the two of them went into the kitchen. Steve got his cell phone out and was about to call General Fury when Gail came back in from the kitchen.

"Steve," she said. He caught a slight tremor in her voice, and saw that she was struggling to keep her composure. "I think we need to get Bucky to a doctor."

Steve snapped his phone shut. "Okay, call an ambulance right now. I need to go outside for one second, but I'll be right back."

He burst out onto Bucky's front stoop and looked up and down the street. Pym's headset didn't have much range, he knew that; it shouldn't be too hard to figure out where the good doctor was. Tomorrow morning was scheduled street sweeping in this part of Brooklyn, and the opposite side of the street was empty except for a single old Chevy Monte Carlo near the corner to the right. Just around the corner from it was a police car. The near side of the street was bumper to bumper except for the standard gap around the block's fire hydrant.

Steve took a closer look at the Monte Carlo. Someone was leaning up against the window. Then that someone took a step back and leveled a gun at whoever was in the car, and Steve was tearing across the street shouting at the top of his lungs for Hank to get down.

23

GOT 'EM, HANK THOUGHT.

He'd run ant survey missions around all of his teammates . . . well, former teammates . . . and come up empty every time. Either the intensity of ambient odors in New York was overwhelming the ants' ability to isolate the Chitauri signature, or the aliens were being more clever than they usually were about disguising their presence.

Or they were following him and making sure that if he was around, they kept their distance. Hank preferred not to think about that possibility, since it led in too many negative directions. If they were watching him, that meant they were figuring out how he was controlling the ants—although they might well already know that from whatever reports they'd received from Greg. Also, if keeping tabs on Hank Pym was one of the Chitauri's ongoing tasks, then he wasn't going to be able to swoop in and rescue anyone with his millions of myrmidons, and Hank wasn't about to lie to himself. A big part of the reason for his commitment to this project was the prospect of being accepted back into the team. If there was any possibility of that, any possibility at all, he was willing to walk around with a target on his back for a while.

And now he'd struck gold. Steve Rogers might think I'm a gutless punk, Hank thought, but he can't deny that I just saved the lives of his friend and the shriveled old version of the woman he loved. Eventually that dog would have taken his true form and invited some friends over for a little Bucky and Gail buffet (although in Bucky's case, being eaten by a Chitauri would probably be an easier way to go than slowly being consumed by cancer). Now, because of Hank, they were safe, and Captain America would have to look him in the eye and say thanks.

He sent the recall command to the ants. On the minicameras he had rigged to a few of them, he could tell that they were wasting their stings on a dead alien, and he could also tell that no one had been killed. They owe me, Hank thought. I screwed up, but they owe me, and they had no right to cut me off like that.

The fact that Janet wouldn't speak to him was less of

a bother. She'd gone through those times before, and she'd probably go through them again. She always came back sooner or later. They were meant for each other.

Any minute now, Fury would show up, Hank was thinking. One more cleanup, one more Chitauri in a jar somewhere in the Triskelion. It was getting repetitious, almost to the point where Hank had entertained the notion that the Chitauri were leading them along. Maybe they were sacrificing one of their number every so often to see how SHIELD reacted, or to cement the impression that they were using particular tactics . . . while planning something else? Something completely different? If so, what? Full-scale assault hadn't worked out for them last time.

There was a sharp tap on his car window. Hank pulled off the headset and looked. It was a cop. He rolled down the window.

"What the hell is that on your head?" the cop asked.

"It's . . . well, it's kind of hard to explain."

"Ah," the cop said. "Would you be able to explain better if you stepped out of the car?"

"I don't think that's necessary, officer," Hank said. "It's not against the law to sit in your car."

"No, Dr. Pym, it isn't," the cop said. "But under the circumstances, it isn't smart, either." Taking a step back from the car, the cop drew his gun. Hank heard a shout from across the street—someone calling his name?— and then the world lit up in flashes from the muzzle of the gun.

• • •

There was someone buzzing around his ear, a tiny man who kept saying *Hank, Hank, get down, get down.* And another little man, a fly with a man's voice, saying, *Doctor Pym, we need you to return to your normal size.*

Return to your normal size.

This is my normal size, he wanted to say. I'm bigger than you, bigger than your judgments, my work is bigger than yours. My other size is like Janet when she's small, giant ambitions and giant personality and giant problems crushed and squeezed down into a size that disguises their true size. This is me, this is me. I have discovered my true size.

He tried to get up, and heard the groan and squeal of deforming metal. Something stabbed him under the armpit, and he was having trouble getting a breath.

Return to your normal size.

No, you fool, he thought. Then I will be small and the wounds will be huge. Then my body will be small and my pain will be huge. Then I will no longer be bigger than Janet, who is tiny tiny tiny and so full of anger that maybe I deserve.

These tiny people, with their bullets and their judgments, no bigger than ants. The ants stung, and it hurt like bullets. Janet, he said. Janet. I drove all night to prove this. I knew it. I knew it. And they knew I knew it, and their bullets sting like ants.

Doctor Pym. This is Nick Fury. If you can hear me, blink twice.

So this is what it takes to get Nick to talk to me again, Hank thought. He blinked. But after the second time, he couldn't open his eyes again.

Get down, get down . . .

Snafu after snafu after snafu, thought Nick Fury. I got a dog who was a Chitauri, and four civilians who saw it lose coherence. I got a cop who was a Chitauri, and a whole goddamn precinct and department bureaucracy who didn't see it lose coherence but who aren't very goddamn happy about SHIELD stepping in and making the body disappear. Granted, two of those four civilians knew about Steve, so they weren't too surprised to find out that there are other boogeymen under the bed. And Bucky wasn't long for the world anyway, so no security problem there. But Grant and Sharon, they were already demanding to know everything about everything, to the point that Nick was beginning to consider sending them on a little vacation until they could reach some kind of understanding about the wisdom of filing lawsuits against the government because their dog was absorbed by an alien infiltrator.

I got one team member in a state of emotional flux because his best and oldest friend suffered some kind of cardiac event when the Chitauri started to lose coherence.

I got one ex–team member in intensive care with four holes in him, who is probably only alive because when he grew, his body put itself back together on the way from Lilliputian to Brobdingnagian.

I got a commanding officer who is in the situation of having an ex–team member in intensive care because that team member knowingly put himself in danger to prove his worth to the members of his former team.

In other words, Doctor Henry Pym is stuck full of tubes because I kicked him out of the Ultimates, Nick thought. And between Bucky and whatever he's doing that involves SKR and someone in Washington he won't tell me about, Steve is about at the end of his rope. And there are Chitauri everywhere, apparently, and Pym's ants look like they're doing a lot better finding them than this fancy tech that somehow was leaked by someone within SHIELD who might or might not occasionally wear a suit with an American-flag theme.

The only thing that had gone right was the fact that Pym had gotten the dog before the Chitauri cop had gotten him. Also Nick was thanking his lucky stars that at least they'd gotten Pym to shrink back to normal size before civilian response teams arrived. The Monte Carlo that Pym had apparently stolen in Skokie, Illinois, now looked like it had been carrying a car bomb, but thanks to the street-sweeping schedule there were no other damaged cars . . . although there were going to be some fence and stoop repairs billed to SHIELD through one of Tony's shell contracting companies.

One problem at a time, Nick told himself.

"Captain Rogers," he said when he saw Steve hang up his phone. "What's the word on Bucky?"

Steve's face was grim. "They say he's still in some trouble, General. He's weak enough from the cancer that they can't treat the heart condition as aggressively as they'd like to, or that's what I understand from the medicalese I keep hearing."

"He's getting the best care he can get," Nick said, which was true. Cardiac care in New York City was about as good as it could be, and Nick had pulled SHIELD strings to get a couple of top-flight military cardiac specialists on Bucky's case.

"General Fury," Steve said. "I waited at least five minutes to call an ambulance because I was taking care of the Chitauri that shot Doctor Pym. If that lag made a difference, I won't be able to live with myself."

"You were saving Pym's life," Nick said, and could hear the answer even before Steve's mouth formed the words.

"That's not a good trade."

"Captain Rogers," Nick said. "I can't order you to stop being so damn self-righteous, or so damn stubborn. But I can suggest it. And I can order you, for the second time today, to take your Chitauri-chewed self to a doctor and get stitched up and checked out. You can't do Bucky any good, and you can't do Pym any good, but you can do the team and this country some good by staying in fighting trim. Now. Go to the doctor. Do not pass Go, do not collect two hundred dollars."

Nick lit a cigar. Steve gazed at Bucky's house.

"Captain Rogers," Nick said. "Go."

Steve went, climbing into a waiting SHIELD limo. The recovery team inside Bucky's house had just finished removing the alien and sterilizing the dining room. Their van pulled away after taking down the SHIELD scene perimeter . . . which left Nick alone to deal with the NYPD investigator, Glenn Owens, who had displayed what even Nick had to credit as superhuman patience while the SHIELD processing had taken place.

"General," Owens said when the white van had pulled around the corner. "I don't know why I'm the only guy here. You want to clue me in to the game?"

Nick gnawed on his cigar and grinned. "'Fraid I can't tell you a thing about why your bosses do what they do," he said. "I have a hard enough time with mine."

"See, the thing is, there should be brass, media relations, union suits, the works," Owens said. "If I didn't know better, I'd think you had something to do with the situation, is all I'm saying."

"Detective, I had a conversation with a man in a similar position to yours out in Illinois a few days ago." Fury's cigar was already going out. He puffed it back to life. "He thought I could do this, and I could do that. The truth is, I go through every day hoping for cooperation from people just like you. I don't get it, my job is that much harder; but there's no good reason for you to give it to me, since I can't give you a good reason."

Owens shrugged. "Have it your way. So tell me again where the body of Patrolman Victor Elizondo is?"

"Patrolman Elizondo's remains are under examination at a federal laboratory for security reasons," Nick said.

"Is that what you're going to say at a press conference?"

"Nope," Nick said. "Because if this gets to the press conference stage, I will already know that I can't hope for any cooperation from you. At a press conference, all you get from Nick Fury is no comment. I can no-comment for an hour straight."

"Understand my position here, General. I catch a case of a cop down, I show up, and there's no team in place, there's no media, there's no nothing. Tomorrow morning I'm going to have to brief the patrolmen's union. What do I tell them? Elizondo had four kids and a wife. What do I tell them?"

Suddenly Nick was tired of the game. "You want to know the truth, Owens?"

Owens didn't say anything.

"Do you?" Nick asked again. "If you want the plain truth, I will tell you. Do you want it?"

After a pause, Owens said, "Yeah, I do."

"Okay. At some point, probably in the last month or so, Victor Elizondo was killed by a race of aliens who can assume the shapes of humans. After they killed him, one of them ate him and took his form. That alien probably went and did regular cop work, came home to his kids, went to bed with his wife, until he got an order from his higher-ups. That order was to track and take out a member of my team." Nick left out the question of Pym's status with respect to the Ultimates; no point in muddying the waters. "Then tonight, he shot my guy four times, and then Captain America killed him. That's the plain truth, as plain as I can make it. I don't care if you believe it or not. And I don't care if you're recording it, because everywhere I go I am shadowed by people whose job it is to make sure that nothing I say or do is recorded by people who should not record it. Now, Detective Owens. Are you glad you have the truth?"

Owens stood for a long time looking up and down the street, taking in the exploded car, the crumpled wrought-iron fences, the broken concrete and masonry on various stoops and stairs. He looked at Bucky's house, dark and empty. He looked at the spot where Patrolman Victor Elizondo had died at the hands of Captain America. "General Fury," he said. "I would like it very much if you could keep me updated as this case progresses. Patrolman Elizondo's family and colleagues deserve a full accounting of the events surrounding his murder."

"Can do, Detective Owens," Nick said, and toasted the detective with his cigar as Owens went back to his car and drove away.

24

SHE KNEW SHE SHOULDN'T DO IT, BUT SHE couldn't not do it, so Janet found herself standing outside the door of Hank's hospital room at Mount Sinai. And she was 110 percent sure she shouldn't have done it when the first person she saw coming up the hallway toward her was Steve. When he caught sight of her, he stiffened a little, but his voice stayed level. "Have you heard how he's doing?"

"I haven't been in, and there's no doctors around that I can see," she said. "But this isn't intensive care, so I guess that's good."

"Yeah," he said, looking around. "I was downstairs looking in on Bucky, and thought I'd . . . you know."

"Softie," she said. Something changed in his face, and she was sorry she'd done it. "Come on, Steve," she said. "You know I'm just kidding."

"It's not a kidding kind of situation," he said.

"I think that's really up to me, isn't it?" she said. "I mean, since I'm still married to him and all."

He took that in for a beat and then said, "Okay. I guess we should talk later."

Janet let him get halfway to the bank of elevators before she said, "Steve. Wait a minute." Steve didn't turn around, but he stopped walking. When she caught up to him, she said, "Maybe we could both use a drink or something away from all of this. How does that sound?"

In the elevator, he was quiet until just before they reached the ground floor. Then he said, "There is no away from all this. You know that. What did you really mean?"

"I meant not here," Janet said. The doors opened and they walked through the maze of hallways and out the emergency room doors. It was a warm night, and they crossed Fifth Avenue to walk on the park side. Steve suggested a walk through the park, but Janet, envisioning him taking off to collar a couple of muggers, wanted to stay on the street. So they ran the gauntlet of hot-dog stands and T-shirt hawkers, cheesy portrait cartoonists and tourists dazed from Museum Mile. Janet wished any of the museums were open, but it was after midnight. Instead she decided on ice cream. Steve didn't want any, so she walked into the first place she saw, got a huge cup of pralines and cream, and savored it while they kept south. When they passed the great granite pile of the Met, it occurred to her that if she was going to go home, she'd need to turn right pretty soon unless she wanted to walk all the way around the park or take a cab. "Hey, Captain America," she said, not caring if he got the wrong impression, "walk me past Belvedere Castle on my way home."

"Yes, ma'am," Steve said, which entitled her to get furious at him for calling her ma'am, and for a little while things were light and easy and okay again.

Then, about the time they were actually passing Belvedere Castle, she screwed it all up again. "I wonder if he's really changed," she said, after a silence had passed between her and Steve.

"You're kidding," Steve said.

"I'm not," she said. "People do change."

"Janet, I'm an old-fashioned guy. I come from a time when nobody would have cared if Pym changed because everyone would have accepted what he did. And even I know he's not going to change. He attacked you with a horde of ants, for Pete's sake."

"And how many lives did he save by finding out about that dog, Steve?"

"What does that have to do with what he did to you?" Steve was trying not to shout, but the way he rounded on her—plus the fact that he stood a foot taller than she did and outweighed her by at least a hundred pounds—made people stop and look.

"It has to do," she said icily, "with the fact that as much as you want to reduce him to a cartoon, he's an actual human being. He does good things and bad things, and I made a choice a long time ago to acknowledge that if I wanted him around, I'd have to take both. Now, the other thing is that I never said I was going back to him. I never said I was not going to divorce him. I never even said I wanted him back on the team. I just wondered if he had really changed."

Janet started walking again. After a beat, she saw out of the corner of her eye that Steve was coming along. "Well, do you?" he asked.

"Do I what?"

"Want him back on the team."

"No, I don't," she said. "But I think it's a little smug of everyone else to have made that decision without even considering what I wanted. What if I thought that Hank would be useful to the team even if every time I looked at him I wanted him to die? Hey, he does great things in the lab. You big men got so caught up in protecting the little woman that you decided to shoot a really promising research initiative in the foot. And you know what? I've had it with being protected."

She stomped off again, and again she watched Steve come after her. This time he came up next to her and put a hand on her shoulder. Instantaneously Janet swore to herself that if he tried to pull on her or spin her around, she was going to sting him until he couldn't see straight, but all he did was pace her with a hand resting lightly on her shoulder. "Take your hand off me," she said anyway.

Steve did, and because he did, Janet stopped. "In the end, it doesn't matter what I feel for him or don't feel for him," she said. "What matters is the Chitauri, and it drives me frankly batshit that some ridiculous leftover chivalry has you and Nick cutting someone out of the team who could make a difference. They want to kill us, Steve, and if they can't kill us, they want to reduce us to zombies. Do you really want to moralize about spousal abuse when the stakes are that high?"

They were across the park, waiting for the light to change at 81st Street and Central Park West because Steve would never jaywalk. The Museum of Natural History—another great granite pile—loomed just to the south. Janet wanted to go in there, too, but now it was one o'clock in the morning and she was close to home, and it was time just to have a glass of wine and go to bed before she got up and had to bathe in Bruce Banner's self-pity for another day while looking for a way to create the latest generation of augmented soldiers like Steve Rogers.

What a job, she thought. Imagine the ad: *Challenging work environment, chance to make a real difference.*

While she was woolgathering, Steve had been looking up at the buildings surrounding the park. "Please don't start telling me about how different it is now," Janet said.

"I wasn't going to," he said. "Although there sure

wasn't anything like that one." He pointed at the new Time Warner building on Columbus Circle.

Janet sighed. "What were you going to say, then?"

The light changed. Steve was quiet as they crossed, but as soon as they got to the sidewalk, he started talking. "When we beat the Chitauri, it's not going to be because some manic-depressive wife-beater with a Buck Rogers helmet on sics ants on them," he said. "It's going to be because human beings—American human beings—prove one more time that they're smarter and tougher and more willing to fight for what's right than interstellar shape-shifting geckos."

"He really gets to you, doesn't he?" Janet asked.

Steve stopped in mid-soliloquy. "Who? Pym?"

She laughed. "You can't even say his first name. Yes, I mean Hank. The fact that he exists drives you crazy."

"No. *Hank* is just loony tunes. A guy like that isn't worth going crazy over, since he's already there. What drives me crazy is that you, who aren't and should know better, are playing right into his games."

"Don't you dare," Janet said.

Steve looked at her like she'd slapped him. "Dare what?"

"Don't you tell me what I'm doing. You and all the rest of the manly men down at the Triskelion look at me like I'm a little girl who needs help learning to ride a two-wheeler. You think you know everything about me, and you walk around congratulating yourselves about how you protected me by getting rid of Hank.

Well, guess what? Maybe you need Hank. Maybe the world needs Hank. I sure as hell don't, but even I can see that anyone who's figured out a way to track the Chitauri belongs in the Triskelion instead of out in the suburbs of for-god's-sake Chicago."

"Ah," Steve said. "We need Hank for his ant gizmo."

"Yes, we do."

"Because he can track the Chitauri," Steve said.

"Yes."

"Come on," Steve said. "I want to show you something."

Ten minutes later they were standing at the dead end of the breezeway between Janet's building and the neighboring building to the south. Steve had a keychain flashlight, and he was using it to show Janet certain things on the ground near the wall. "Recognize this?" he said, holding the light over a series of discolorations on the concrete. No, they were marks.

She was looking at a series of faded evidence notations of the kind made by SHIELD post-operation investigation and recovery teams. One string of letters, repeated over and over, stuck out: CTT.

Chitauri tissue.

"One of them was here," Janet said softly. She looked up, to the third floor, where her small bathroom window looked out over the breezeway.

"Yeah. One of them was here. Two, actually. An armed-services black-ops team took one of them out, and the guy who runs it brought me back here to show me how it happened. He was also showing me a hand-held version of Tony's screener. It sniffs around and detects shed cells carrying Chitauri DNA." Steve pointed at the window grates, one after another. "The sniffer lit up there, and there." Then he pointed at the wall. "And there."

"Oh my God," Janet said.

"I caught it on the fire escape just below the third floor, and I killed it by the wall at the back of the courtyard." Steve's face was hard in the wash from the flashlight. "*Hank* wasn't here for any of that. I just thought you should know."

He started walking back toward the street. "I'll stand here and make sure you get inside safe."

"Steve," Janet said.

"I don't want to talk anymore," he said.

Janet looked at the notations for a long time. Then she found her keys and went around to the front door. "Steve," she said.

"Good night, Janet," Steve said.

She opened and closed the door. When she was inside, in her lobby in her new building unshadowed by memories or the presence of Hank, she leaned against the bank of mailboxes and said, in a voice barely above a whisper, "Steve. You don't get it at all. You're missing the point."

25

Status Report

Unplanned loss of assets has occurred in <New York City>. Further complications include the apparent reintegration of <Henry Pym> into the operational structure if not member circle of the <Ultimates>. Assessment of the <Pym> situation continues.

Assimilated nonhuman asset tasked with surveillance and infiltration of friends and associates of <Steve Rogers> lost .000456 solar year ago. Assimilated asset in <New York City Police Department> lost .000451 solar year ago after undertaking mission to track and eliminate <Henry Pym>. Events appear to have combined unfortunate timing and unanticipated improvisation on the part of human/augmented human opponents. Revisions to operational planning continue to incorporate this new information. Suggestions that <Henry Pym> deliberately put himself at risk to provoke response from <Steve Rogers> and other <Ultimates> seem to overestimate human capacity for risk assessment, as well as <Henry Pym>'s capacity for behavior in the mode of altruism. It is considered more likely that the operation of chance was decisive in this case.

Operations within media conglomerates proceed at a pace short of projections, and will be discontinued. Available broadcast technologies fail to meet necessary standards for proposed component of human ordering project. Abandoned initiatives involving application of psychoactive substances to municipal water supplies are undergoing renewed study, but prospects for implementation remain uncertain. More promising are assets and initiatives existing and developing in <Washington, D.C.>.

Assets within <Stark Industries> report technological advance bearing strong implications for success of human ordering project. Few details are currently available; investigation ongoing. Planning for countermeasures will continue on an expedited schedule, as necessary and possible given new information and changing circumstances in the field.

All assets are instructed to be watchful for the presence of invertebrate order <Hymenoptera>. If assimilated circumstances permit, assets should avoid locations commonly inhabited by <Hymenoptera>. If such avoidance is impossible, curtail the number and duration of visits to such locations. This directive is issued with full cognizance of <Hymenoptera>'s wide distribution and near ubiquity.

Efforts to degrade human capacity to control <Hymenoptera> are ongoing. Prospects of success impossible to determine at this time. Expenditure of assets is deemed highly probable in the event of a direct operation to degrade or eliminate <Pym-Hymenoptera> technology. In anticipation of this necessity, until extent of development of <Pym-Hymenoptera> technology is more fully understood, asset conservation will be prioritized.

Intelligence regarding imminent human/augmented attack, location <Saxtons River, Vermont>, should be considered unsubstantiated at this time. However, considering events of the previous .000456 solar year, assets in the area, or with operational connection to <Noofie Acres>, will proceed on maximal alert status.

26

ON THIS FINE SUMMER THURSDAY, THOR HAD been planning to attend a retreat organized by a new anti-globalization collective called CAREFIST. Instead he found himself in the bowels of the military-industrial beast called Triskelion, listening to Nick Fury expound on the latest developments in the Chitauri saga. We know how this is going to end, Thor thought. We'll run them to ground somewhere, and kill them; and then, sometime later, we'll find out that we didn't kill all of them, and we'll have to do it again.

Or, one of those times, fate will swing the other way, and the Chitauri will win.

The conference room—the same place where Tony had originally demonstrated his screener—was full. All of the Ultimates were present, including poor Banner via monitor. In addition, several tech-support staffers milled around in the back of the room tinkering with some kind of gadget that, Thor assumed, would be the centerpiece of a glamorous demonstration whenever Nick finished his speech. At least Thor had the good fortune to be sitting next to Clint, who was the only other member of the team, in Thor's opinion, with the right (which was to say, cynical) attitude toward the Ultimates and SHIELD as a whole. Perhaps it was because Clint had come out of the dirtiest of dirty worlds, deep-cover black ops. *We have both seen the worst behavior of human beings,* Thor thought. *He has been a slave of the globalist hegemony, and has killed for it; I have always fought against it. But we have both seen its worst excesses . . . and I have a little history that he does not.*

Nick stood near a display screen at the head of the conference table. "It looks like everything is about to come to a head, Chitauri-wise," he was saying. "We have new technologies for identifying and tracking them, and they know it. As a result, they're becoming more aggressive. The actions of Doctor Hank Pym have both helped and complicated the situation, since he has been able to direct ants to attack Chitauri, but he has also revealed this ability to them, which may cause them to rethink their tactics."

Thor saw Steve and Janet exchange a sharp glance.

He wondered what was happening there; he'd heard about the Chitauri caught near Janet's apartment, but didn't know why the two of them looked angry. Lovers' quarrel, he decided. Not worth pursuing.

"Most recently, a Chitauri was found in the form of a Newfoundland dog belonging to the nephew of an old friend of Steve's. Obviously this Chitauri was there to observe what Steve was up to, and be in a place where it could act immediately if it needed to. We must assume that other such disguised agents exist."

"Sic ants on all of us," Tony said with a smirk.

"It may yet come to that," Nick said. "We found out where that dog was bred and ran a little operation out that way, in southern Vermont. Town called Saxtons River, and the breeder was called Noofie Acres. Bagged forty-six Chitauri, the biggest single concentration since before Arizona. Plus now we've got about sixty Newfoundland puppies that are verifiably not Chitauri. Anyone here who wants to go into the dog-breeding business after we rid the world of our latest alien menace, let me know."

A ripple of laughter. Sixty Newfoundland dogs, Thor thought. You'd need an island of your own. A nice northern island, granite and tall pines and deep azure fjords . . .

"According to tax and license records, Noofie Acres has been there since 1981, and hasn't changed owners. So the Chitauri are getting a little bit cleverer about where and how they settle in. What with this, the attack on the Triskelion, and the various lone wolves we've smoked out—some thanks to Dr. Pym's work with ants—a picture is emerging of an enemy that's learned it can't defeat us in a direct fight, so it's adapting its tactics to the resource differential. Settling in and keeping a low profile at a place like Noofie Acres indicates that they're planning long-term; but something like the suicide attack on the Triskelion means that they've got short-term plans as well, most likely meant to provoke a specific response."

Fury looked directly at Steve Rogers. "And unfortunately, I believe we have in certain cases done exactly what they wanted."

Hmm, Thor thought. He glanced over at Clint, who returned the glance. They'd both seen it. "Times like this," Thor said softly, "make me glad I stayed on the outside of all the power struggles."

"Yup," Clint said.

At that moment, Thor saw Loki on the other side of the room. Ah, he thought. So the complications have not yet finished complicating. Loki stood in the guise of a slightly built female technician helping to put together the display for Tony's presentation that was to come after Nick brought them all up to speed.

Brother, Loki said.

Thor nodded.

This is a delight to observe, brother, Loki said. *It's so rare that I get to merely watch chaos instead of having to create it myself.*

You've had nothing to do with this? Any of it? Thor wondered.

Solely as spectator, Loki said. *But aren't we in a quantum world? Do we not know that the observer alters what he observes merely by observing? Ha ha ha!*

You're not going to get me to come after you in the middle of this meeting. Thor shook his head. *They don't need another reason to think I'm crazy.*

Oh, Loki said. *Worried about what they think now? Worried about the perception of you among the humans? How very Ultimates. How very image-consultant and focus-group. Our father would gouge out his good eye if he heard you say that.*

We'll settle this another time, Thor said.

And your little comment to Hawkeye there, about power struggles? Oh! Loki laughed. *Yes, you've never taken part in power struggles. No, no. The Aesir are so innocent of turf battles and petty feuds. We could give lessons. Ha ha ha!*

"What are you looking at?" Clint whispered.

At that moment, Thor didn't care what anyone thought. "Loki is here watching."

"No kidding. Where?"

Thor waited until Fury was looking the other way, then pointed. "Looks like a tech to me," Clint said.

"That's what he does," Thor said.

"Well, shit," Clint said. "Bad sign?"

"Bad enough."

"Can we do anything about it?"

"Probably not right now."

"Ah. Well, hell with him, then." With that, Clint

went back to listening to Fury. What a skill, Thor thought. To be able to track and untrack your mind in that way. To be able to just stop thinking about something . . .

A sharp shriek cut through the room, ending as quickly as it began. Everyone around the conference table leapt to their feet; various weapons were unlimbered and fighting stances assumed. All of them focused on the source of the sound: Loki, in his Stark Industries coverall. He had a hand on the side of his face, and Thor watched him quickly adjust it to rub at the side of his nose. Something gleamed in his left ear.

"Sorry, everyone! I know that didn't sound like a sneeze, but it was one. Sorry. I've always had a weird sneeze. Got kicked out of class for it in high school. Dust gets me every time." Loki smiled, and Thor wondered what had really happened.

Clint winked at him. "Can't stand a sneak," he whispered. "Especially a sneaky Norse god. I mean, if you're a Norse god, show yourself."

"What did you do?"

Clint held up a paper clip, bent straight except for a single curl at one end. He made a flicking motion with the fingers of his right hand. "Sent him a little greeting card, is all."

"Careful," Thor said, even though he couldn't help but smile. "Loki has a long memory, and he carries grudges."

"So do I," Clint said.

"General," Steve said, and Thor turned his attention back to the front of the room. "How exactly have members of this team acted in ways that the Chitauri would have wanted us to?"

Steve's directness surprised Thor. It wasn't like Soldier Boy to bark back at his superiors.

Nick looked a bit surprised, too, but he didn't let it show for long. "The Chitauri mean to cause chaos and division," he said. "If that's what they want, then one responsibility of this team is to show a united front. We all need to be pulling in the same direction."

"Classic guerrilla tactics," Steve said. "We all understand that, General. And isn't one of the classic problems faced by conventional forces in a guerrilla war an inability to adapt to the guerrillas' way of fighting because that conventional force is overconfident by virtue of numerical superiority?"

"Captain," Nick said. "This isn't the war college. You can write your dissertation after we've taken care of the Chitauri. Unless you're trying to make a specific point about SHIELD operations?"

How interesting, Loki said. *I believe we're witnessing a proxy battle here. On the one hand, the intrepid Steven Rogers; on the other, the indomitable Nicholas Fury. Both of them too stupidly proud to focus on what's really happening. I love this.*

"Can you put one of those paper clips in his eye?" Thor whispered.

"Sure," Clint said. "But he wouldn't be able to pretend he was sneezing."

Too bad, Thor thought.

"I don't think any more needs to be said about this."
Nick held out a hand toward Tony Stark. "And now
Tony's going to show us the latest Stark Industries toy.
Before he does, I'll just say that we are all indebted to
the work done by Henry Pym. Pym will not be returning to the team, but his independent research has
proved very useful, so credit where credit is due."

Thor looked around the room, and saw that Loki
was still sitting, still watching. As if he felt Thor's gaze,
Loki looked over and gave his half brother a little wink.
His new paper clip earring showed through the dark fall
of his hair.

This isn't over, Thor thought.

27

"OKAY," TONY SAID, STANDING UP AND LOOKING around the room. "I'm going to try this one more time. And Nick, this time I promise I won't use you as a guinea pig." He caught the eye of his lead tech. "Carlo. We ready to go here?"

At the thumbs-up from Carlo, Tony said, "This is another case of me getting a little far afield from the initial purpose of a contract. At one point in the not-too-distant past, Stark Industries was asked by parties who shall remain nameless to investigate the possibilities of using wireless-enabled consumer products as a kind of distributed surveillance or information-gathering network. I worked on that for a while, but I'll tell you the truth. The Chitauri problem makes it difficult to focus on basic research, and it also makes it difficult to stay within the parameters of a research contract when I see a possibility that might have application elsewhere." He grinned and shrugged. "Call me scatterbrained, I guess. Carlo, start the movie."

The lights in the conference room dimmed as a projector started up. A map of the United States appeared. "After Arizona," Tony said, "we all decided to believe the Chitauri were gone. But in the last couple of weeks, we've had confirmed sightings in Illinois and New York."

"And Washington, D.C.," Steve said.

There was a moment of silence.

"Is that so?" Tony said. "Hmm. Seems our intelligence sharing isn't what it could be. Okay, and Washington, D.C. Carlo, next time we show this, bring a Sharpie in case anyone else has a Chitauri sighting to add."

Nobody laughed. Oh well, Tony thought. There are occasions when even I can't lighten up a situation with a joke. Keeps me humble.

"In any case, confirmed sightings, and in situations that indicated they weren't just hanging around. They were tracking us. They infiltrated Hank Pym's lab, they carried out a suicide bombing on the Triskelion after figuring out exactly how our freight intake was handled, they tried to get into Janet's apartment, and they even assimilated a dog to keep an eye on Steve. Last time around, they went for big clusters and grandiose gestures. This time, it looks like they're taking a much more subtle approach . . . focused on us."

As Tony listed each Chitauri action, the projector showed a related image: Hank's wrecked lab, the aftermath of the Triskelion bombing, the recovery team in the breezeway next to Janet's building, the destroyed Monte Carlo where Hank had been shot. That final image remained as Tony went on. "And especially focused on Hank, even though he's not on the team anymore," Tony said. "Why? Because—and this is hard for me to admit—Hank found the silver bullet."

The screen image flickered and became an ant.

"Bullet ant, I should say. Chitauri under great physical stress begin to lose their shape-shifting ability. This ant packs possibly the most painful sting in the insect kingdom, and a little cluster of them can ruin a Chitauri's disguise in no time flat. How do we know this? Because Hank Pym figured out how to tell ants to search for and attack Chitauri."

Tony paused for just long enough to let that sink in, and then he said, "Kind of makes me wish I'd never wasted my time on those screeners. They'll do some good, but if the Chitauri don't want to be spotted that way, they'll just avoid airports and the other places where screeners like that get installed."

On the screen, a reproduced newspaper headline, clearly from a small-town weekly: *Local Woman Attacked by Fire Ants.* More headlines followed, all variations on the same theme.

"Apparently Hank couldn't always get bullet ants, so he practiced with whatever species he had around. But his results, ladies and gentlemen, are impeccable. Hank Pym has designed broadcast commands for twenty-odd different species of ant, all of which can now be made to hunt and attack Chitauri on command. How are we doing so far? Questions?"

"What about—" Steve started to say.

Fury shot out of his seat. "Captain Rogers. You will not waste Tony's time. Is that understood?"

Steve looked straight ahead at nothing and folded his hands on the tabletop. "Yes, sir," he said.

"Good. Tony, please continue."

My goodness, Tony thought. A more obvious bitch-slap has probably never occurred in this room, or at least not between members of the team. Wonder what that's all about. "Okay, well, the great thing about what Hank did is that ants live nearly everywhere in the world that people do. So we could see a solution: put the world's ants on high alert for Chitauri presence, and have rapid-response teams in place to act whenever the ants turned one up. The problem, as you have all doubtless already figured out, is that Hank Pym doesn't work for SHIELD anymore, and anyway, how is one guy going to run around the world with his ant-controlling helmet on all the time?"

The image changed back to the map of the United States. After five seconds, splotches of color began to cover it. "These are maps of cell-phone coverage," Tony said. "All the major companies, including mine." Most of the map was covered, but there were large empty spots, mostly in the Rocky Mountain West.

"This is pretty good, right? But not good enough. So we kept looking, and I even tried to buy a couple of AM radio stations to fill in some of the holes, but the FCC doesn't move that fast for any man. I tried to pick up an XM satellite frequency, but it turns out that none of the ones that are available would work for the ants. Then I had an idea. What if we could piggyback on consumer electronic devices? GPS handsets, cell phones, PDAs, everything. They all send out signals to their networks, just to keep in touch, and if we can add just a little packet of data to those signals, we can suddenly have literally trillions of sentinels on the lookout for Chitauri everywhere. All the time."

"I'm going to step in real quick and ask a question, Tony," Nick said. "Which is: but how does this work? I mean, you can't wave a sample in front of the ants and tell them to go look for something, right?"

"No, but you don't have to. One of the smart things Hank did was figure out how to turn one chemical signature of Chitauri tissue into a set of electrical impulses. It's like talking on a phone. Sound becomes electricity becomes sound. In this case, an odor becomes a kind of algorithm, which when broadcast into the ant's brain becomes the sense of an odor together with the pheromonal signal to attack. Put another way, Hank figured out how to actually broadcast thoughts into ants' heads. I've got to tip my hat to Hank on that one. It's good stuff. Stark Industries is stealing it without shame. And the best thing about the whole project is that it works like SETI@Home, or any one of those other geek-nirvana projects," Tony said. "It'll broadcast on any wireless router, and pretty much any other Bluetooth device. If you're driving across the Mojave and there's not an Internet café within a hundred miles . . . as long as you've got cell service, you'll be helping us out. Or if your car has GPS, or whatever. Carlo, we ready?"

"We sure are," Carlo said.

"Okay, everyone," Tony said. "Turn around so you can see where Carlo is, and let's watch."

Amid the shuffle and scrape of chair legs, Tony thought he'd talked too much. Always better to let people come in once in a while, and use their responses to drive things forward in a way that made them feel like they'd contributed. Nick had kind of put everyone on alert with his takedown of Steve, though; no wonder the room had been so quiet afterward. What the hell was going on with those two, he wondered? Was this still about the leak? Did Nick think—or know—that Steve was the culprit? Was that why he was keeping Steve on a short leash?

Spare me the intrigue, Tony thought. I've got brain cancer, and there are aliens among us. Let's get this done.

Carlo uncovered a large Lucite terrarium, approximately one-third filled with earth. The rest of it was filled with a standard assortment of leaf litter, pieces of fallen trees, and so forth. Your typical pocket ecosystem ant farm. "In there are about twelve thousand average harvester ants," Tony said, "and a single half-gram sample of Chitauri tissue. And this," he went on as he held up a small black rectangle about the size of a remote-entry car key, "is a little voice that will speak to the ants. Everybody turn your cell phones off."

When everyone had done so, Tony set the black rectangle on the table in front of him. He switched it on and said, "Now look at the ants."

The ants weren't doing anything unusual. "Here's the good part," Tony said. "Someone—ah, how about you, Janet?—turn your cell phone on."

Janet looked annoyed, but she got her phone out of her coat pocket again and turned it on. "The phone is going to start looking for its network," Tony said. "When it does that . . . hey, look at those ants."

Everyone turned, and it was perfect. The ants came churning up out of the earth and converged on a spot near the end of a length of decomposing birch. Almost instantly, the birch disappeared under the swarming ants. "Anyone care to guess where I put the sample?" Tony asked.

"And this would have worked no matter which of us turned on a phone?" Janet asked.

"It would have worked no matter who turned on a phone, or any other personal accessory that broadcasts its presence to a network," Tony said. "There's one other thing, too. Stark Industries owns a number of communications satellites, and I believe I'm going to be able to slip this message into their signals. If that works, then we'll have coverage of the entire world, just like that. But if it doesn't, I still have this."

The projector showed a roughly cylindrical metal machine sitting on a tripod, with antennas fanning out around its midsection. It looked like a satellite, but the framing of the image made clear that it was small enough to sit on a table. "I thought you said you hadn't gotten the satellites up yet," Janet said.

"Janet, my darling, getting things up is never my problem. I said I hadn't worked out the signal yet, and this isn't a satellite. This is an amplifier, which if attached to an aircraft at a sufficient height should be able to bounce a signal to the ants all over a line-of-sight area. Say, a time zone at a time. If I can get a dozen old U-2s, or even a secondhand fleet of Airbus 320s, these amplifiers will give what we call blanket coverage."

"Meaning," Nick said, "that there's nowhere in the world—or at least the parts of the world inhabited by ants—that a Chitauri will be able to hide."

"And without them, we'll have to rely on one phone, one BlackBerry, one GPS at a time. The amplifiers are the trump card."

"So what, we get the amplifiers deployed and the Chitauri just pull up stakes and head for the North Pole or the Himalayas or somewhere?" Clint asked.

"Well, this is where Homeland Security's data-mining operations are going to be very useful," Nick said. "Some of you have made no secret of your distaste for how closely SHIELD has to work with Washington, but in this case that cooperation is going to come in handy. We'll have access to everything they know about sudden movements of population, and we've already got surveillance satellites on the lookout for new populations in areas unoccupied by ants."

"Already?" Clint repeated.

Nick looked a little less confident when he answered. "In the event that the Chitauri have already figured out what Hank has been up to. If their agent in Hank's Illinois lab was able to report back, then the Chitauri might already have gone to a worst-case scenario and figured that they should head for the hills. I don't think that's the case, but we've got to include it as a possibility."

"And if they have, then what?" Thor boomed suddenly. "Another little incursion into a sovereign nation? Will we be nationalizing any oil assets along the way?"

"Keep your pinko politics out of this room, mister," Steve growled. "You're not even American. We're under attack. They want to kill us. If you don't want to fight back, then there's the door."

"Captain Rogers," Nick said. "Team unity is very important here. When the enemy is not obviously identifiable, it's natural to start suspecting everyone's motives. But we don't need that. What we need is everyone on-board. You can fight about multinational corporate hegemony some other time."

"As much as we'd all love to talk about it now," said Tony with a roll of his eyes. "Being a hegemonic corporate presence myself, I can't wait to have that conversation."

"Are we going to be clearing this project with people in Washington? The ant part of it, I mean." Steve glanced over at Nick, but for once Nick let him run. Curiouser and curiouser, Tony thought. "Is Homeland Security just mining data and taking pictures for us, or are we supposed to be working together? They killed the screening tech, remember."

In the silence that followed, Tony looked around the room, just sort of to take everyone's temperature. A serious confrontation was brewing between Steve and Nick, that was clear. As far as Tony was concerned, the two of them deserved each other, but everything needed to be kept on less than a full boil until this little problem with the alien invasion was taken care of.

"They did kill the screening tech," Nick said. "But it didn't stay dead, now, did it? Which is a good thing. I'm not a tremendous fan of leaks and other security breaches, but that one seems to have done the job. My point is that Washington is Washington. Sometimes they do the right thing, sometimes they don't. So when they don't, we need to be flexible enough and smart enough to figure out a way to do our jobs even when the people who are supposed to be helping just get in the way."

"So we are taking this to Washington," Steve said.

"No, we are certainly not," Nick said. "Officially, SHIELD doesn't know a goddamn thing about any ant project. Hank Pym is not a member of this team, and Stark Industries operates under all kinds of defense contracting protocols, very few of which have anything to do with me or with SHIELD." Nick cracked his big action-hero grin. "That, ladies and gentlemen, is what is known as plausible deniability."

28

STEVE WENT STRAIGHT FROM THE UNVEILING OF Tony's amplifier tech to a scheduled meeting with Garza, which was the last thing in the world he wanted to do right then. Didn't it just figure that General Fury would throw a monkey wrench into the whole works by doing the right thing? How was a guy supposed to move ahead when nobody around him would stay consistent?

Face it, he told himself. Your real problem is that you thought you had everyone pegged, and now that they're not fitting into the holes you made for them, you're second-guessing yourself. No time for that. The Chitauri aren't second-guessing themselves, you can bet on it.

So the thing to do was stick with what he knew. There was a threat; there was a way to deal with the threat. That was all anyone needed to know about the situation. The complicating factors—idiots in Washington and the bureaucratic self-preservation instinct that infected people who had to work with idiots in Washington—were part of the equation, but they weren't the primary factors. Stay focused, Steve thought, and got into the now-familiar black limousine waiting in Battery Park City. Before he could say anything, Admiral Garza said, "We've got a problem, Steve."

Tell me about it, Steve thought. But we've got a solution, too, if people would just stay out of the way.

"What is it, sir?"

"We've had to shut down production at SKR. In the past forty-eight hours we've discovered nine employees who were Chitauri." As he said it, Admiral Garza looked angry and embarrassed. "I don't have to tell you that this is a black eye for me. We have to assume the Chitauri know the location of every screener, and will plan to avoid them. There's a minimal benefit to knowing that they won't be going through security at La Guardia, but it's not nearly what it would have been if we could have had them believing they were free to move about. Goddammit," Admiral Garza said. "I'm furious at myself."

What Admiral Garza hadn't mentioned was that Chitauri discovery of the screener tech was exactly the reason Ozzie Bright had given for not wanting the screeners publicized and privately manufactured in the first place. "I guess Ozzie Bright had the right idea," Steve said.

"Ozzie Bright can go to hell," Admiral Garza said. "You know the old saying. Even a blind hog finds an acorn once in a while."

"What do we do?" Steve asked. "You still have the handheld screeners. Do the Chitauri know about those?"

Admiral Garza shook his head. "We're building those in-house. Right now we're hammering out the interagency cooperation protocols to equip all Transportation Security Administration personnel with them, and also begin handing them out to federal law enforcement. You know these Beltway types, though. Anything that really needs doing takes forever, and is usually screwed up from the beginning." Looking at his watch, Admiral Garza opened Steve's door. "Listen, we're going to need to touch base again tomorrow. I've got an urgent meeting to get to, and I need you to do a little listening around SHIELD headquarters. Don't spy for me, Steve. You're not cut out for it, and it's low work for a man of your beliefs and integrity. If anyone asks you anything, tell them. Don't keep secrets for me anymore, either. But do tell me what people are asking you. I'm in a tight spot right now between Washington dumbasses and Triskelion paranoids. It's not an easy place to be. We know the aliens are out there, and we know how they work. So what we need is enough resources and enough time to put that knowledge to use. I'll put together the resources. You help me gain the time to use them."

"Yes, sir," Steve said, although the truth was, he'd followed very little of what Admiral Garza had said. Everyone, it seemed, was having trouble being coherent and consistent today.

His phone rang. "Go ahead and take that," Admiral Garza said. "I'll be in touch. And you can tell Nick about the SKR problem. I'd do it, but he and I haven't been getting along lately. Maybe you can soften the blow."

"Yes, sir," Steve said again, and got out of the car. He flipped open the phone and found Tony Stark on the other end.

"Listen, my friend," Tony said. "I was just downstairs in the lab with Janet and she said you told her something about a handheld alien detector. Is that right?"

"I'm not at liberty to tell you about that," Steve said.

"Okay, so you did say it. Don't pussyfoot around with security and chain-of-command crap, Steve. Where were you when you saw it, and who was using it?"

"I'm not at liberty to tell you—"

Tony exploded. "Goddammit, Steve! It was Janet's building, in the breezeway around the side, and you were with some of the goddamn spooks you spend all your time with! You're a terrible liar, Steve. Even when you're not trying to tell a lie, you might as well be walking around wearing a sign that says I Have Secrets. You can't bullshit a bullshitter, and you're talking to the best. Now are we going to have a conversation here, or do I have to go and tell Nick about all the time you're spending with Esteban Garza?"

"We had a word for people like you," Steve said.

"You had a lot of words for people like me," Tony shot back. "*Fink, stool pigeon, snitch.* I don't care. *Drunk? Lush?* Whatever. Call me whatever you want. Just tell me about this supposed miniature screener."

"If you know I talk to Garza, General Fury does, too," Steve said.

"Could be. You want to find out for sure?"

I can't risk it, Steve thought. If Janet told him, Tony's got no reason to think she's lying, and he's right. I've got a lousy poker face.

"I saw one of the people I was there with use it," Steve said.

"Ah. Honesty. How refreshing. Well, let me tell you something. I optimized that design, size-wise. It doesn't work any smaller because you need too many sniffer points for the processor to come up with a faultless result. If the screener doesn't have enough different sources for its samplers, the computer doesn't get enough data fast enough to figure out where the source of a particular odor or chemical signature is. So they're spaced out along the frame."

"Tony," Steve said. "I saw this thing work."

"Steve, if a handheld version of this thing was possible, I'd have invented it already and I would also have made sure that it was in every cereal box in the country by this week. I know you're not going to believe this, but you're being suckered. Plain and simple."

"You think you know everything? Maybe someone just figured out something that you couldn't."

"About this? Yes, I do know just about everything. One of the things that I know is that miniaturization has serious limits when you're talking about screening tech that has to pick out and process something as small as DNA within an operationally meaningful time frame. It's not possible. It's like someone was telling you that they invented a perpetual-motion machine."

"I'm telling you, I saw it work."

"Steve, don't take this the wrong way, but you're not a scientist. You saw what, exactly? You saw someone wave something around and then you saw a little light go on. That's how Janet described it. Pretty accurate?"

"You're leaving out the part about how there really was a Chitauri in the backyard about to climb into Janet's window. The thing worked, Tony."

"My God, are you gullible," Tony said. "They sent suicide bombers to the Triskelion, and you don't think they'd throw one soldier under the bus if it meant they could keep you barking up the wrong tree pretty much forever?"

Steve hung up the phone. He had a country to defend, and he didn't need Tony Stark's alcoholic ramblings to distract him. Three minutes later, someone called back from Tony's number, but Steve didn't pick up. Three minutes after that, he got—of all things—a text message. "Oh, for Pete's sake," he said, hating text messages and the whole of youth culture. But he opened it. GET TO A TV, WATCH CNN, it said. It was from Tony.

Battery Park City was crammed with chain restaurants, all of which had TVs on in their bar areas. Steve walked into the first one he saw and glanced around for news. What he found was mostly baseball games, but there was one TV in the back of the bar tuned to National Geographic, and nobody seemed to be watching it. "Mind putting on CNN?" Steve asked a passing waiter. It took the waiter a couple of minutes to find the remote and get the channel changed, and then a seeming eternity of dumb celebrity news that Hedda Hopper would have been ashamed to print . . . and then Steve figured out what Tony had meant.

A news anchor was saying, "Early indications are that Undersecretary of Defense Ozzie Bright went into anaphylactic shock upon being stung by fire ants while walking across the Mall to get a hot dog." The image cut to a full screen of the Washington Mall, full of people taking in the summer sun, the white obelisk of the Washington Monument in the middle distance. "Hospital staff are being very closemouthed about details of

Bright's condition, but witnesses report seeing him being stung by a large number of the ants."

Steve watched in shock. Ozzie Bright, he thought. A Chitauri. How does it all fit? Variations ran through his mind. Bright a Chitauri, so Altobelli and Garza weren't; or all of them were, and the outbursts General Fury had told him about had been an elaborate charade; or Bright and Altobelli were, but not Garza . . . but then Tony's parting shot rang in Steve's mind: *You don't think they'd throw one soldier under the bus if it meant they could keep you barking up the wrong tree?*

A teenager wearing a Baltimore Orioles cap filled the screen. "I saw him, man. He had them ants all over, and he was screaming . . ." The kid shook his head. "Almost didn't sound like a man."

It wasn't a man, Steve thought. And I fell for it hook, line, and sinker.

"And then did an ambulance come?" came the question from an offscreen reporter.

"No, it wasn't no ambulance. About six men come piling out of a big black Escalade, drove right out onto the grass, and they grabbed the man and took him away."

Back to the anchor, who said, "Mall staff sprayed the area immediately after the attack, and spokesmen say they'll keep that part of the Mall cordoned off while they investigate. We turn now to Doctor Leslie Armentrout of the Centers for Disease Control and Prevention. Doctor Armentrout tracks incidents involving venomous insects, and is here to give us a little background on this phenomenon. Doctor, it seems like all we've been reading about in the papers lately are ants stinging people. Is it really happening more often, or is this a case of the media latching onto a previously unreported story and making it news?"

"Well, Bob, there's no question that there's been an uptick in the number of serious ant-sting incidents. Could be it's climate change, could be just that the ants are tired of waiting for crumbs to fall from the picnic tables and now they're just going to take the whole picnic, you know what I mean?"

Steve didn't stay to hear any more. He charged back out onto the street, calling Tony back. Tony's phone cut immediately to voice mail. "Tony, it's Steve," he said, and hung up. Next he tried General Fury, but there was no answer at all there. Then he got an alert: another text message, from a number he recognized as the automated Red Alert line used for SHIELD emergency messages.

ATTACK UNDER WAY STARK INDUSTRIES, it said, and nothing more.

29

Status Report

Circumstances, and prospects for success of the human ordering project, have undergone a radical change from -.005476 solar year to present. Under consideration once more is the surgical option. Unfortunately current assets do not include the same caliber of ordnance brought to the last open confrontation with human defenders. It remains possible, however, that assimilated assets in place could cause profound damage to human centers of population. Whether the amount of damage inflicted would, in the end, precipitate ecological upheaval on the scale necessary to bring about the ordering of *Homo sapi-*

ens via its elimination rather than its alteration remains uncertain. Choices will have to be made whether the remote possibility of such ecological transformation is enough of a potential reward to offset the certain loss of all existing assets in the effort to catalyze it. Another possibility is a degradation of human civilization to its state of approximately -1000.00 solar years. This degradation could possibly be accomplished through a small number of carefully targeted actions to destabilize food production, clean water availability, and similar resource arenas. Simultaneously, ethnic, national, and religious tensions could be inflamed in flashpoints such as <South Asia>. Simulations and projections related to the possibility of success in these and like ventures have thus far yielded unclear results. Further analysis is ongoing. The ordnance challenge after the events of <Arizona> is formidable, and the possibility exists that a large-scale operation designed for pervasive and long-term degradation of human civilization is beyond the scope of current assets.

If so, current asset and command structure will refocus around mission of eliminating augmented human assets such as the <Ultimates>, with a view to future reinforcements and redevelopment of the human ordering project. Timeline of the project should perhaps be viewed as more flexible than was previously considered desirable.

While this ultimate decision is analyzed and taken, all available assimilated assets are to review their orders. Mission to reduce or eliminate Stark Industries amplifier technology commences .000273 solar year from broadcast of this report. Primary focus of mission will be capacity of Stark Industries to disseminate software via existing public networks. Secondary objectives are contained in individual unit orders.

Appendix

Unless otherwise noted, asset losses delineated below are the result of action of arthropods, order <Hymenoptera>, presumably directed by <Henry Pym>.

Assimilated human asset lost in <Fort Bragg, North Carolina>.

Assimilated human asset lost in <New York, New York>.

Assimilated human asset lost in <Miami Lakes, Florida>.

Assimilated human asset lost in <Dania, Florida>.

Assimilated human asset lost in <Fort Hood, Texas>.

Assimilated human asset lost in <Atlanta, Georgia>.

Assimilated human asset lost in <Antelope Valley, California>.

Assimilated human asset lost in <San Diego, California>.

Assimilated human asset lost in <Imperial, California>.

30

EVEN A GUY WITH THE UNCANNY ACCURACY OF Clint Barton needed quality equipment. And for his equipment he had once gone to a seriously top-secret NSA lab in West Virginia. But then he came in out of the cold, so to speak, and ended up with the Super Hero Ultimates gig, and now he went shopping for his gear at Stark Industries, which occupied a fine-looking skyscraper near Bryant Park. Nothing big or flashy by Manhattan standards: fifty, maybe sixty floors, glass and steel construction. It was underground that the place got exciting, because Tony had figured out some way to engineer a whole lot of subbasements that avoided subway tracks, utility conduits, and other existing basements. The whole setup was a marvel of engineering vision and ruthless graft. Clint often wondered what a three-dimensional schematic of the subterranean parts of Stark Industries would look like. Swiss cheese, maybe. Or, to use a comparison more apropos to current events, an ant farm.

Clint had come to the ant farm to test out some new arrowheads and miscellaneous other doodads that the tech underlings at Stark were constantly working on whenever Tony freed them from their government projects. It seemed to Clint that the underlings had quite a bit more enthusiasm for Ultimates-related gimcrackery than for their standard cluster bombs and cruise missile gyroscopes. Today he was there to look at a prototype arrowhead that would, if it worked as advertised, deliver serious armor-piercing value even at the relatively low velocities an arrow could reach. This was apparently achieved by an extraordinary rotational velocity that caused initial penetration even into hardened steel, after which a high-explosive charge did the rest. It was the kind of battlefield performance fairly easily reached by a rocket-propelled grenade or high-caliber depleted uranium bullets, but you didn't always want to make your mark with those munitions. What if, say, you wanted to punch a hole through the door of a hardened limo, but you didn't have any way to set up with an RPG or .50-cal?

And what if you just plain loved the feeling of the bowstring tautening as you held it back, and then back a little more . . . and then let fly?

Hell, I can shoot guns, Clint thought. I've spent more of my life looking through crosshairs than most people have spent eating cheeseburgers. But the bow. The handheld projectile. That was where his body found its true union with the weapon.

"So show me the new toy," he was saying to Arjun, the lead weapons tech in Stark's Low-Velocity Research Facility.

"You got it," Arjun said, and started a complicated sequence with a keypad to get them through a door, and that's when the first bomb went off upstairs.

Clint and Arjun looked at each other in shock. "Arjun," Clint said, "I don't care if they work to specs or not. Give me some goodies."

Another explosion shook dust from the ceiling. Arjun finished the keypad sequence and stood back as the door opened. "Locker's the first door to the right," he said. "Take what you need. I'm getting the hell out of here."

Which is as it should be, Clint was thinking as he headed back up toward ground level, bow in his left hand and forty-eight arrows in three quivers slapping against both hips and his left shoulder blade. Get the civilians out of the way. If there's fighting to be done, leave it to the soldiers. He wished he had some regular old arrows. If he was going to be shooting Chitauri with these armor-piercing shafts, they'd likely be sticking out the other side before the explosives got around to detonating.

Gunfire to his left. Clint turned and shot before his conscious mind had identified a target. The arrow drilled through the head of the guy with the gun, right behind the hinge of the jaw, and then the charge went off and the guy's upper body turned into a big bloody loogie on the wall. "Yikes," Clint said. He was loaded for bear here, and maybe only hunting squirrel. For a would-be perfectionist like him, being overequipped was almost as bad as being underequipped.

He took a second to raise Nick on the cell. "Nick," he said. "I just shot somebody in Tony's basement."

"Keep it up," came the reply. "We're on the way, but you and Tony are the only ones there right now, and he's not sure he can get to the suit."

Suit, Clint thought dismissively as he clicked off. Anyone can be a hero inside a robot skin. And anyone can be a hero if he can grow to be sixty feet tall, but Hank Pym is still a loser. Me, all I have is the hand and the eye and the tool. And that's all I need.

He found a fire stairwell and got on the cell again, looking for Tony this time. "I'm a little busy," Tony said when he picked up.

"I'm in your basement," Clint said. "What should I be looking for?"

"Outstanding," Tony said. "Can you get to 2-B?"

Clint looked up the stairs. "I'm at 4-B," he said.

"Then go up two flights and kill anyone who might be an alien," Tony said. "I'll be there as soon as I can."

• • •

Clint walked through his daily life with a part of his brain constantly assessing the manner in which he could kill anyone who passed through his field of vision. It wasn't a character trait he took any pride in, but it had kept him alive and made him invaluable to a certain type of unscrupulous or ideological bureaucrats until he'd woken up one morning, realized he'd killed nine people the day before without ever knowing what they'd done to deserve it, and felt nothing. He was out of black ops the next day, and what kept him alive was that all of the people in his former areas of employment were too scared of him to try to take him out. This was the only compliment any of them were ever likely to pay him. He got the all-hands-on-deck text message when he was waiting outside the door to 2-B. "Hmm," he said to the stairwell. "Wonder how long it'll take the gang to get here. All I got is forty-seven arrows left."

The door was locked, and Clint cursed Tony loudly and without reservation until he decided just to blow the goddamn thing off its hinges. Which he did, the AP-HE arrowhead working admirably when it had a little more than human bone and tissue to work with. The doorknob and about eighteen inches of the jamb disappeared in a poof of smoke and a singing haze of shrapnel, and then Clint was into Tony's private lab, where Tony worked on the Iron Man suits. Clint had forty-six arrows and no idea who he was supposed to be killing. People were running in every direction, there was a hell of a lot of shooting, and smoke from a hole in the wall made it hard to see and breathe. During the hit on the skyscraper last year, they'd known everyone in the building was Chitauri. This was different. Who were the bad guys? Chaos, man.

The hole made one aspect of target selection easier; anyone who came in through it got an arrow. Then anyone who reacted to that got an arrow. The explosions were outright deafening in the closed space of the lab, and something about the constant impacts on his eardrums slowed Clint's thinking just a touch. It took him much longer than it should have to figure out that the infiltrating Chitauri weren't going after Tony's suits. The ones already in the room were laying down suppressing fire to get the others through the lab and into the stairwell.

They want the amplifier, Clint thought. Shit. Here I am trying to save Tony's suits, and they aren't the objective. Dumb, dumb, dumb.

He'd been firing from behind a lab table near the stairwell door where he'd come in, and now he ducked under the table and sprinted through the smoke and chaos to a bank of monitors and testing equipment, from which he had a better angle on the other stairwell door.

From somewhere overhead, a big explosion shook the building. Clint saw the shock wave propagate through the hanging smoke in the lab. What were they after? He fired until his arrows were gone, and then he swept two AK-47s up from dead Chitauri and switched them to single shot.

God, the world was slow. It was a hundred feet or so from the hole in the wall across the lab floor to the stairwell door. A fast Chitauri in human guise could cover that distance in less than five seconds. Clint could draw a bead on a running target, squeeze off, and go to the next in a hundredth of that time. By the time the clips in the AKs were empty, the room was quiet except for the ringing in his ears and the panicked yelling of the techs who had survived the initial assault.

Clint snapped open his cell and called Tony. No answer. "Shit," he said. Next he tried Nick, and got him on the first ring.

"The lab is clear," Clint said. "But they weren't after the suits."

"We know," Nick said. "You still on 2-B?"

"Yeah."

"Load up and head for the ground floor. Fastest is through the subway tunnel."

"Subway tunnel?"

"The hole in the wall that goes to the subway. Follow it to your left until you see a hole in the ceiling. Come up that way and you'll know what to do from there. Haul ass, Clint."

Fury hung up, and Clint headed for the hole, scavenging clips where he could find them. They didn't fit very well in the quivers he was wearing, but sometimes a man had to improvise.

He poked his head into the tunnel just as an outbound Long Island Rail Road train was roaring by, not nearly close enough to hit him but not nearly far enough away that he could avoid an instinctive flinch back into the lab. As the train's clack and thunder echoed away east, Clint wondered why the Chitauri hadn't blown the subway tracks, or one of the trains, if what they were really after was widespread chaos. Goddamn aliens, even when you understood what they wanted you still couldn't figure out how they'd go about getting it. "The world," Clint said, "was a better place when we were the only ones screwing it up."

Out in the tunnel again, he raced down a long-abandoned catwalk, finding a hole in the ceiling about seventy-five yards west. Hoisting himself through it, Clint came up into a supply closet with a nice clean hole blown through its west wall into what must have been level 1-B in Tony's building. He was in a long, white hall, lit only by emergency bulbs near the floor. A large number of dirty footprints, tracking in subway grime, led off to his left. It was suspiciously quiet, and when his cell phone pinged with an incoming message Clint had a moment of intolerable paranoia, imagining every rifle muzzle in the world picking out this one sound in the dim and silent hall.

He opened his phone and saw the message from Nick: STAY THERE. DON'T LET ANYONE OUT.

Part of Clint was furious. He wanted in on whatever was happening. His blood was up, he'd logged maybe

31

STEVE GOT TO STARK INDUSTRIES THE FASTEST
way he could on a weekday afternoon. He ran. The
four miles between Battery Park City and Tony's
headquarters melted away, and the only reason Steve
didn't run right on in the front door—through the
cordon that had already formed outside on 34th
Street—was that General Fury called his cell. "Steve,
find the closest subway grate. Go through it and call
me back."

Fires burned in several of the building's lower floors,
and Steve could hear small-arms fire through broken
windows. As he watched, another window spider-
webbed and then disintegrated under the impact of bullets. Fire crews were starting to respond, and there were

so many sirens going off that it sounded like the last time Steve had been in an air raid over Germany.

"It's kind of loud out here, sir. Did you say to go through a subway grate?"

"That's what I said." Fury hung up.

Steve had gotten some odd orders in his time, but this one was right up there. "Yes, sir," he said, even though he was talking to himself, and he flipped up the first grate he saw. Dropping into it, he landed in a thick sediment of cigarette butts, falafel wrappers, tourist flyers, and the miscellaneous muck and scum that washed through the grates every time it rained. It smelled like the floor of a Coney Island bathroom, if that bathroom had recently been on fire. He called General Fury back.

"Okay, get down into the tunnel," General Fury said. "Cross to the north side of the track that runs under 34th Street and head east until you see a hole in the ceiling. Go through it, but sing out first."

"Am I hearing you right?" Steve asked. "You want me to announce my presence?"

"Are you going deaf?" General Fury snapped. Static flared over the phone, and Steve heard a boom from the street above. Some of the assembled crowd of gawkers screamed. "Yes, I want you to announce yourself, unless you want seven or eight bullets in your head. Clint's down there, and he's pissed off and jumpy."

Which turned out to be a fairly exact description. Steve found his way through and past holes in a couple of train tunnels, and when he got to the one in the ceiling where General Fury had told him to look, he called softly. "Clint? Steve here."

"Left hand through the hole, pinkie and thumb extended. Now."

Steve did it.

"Huh," Clint said. "You're pretty fast. If that had been a normal reaction time, I was going to take off the thumb just to be sure."

Steve came through the hole and settled next to where Clint lay in a sniper's prone firing position.

"Been a long time since someone said I was only pretty fast," he said.

"All in your frame of reference," Clint said, never taking his eyes off the hallway.

"Okay," Steve said. "Where do we go?"

"Not we."

"No?"

"No," Clint said. "I've got orders to stay right here. Nobody's supposed to get out this way. Good thing you're trying to come in. Nick didn't say anything about that."

"So where do I go? And is that a Russian gun?"

Now Clint did look away from the sight of his rifle. "It's a cheap-ass Chinese knockoff of a Russian gun, and no, I'm not happy about it. But what you're supposed to do is follow those tracks, Sherlock. And do me a favor. Whatever's on the other end, see if you can flush some of it back my way. I don't want to lie here all day and have nothing to show for it but a headache."

"Will do," Steve said. "By the way, I should have taken you more seriously the other day."

"About what?"

"Cynicism," Steve said. He started walking down the hall, thinking of how very much he would like to kill the alien masquerading as Admiral Esteban Garza. "I've got a lot to learn about it."

"You're talking to a Ph.D.," Clint said from behind him. "Stop on back anytime for a lesson."

Around the corner, the boot prints divided. Some went through a fire door, and some kept going until they came to the blown-apart remains of what had been a vestibule between two heavily secured steel doors. Both of the doors were now lying bent and scorched on the floor, and the bodies started to pile up there as well. The acrid stink of gunfire hung heavy in the air. Steve went through the vestibule unarmed and alone, passing into a computer lab that looked as if the invading force had dedicated itself to demolishing each and every terminal, server, and peripheral. Several low fires burned, adding their fumes to the already-fouled air. The sprinklers, it appeared, had come on and then cut out; everything was wet, but not wet enough to put out the fires. Steve sneezed. Among the bodies of human lab techs and code monkeys, he saw a number of Chitauri beginning to decohere. It was hard to tell which were invaders and which had infiltrated Stark beforehand.

Which, of course, they had. It was plain idiotic to think that they hadn't. If they could get into the Joint Chiefs of Staff, they could get into Stark Industries. And if they could do that . . .

The truth is, Steve thought, I'm the only guy I know who I'm sure isn't a Chitauri.

Fresh gunfire erupted ahead, on the other side of another set of blown security doors. Steve hunkered down and called in, using the number that would link into General Fury's SHIELD comm. "General," he said. "I'm in a lab on the target floor. There's small-arms fire ahead. Orders?"

"We're out in the main lobby, about to push straight into the lab where you're hearing shooting. That's where the amplifier is, according to Tony. No idea of enemy strength on the inside, but Clint reports upwards of fifty kills on their way in and he just caught the end of the break-in. So look for . . . hang on." The line went dead for a moment. When General Fury came back on, he said, "Go, Cap. We'll meet you inside."

Steve went in shooting, like he was an old-fashioned commando again in an old-fashioned war. At about the same moment, General Fury's platoon of next-gen super-soldiers came in the front door. The Chitauri forces had anticipated the frontal assault, but their rear guard was thin and distracted by something out toward the center of the enormous lab space, which appeared to have a hole in the floor surrounded by six-foot railings. Glancing up, Steve saw that the floor above was the same. One of those labs that occasionally had to work on something tall, from the looks of it. But why Tony's amplifier was in here was anyone's guess. He'd said it was small enough to fit on the meeting table in the Triskelion.

Picking off two Chitauri trying to cover their rear, Steve circled around along the wall, trying to stay out of Fury's field of fire while still doing some good. This was one of those times when he wished he had the suit and shield instead of jeans and a Brooklyn Dodgers T-shirt he'd paid forty dollars for. Incredible, he thought as he nailed a Chitauri about to throw some kind of grenade into the shaft cut through the middle of the floor. Forty dollars, and the clerk called it retro and rolled his eyes. The grenade rolled about three feet and went off, demolishing a bank of what looked like chemistry equipment. A beaker, miraculously unbroken, came skipping across the floor in Steve's direction, looking so alive in its motion that he almost shot it.

Thor appeared in the middle of things. He was singing some Nordic song in a hearty baritone, slinging alien bodies all over the place and—if Steve was not mistaken—not being overly careful with his backswing when it might damage some expensive goodies belonging to the global corporate hegemony. How many people on the team were crazy, Steve wondered? Thor, Banner, Pym . . . heck, how sane was Steve, if by *sane* you meant *well-adjusted to your surroundings*?

Screw it, he told himself, and fought his way over toward Thor. "Ah, Steve!" Thor shouted. "Enjoying our little service to humankind and its multinational overlords?"

"Can it," Steve said. "Where's the amplifier?"

Thor actually did a double take. Steve thought that as long as he might live, he would never see anything quite so strange as a Norse god doing a double take . . . if, that is, he was going along with the proposition that Thor was a Norse god.

"Amplifier?" Thor said. "So you don't know?"

"Know what?"

"According to Loki, there is no amplifier." Thor held Mjolnir aloft and brought a stroke of lightning down through the shaft to incinerate the Chitauri against the railing.

Great, Steve thought. According to Loki.

"So where's Loki now?" he asked, laying down cover for a pair of next-gens pinned behind a tool cart. They scampered back to more substantial cover with the main body of General Fury's unit.

"I haven't looked for him," Thor said. "But you can bet your flag he's somewhere watching the show."

"Bring down the lightning again!"

"I'm not sure I can," Thor said, looking up the shaft. "It's hard to keep it small, and you don't want to see what would happen if it got a little too big inside a nice skyscraper like this."

The look on his face said different, though. "You're

nuts," Steve said. "You do want to see what would happen, don't you?"

A grin spread across Thor's face. "Well, now that you mention it," he said. "What a show it would be." He glanced over at Steve and shrugged. "What can I say? Us gods are capricious, you know? All the stories say so."

The two of them were wedged into a narrow space between an industrial-sized refrigerator containing God knew what, and the railing around the shaft. Bullets hammered into the fridge, and Steve wondered what was leaking out. He was about to say something to Thor, along the lines of *give me a break,* when three people in Stark Industries lab coveralls appeared along the railing on the next floor up, directly over Steve's head. A cold feeling came over him. They were too calm, and he had no angle to get a good shot, unless . . .

Before he could complete the thought he was up and running, and then he leapt up and out over the shaft, pirouetting in midair to empty the clip of the junk commie AK-47 he'd liberated from a dead alien . . . all just an instant too late. The three targets crumpled and died in the split second after each had shouldered and fired a rocket-propelled grenade into the heart of General Fury's position. The explosions, nearly simultaneous, drove through Steve like a punch from the Hulk, and he fell.

32

IN THE SIXTY SECONDS BETWEEN WHAT NICK hoped would be his final conversation with Tony and what Nick hoped would be a quick and decisive elimination of the Chitauri force that had gouged its way up from MTA and Long Island Rail Road tunnels into one of Tony's main testing laboratories, Tony—being the finicky CEO type—found a reason to call back.

"Say, Nick," he said over the SHIELD comm, which only Tony and Nick were wearing. "It occurs to me that Clint's little massacre down in 2-B has given me an opportunity. How about I go downstairs and get my suit on?"

"Be my guest," Nick said. "If you can get there."

"Oh, I can get there. I've got an elevator line, powered separately, that takes me straight from home to lab. So go ahead and cut the power or whatever the SWAT manual says you should do. I'll get along fine."

"So why are you calling? I got aliens to shoot."

"Right, I know. Do you think they've figured out yet that there's no way they can get what they came for?"

"Tony, I have to go. If you're going to go get the suit, go get the suit." Nick hung up as something exploded inside the lab. "Wait a minute," he said, before he remembered that the phone was dead.

What did Tony mean, they couldn't get what they'd come for?

Don't go there, he told himself. "Boys," he said to the assembled dozen or so next-gens, and also to Thor, who had happened to be at the Triskelion when the call came in, "I don't know exactly what we're going to find in there, because the management won't tell me." A smirk from Thor. "But I do know that the enemy cannot go back the way he came in. We've got that sealed off. He may or may not know that. If he does, they may fight just to get out through us, and I can't let that happen, so we're not going full penetration. Get positions as close to this door as you can, hold them, spread gradually through the room only when Thor has softened up areas. We can expect reinforcements from Captain America fairly soon."

Annoyed looks among the next-gens at this news.

They didn't like Steve, considered him out of date and ridiculously naïve. The next-gens were super-soldiers for this time and place. To them, Steve was their own origin myth, alive when he shouldn't be, walking the earth that rightfully should have been theirs.

"Was that Tony on the comm again?" Thor asked. Nick nodded. "He planning to join us, or is he in a meeting?"

"I think," Nick said, "that you might be in for a surprise." Surveying his troops, he said, "All of us might be. Okay, on my go."

Boom, through the door with the pieces still flying from the set charges. Return fire came immediately, from well-defined and well-chosen points through a space that Nick assimilated all at once: broadly rectangular, with their access point near one corner. The center of the room had no floor, and no ceiling, as if it had been designed with a missile launch site in mind. Diagonally across the room was another exit door, destroyed along with part of that wall. Nick counted a dozen workstations, and more kinds of equipment than he could recognize. The next-gens were doing their thing the way they'd been trained, concentrating firepower on specific areas to enable a small advance, then consolidating that gain. Thor surged straight out into the mass of Chitauri defenders, leveling anyone who got within arm's length. There were no worries about target differentiation; whichever members of Tony's staff hadn't already gotten out were dead or dying on the floor.

Thirty seconds after insertion, Steve Rogers came in through the back door, and the dynamic of the fight changed. Thor had already cut a swath through the Chitauri almost all the way across the lab, leaving both bodies and wreckage in his wake, and when he and Steve met up, Nick thought, *Good.* Now we squeeze.

And then he saw Steve look up. Following Steve's line of sight, Nick spotted the three Chitauri and their RPGs, and in the instant before they fired, too many things happened in his mind for him to be able to keep track. Hell of a move by Steve, he thought as Steve danced out over the central shaft and drew a bead on the shooters. At the same time he was thinking how bizarre it was that the Chitauri had gone from emulating the Third Reich to adopting the tools and tactics of every insurrection from the Viet Cong to Iraq. And then he was ducking for cover as the three Chitauri fired, the heavy whoosh almost swallowed by the din of automatic-weapons fire, and the world around Nick went up in flames.

Things were a little scattered when he'd come to his senses. There was blood in his eyes, and he could tell that he was deaf. He tried talking into the comm to see where Tony had gotten to, but although he could tell he was making words, could feel the vibrations in his throat, Nick knew that he wouldn't be able to hear whatever Tony said in response. Cap was gone, Tony was God knew where, most of the next-gens were in bad shape . . . there were more holes in the floor. Nick's left leg was dangling over one. Could be one of the RPGs had dug through the floor before going off. Where was everyone? Dimly he could tell that his eardrums were registering sound, but he couldn't hear, dammit, and when he wiped his good eye it hurt like a son of a bitch. I don't want to be blind, he thought, and wiped again and again until he could sort of focus on what was around him.

The Chitauri were coming down from the floor above. Thor was killing them by the ton, but more were coming. Where was Steve? Where was Tony? They couldn't actually be losing here. They'd gone in with three Ultimates—four, if Tony ever got around to showing up—and two dozen next-gens, and Nick could not believe they were going to lose this battle. They could not lose this battle.

Then a light flared in the central shaft, so bright that at first Nick thought Thor had called down lightning again, and out of the light rose Iron Man. With a sweep of his right arm, Tony brought down the entire far side of the floor above, and with it the bodies of Chitauri crushed by the force beam and falling wreckage. From Tony's left hand hung Steve Rogers, and Steve flipped into a somersault that carried him back over the railing and into the fray once more. With both hands free now, Tony turned the force beams on what remained of the floor above, and then he went to work on the floor above that, and Nick blacked out for a bit. When he'd come to again, Thor was carrying him back out into the lobby of Stark Industries, where a SHIELD medic whose name Nick could usually remember was mouthing words that Nick thought were *Sir, can you hear me?*

"I sure as hell cannot," he said, and blacked out again.

The next time Nick woke up, he was in bed, and he could hear. Two improvements over his previous attempt at consciousness. A doctor came in and informed him that he'd be able to go home the next day. "I will be leaving here in one hour," Nick said, "and I'm only giving you that long because I know you'll never get the paperwork done sooner."

One hour later he was leaving the hospital. One hour after that he was back in his office in the Triskelion, going over mission reports. The first thing he did upon sitting down at his desk was put in a call to Tony Stark. He got voice mail, and said, "Tony. I'm expecting an explanation of your last comment, and I mean soon." Then he hung up and started poring over initial results of Homeland Security tracking to see if there had been an unexpected influx of new residents into any of the populated areas of Earth's landmass where ants didn't live. Nothing showed up in the numbers, and Nick leaned back, thinking the situation over. The Chitauri had clearly put all they had into the attack on Stark Industries, which meant they still thought they had something to fight for . . . which in turn meant that they didn't think the ants were going to be decisive.

Nick went back over the reasoning. An alternate possibility was that this had been an all-or-nothing attack because the Chitauri knew they were already beat, and Stark Industries had been a Hail Mary. Nick couldn't quite make himself believe that, though. They were too cautious, and too good at planning for the long haul. If that hadn't been a last-ditch effort at something, though, the waste of manpower was huge . . . which meant the Chitauri had lots of bodies to waste.

Each line of thought turned itself into its opposite, and Nick gave up after spending the afternoon plowing the same furrows through his mind. He checked in at the lab downstairs to see if any of the Chitauri had survived, and could be interrogated, but according to Janet there had been no survivors. "And, Nick," she added, "just how the hell am I supposed to interpret the fact that everyone on the team was called in except me?"

"I sent out an APB to all team members," Nick said. "You're on the list. I'm not going to take responsibility for anything beyond that."

Over her shoulder he could see Banner looking out of his glassed-in cell with keen interest. Wonder if anyone's doing the kind of psych profiling on him that could tell whether his isolation is changing the way he gets interested in other people, Nick thought. Not that it mattered. Looking back at Janet, he saw that she didn't believe him. "Janet," he said. "I was damn close to calling Hank there at the end of that fight. I mean, look at me. You think I'd have just left you out?"

Wrong thing to say, Nick thought as her soon-to-be-ex-husband's name left his mouth. "Oh, you were," Janet said. "Funny. Does the SHIELD moralizing have some kind of emergency threshold? When the chips get down, we call back in the abusers that we cashiered even though we ignored all of the other things other members of the team had done? That must be one of those situational ethics things they teach you when you're in military college."

"It was a joke, Janet. An exaggeration. We were never going to call Hank," Nick said.

"Go to hell, Nick."

Janet turned and walked off, and Nick saw that Banner was still looking at him. When Banner noticed Nick's attention, he shifted his gaze to Janet and followed her all the way to a specimen locker at the other end of the lab. Psych people would have no trouble figuring that out, Nick thought. He sighed, went back upstairs, and put in a work order for a tech team to figure out if there was something wrong with Janet's phone or SHIELD comm, if she'd had it available.

It was five o'clock, his head was killing him, he had stitches all over his arms and shoulders from a menagerie of shrapnel, and he still hadn't begun to deal with the biggest problem of yesterday. Some combination of Ozzie Bright, Vince Altobelli, and Esteban Garza was Chitauri. Nick's guess was all three, but he wasn't sure about Altobelli. He also wasn't sure how the Chitauri would be reacting to Bright's outing as one of them. They had to know that SHIELD would realize that Bright had been assimilated, and they had to know that Steve would put together the relationship between Bright and Garza. Bright played bad cop. Garza played good cop, and Nick Fury bought it hook, line and sinker. So had Steve, until Tony laid out for him the impossibility of a handheld screener. It was all elementary misdirection, exposed as soon as Steve started telling even a fraction of the truth to his nominal superiors.

Emphasis, Nick thought, on the nominal. Time to put that to rest. He put in a call to Steve, just to run through the facts one more time, and then made one of the most difficult decisions of his service life. "Steve," he said for the second time in a month, "how about we get us a beer together?"

"You know I don't drink, General," came Steve's response.

"I also know that you've been lying to me, that you don't trust me, and that this team is going to fly apart if you and I don't clear the air. So you will meet me at the same place as last time, and we will have a beer, and by the end of the night we will understand each other better than we do now."

"Is that an order, sir?"

"All of it's an order. Meeting, drinking, understanding. You are ordered to do all three." Fury hung up and started contemplating what a pain in the ass it was going to be to get to Brooklyn. He hated taxicabs. On the train, the ride was fairly short, but that was only because it left you with quite a ways to walk. Nick didn't know if other people felt this way, but if he was going to walk somewhere, he'd just as soon walk there; if he was going to take wheeled transportation, he wanted it to drop him off within sight—preferably within arm's reach—of his destination. Mixing the two was not his style.

And thinking about it was starting to make his battered body feel worse. Here I am with a building full of engineers and geniuses, man, Nick thought, and all I really want is one of them to teleport me to a bar. What the hell good is science, anyway?

The only good thing to come out of the day so far was that SHIELD's news-culling service was starting to spit out increasing numbers of headlines about ant attacks. Somewhere out there, Hank Pym was doing his thing, and the Chitauri were responding. This led to a new set of problems, since there was no mission coordination. Hank wasn't answering Nick's calls, which Nick could understand on a personal level, but this was no damn situation to let feelings get in the way of what needed to be done. Hank was a liability, team-wise, and he knew it; he also must know that the ant research could be done faster at Triskelion laboratories than at whatever thrown-together facility he could get together. None of that would make any difference to Hank, because he carried around an inferiority complex big enough to make anyone paranoid—even if that anyone wasn't bipolar to begin with. So Hank was at the mercy of his brain chemistry. All of them were.

I got a guerrilla ant army out there, Nick thought, but no way to control it until Tony gets his voice of God networking thingamajig set up. I sure hope he didn't blow the shit out of his own building to the extent that he can't go ahead with that little project, which might save all of us. Be just my luck if suddenly there's some kind of continent-wide spraying program that wipes out all the ants. If Steve was right about Bright and Garza, it wasn't out of the question. They had to move fast.

Life, Nick thought, would be easier if I was as stone-cold a human being as Janet appears to think I am.

Since he wasn't, he was going to go have a beer.

33

Status Report

The <Pym-Hymenoptera> technology begins to cause consistent asset loss, and has resulted in difficult curtailment of standard surveillance activity and regular mobility. At this time no viable countermeasure is available. Frequency jamming fails due to the constant band-switching of <Hymenoptera> signals, and the limitless number of possible sources of such signals now that the <Stark> modification to the <Pym-Hymenoptera> technology is operational.

Planned elimination of the <Stark> modification by means of assault on manufacturing and design facility in <New York City> proved unsuccessful. Mission timeline and analysis follow. Due to mission results, retrenchment will occur as of receipt of this transmission.

Mission Timeline

-.010954 solar year: Initial reports that <Stark Industries> has developed a device capable of tremendously enhancing human detection and counter-infiltration activities.

-.010713 solar year: Preparation of mission plans. Reconceptualization of possibilities for success of human ordering project. Selection of mission plan according to primary objective of eliminating or delaying deployment of <Stark Industries> amplifier technology.

-.005422 solar year: Mobilization of assets. Planning for redeployment of assets to minimize impact of <Pym> technology for control of <Hymenoptera>. Two plans constructed, one subsequent to planned <Stark> mission success and another envisioned as retrenchment in the event of <Stark> mission failure.

-.002825 solar year: Assets within <Stark> secure laboratory where amplifier is believed to be designed and where prototypes are believed to be housed. Penetration of <Stark Industries> headquarters by means of subterranean demolition.

-.002813 solar year: Destruction of utility and network lines in and out of <Stark Industries> headquarters. Reserve power systems prove resilient and problematic.

-.002795 solar year: Laboratory in which <Tony Stark> designs <Iron Man> exoskeletons provisionally secured. Forces moving through to next mission objectives.

-.002793 solar year: Unexpected (and believed coincidental) arrival of <Clint Barton> in <Iron Man> lab. Consequent failure to deliver full amount of assets to next set of objectives. Unexpectedly high losses of assets.

-.002754 solar year: Penetration of laboratory previously secured by assets within <Stark Industries>. Thorough destruction of laboratory, penetration of attached facilities on adjacent floors.

-.002749 solar year: Intelligence of <SHIELD> rapid-response team. Preparation for counterattack. Continued degradation of laboratory capabilities. Numerous amplifier prototypes destroyed.

-.002733 solar year: Arrival of <Steve Rogers> through ingress previously believed controlled by rear-guard assets. Near-simultaneous penetration of laboratory by <SHIELD> rapid-response team, including <Thor>.

-.002723 solar year: Degradation of <SHIELD> rapid-response team, with exception of <Thor>.

-.002720 solar year: Arrival of <Tony Stark>, in <Iron Man> exoskeleton previously believed secured. Near-total destruction of amplifier laboratory and adjacent floors.

-.002711 solar year: Loss of mission assets reaches 85 percent. Retreat executed. Egress controlled by <Clint Barton>. Near-total loss of mission assets.

Analysis of <Stark> Mission

Mission failures included redeployment of assets away from surveillance of <SHIELD> team members. Lack of surveillance resulted in unexpected combat circumstances and unsustainable losses of assets. Retrospective analysis indicates that mission planning was reactive and too narrowly focused, as well as insufficiently respectful of alternatives and possible consequences of asset redeployment.

A more decisive shortcoming was failure to credit possibility that the <Stark> amplifier was a decoy, of similar nature to the <Micronesia> operation carried out against <SHIELD> forces with notable success in the previous solar year. Available evidence indicates that <Tony Stark> alone among the <Ultimates> knew that the amplifiers were fabricated; the only possible conclusion is that <Stark> deliberately endangered his comrades and engineered the partial destruction of his headquarters in order to inflict heavy asset loss. The irrationality of this initiative needs no explication. Its success demands consideration.

The <Stark> entrapment appears to have been made possible by the human tendency toward strong personal identity, without which a single individual—in this case <Tony Stark> himself—would have been unable to conceive of and execute an operation in which his colleagues and superiors were deceived to the same degree as our assets. A heterodox possibility presents itself: perhaps, due to ecological quirks on a local scale, <Homo sapiens> is better served by individualism, traceable to primate ancestry, than other dominant species have been by the more common trait in successful civilizations of mass identification. Millennia of documented ordering projects militate against this possibility, but the human ordering project has been unusual in a number of ways. A flexible and committed project guidance hierarchy would take into consideration this strong variance from the norm when future ordering projects are being planned.

At this time, prospects for success of the human ordering project are highly uncertain. Arrival of reinforcements from other sectors would positively influence the equation; however, lack of consistent communication with other sectors would seem to indicate that events elsewhere are unfolding in a manner unlikely to yield significant asset redeployment to <Earth>.

Given results of <Stark> mission, existing redeployment plans for minimizing impact of <Pym-Hymenoptera> technology are to be implemented as of receipt of this transmission.

years he'd missed. He ordered a ginger ale from the Chinese bartender, whose name—Steve discovered when the other bartender asked him where something was—turned out to be Steve.

Go figure. *There sure weren't any Chinese named Steve when I was growing up around here*, Steve thought.

While he waited for General Fury to get there, Steve wondered how often in the history of military operations a soldier had been ordered to sit in a bar and wait for his superior so they could have a drink. Probably it happened fairly often to spies, but Steve Rogers would sooner have worn a hammer and sickle than considered himself a spy.

Whoa there, he told himself. *What have you been doing this past couple of weeks? Keeping secrets, executing plans that directly contravene your orders . . . if that wasn't spying, it was sure in the same territory.*

Steve's father had always drilled into him the importance of being a man when you found out you'd been wrong about something. A real man admitted his errors and would move heaven and earth to make them right. Now Steve found himself in the position of having to do that. General Fury had called him out.

The jukebox abruptly switched from some kind of incomprehensible noise to music that Steve recognized, even if he'd never learned to appreciate it: the Delta blues he'd never known anything about until he'd gone into the service and heard it coming from the kitchens and maintenance yards where most of the black soldiers were assigned. The only black person in the bar was wearing a leather cowboy hat and long braids. Not a blues type, that was for sure. And now here came General Fury through the door, more walking evidence that Steve was a man out of his time as surely as Rip Van Winkle. A black general. With a flush of embarrassment, Steve remembered breaking General Fury's nose, and later apologizing about it. When you made a mistake, you made it right, no matter how hard or humbling it was.

"General," Steve said, standing up as General Fury approached his booth.

"Sit down," General Fury said. "We're off duty here. You want that freshened up?"

"Thanks," Steve said. When General Fury had come back with another ginger ale for Steve and a beer for himself, Steve said, "Okay. I have three orders, and I've completed one. Can I get a pass on the second if that makes it easier to fulfill the third?"

"You mean I'm not going to be able to get you drunk?" General Fury said. He did not smile, which put Steve off balance right away.

"I got drunk once in my life, when I was sixteen," Steve said. "That was enough."

"Fair enough. Consider the second order rescinded. Now let's get on with the third. I need you to lay out for me exactly what you've been doing with Esteban Garza. Has he been in touch with you since Ozzie Bright had his little accident?"

"No, sir. I haven't heard from him. I imagine that I won't be hearing from him." How did you say it, Steve wondered? When you were Captain America, how did you admit that you'd been suckered because you were so hungry for action, for the grim self-satisfied thrill of deciding what was right and then doing it, that you decided to ignore the oaths you'd sworn? He couldn't make the words leave his mouth. Pride, he thought.

"Did he ever ask you to report on SHIELD activity?" General Fury asked.

Steve remembered Admiral Garza saying something along the lines of *I'm not asking you to spy for me, but I am asking you to listen.* "Not directly," he said. "He did ask me to pay attention to how you were dealing with Washington."

"And did you?"

"I—" Steve caught himself. He was only going to get one chance to say this, and he had to both tell the truth and make sure that it sounded right. But he spoke quietly, both because there were civilians around to hear and because he was going to be saying words he never thought he would have to say. "I never told him anything that compromised any mission or SHIELD security, sir."

"Okay. What did you tell him?"

"Mostly that I was angry and dissatisfied with the way SHIELD was approaching the Chitauri threat."

"Was this after Garza used you to leak the screener to SKR?"

"Yes, sir."

"You know that SKR was shut down."

"Yes, sir. Admiral Garza told me."

"He make a big show about how embarrassed he was?"

Steve nodded.

"You realize," General Fury said, "that he flew you like a flag. I sent out a test crew with Chitauri samples, and they walked right through every single SKR screener they tried. You got up on TV to tell everyone about terrorism and how SKR was going to make them safer, and what happened was that they made goddamn placebo screeners, and now the Chitauri know exactly where they can go, unless we're going to fill every airport and federal building in the country with ants. Let me put this as clearly as I can: if you weren't who you are, you'd be in jail. In some situations, you'd be in a grave. I never thought I'd say this, but Hank Pym's been a damn sight more useful to us the past few weeks than you have."

Steve could feel his face burning. Still he did not speak, because he could not defend himself. What he could do was sit and take his medicine, and wait for his chance to make it right.

"Now," General Fury said. "Am I wrong?"

"No, sir," Steve said. "You're not wrong."

"I'm glad we agree. Now would you like to get started on fixing this mess?"

"I very much would, sir."

General Fury killed off his beer. "I thought you might. Find Garza. When you find him, call me so we can bring him in. Under no circumstances are you to take him down yourself. Are all parts of those orders understood?"

"Yes, sir," Steve said. "May I ask a question?"

"You sure may."

"Will I have SHIELD resources available to me while I'm looking?"

For the first time since he'd walked into the bar, General Fury cracked a smile. "Oh, *now* he wants to work with the team. Yes, Captain. They're waiting for you at the satellite tracking lab right now."

It took less than six hours. Garza had been smart enough to ditch his cell phone—which pinged from a Dumpster on Great Jones Street—and nobody at the Pentagon would allow SHIELD to piggyback on the homing beacon they had in all high-level staff cars. Initially that was a problem. Then Steve realized that the Chitauri might not know that SHIELD had pegged exactly the way in which SKR had faked the screeners, and he commandeered security footage from Washington and New York airports. Presto. Either Garza hadn't had time to consume and assimilate a new identity, or he hadn't thought he needed to. Whichever was the case, a lab tech caught him via facial-recognition software coming out of long-term parking at JFK. With that hit, they tracked him into his terminal, through a gate with a brand-new SKR screener, and to the gate where he boarded a flight . . . for Buenos Aires.

Back to the Pentagon, where after some wrangling Steve was able to get a look at tapes from Ezeiza Airport in Buenos Aires. Again the techs went to work, and they pegged Garza getting on a chartered flight. Using the gate number, they cracked Ezeiza's records . . . and found that there was no record of any flights taking off from or landing at that gate on the day in question.

"Hmm," Steve said. "Looks like our lizard friends have gotten into the airport before us."

"You want my guess?" said one of the techs. "Heading through Argentina, plus no ants, equals Antarctica."

Steve watched the map, wondering how he might test that hypothesis. "Could be you're right," he said. "Let's nail that down."

Ninety minutes later, armed with satellite tracks of a private jet leaving Buenos Aires at the right time and then landing in the Antarctic interior, Steve was on his way by helicopter to McGuire Air Force Base in New Jersey. An hour after that, he was thundering south in an F-16. He left a message for General Fury: GONE ICE FISHING.

35

IT ALL COMES TO A HEAD, NICK THOUGHT. ONE last meeting, one last set of orders, and one more time we set out to take care of business. Normally he was starting to get jazzed up about a mission by the time it came to this point—knowing combat was on the way was the second-most powerful buzz in the world, combat itself being the first—but for some reason he was coming into this final briefing annoyed and out of sorts because they should have put the goddamn Chitauri away the last time.

Which is what he told the team right off the bat. "What we're doing here," he said, "is cleaning up a mess that we never should have made. We had the Chitauri on the ropes in Arizona, and we got distracted by other things, and look where that got us. Today or tomorrow, we finish the job once and for all." He looked around the room, from Janet to Clint to Thor to Tony. Banner hadn't been invited today. They would also be using several squads of next-gens, but Nick planned to brief them separately later.

"Okay," Nick said. "Steve is en route to Antarctica right now. It looks like the Chitauri have decided that the ants are their biggest problem, so they've cleared out to where ants don't live. Unless Hank comes up with a way to control penguins, we're working with a whole new set of circumstances on the ground."

"Sounds a little like Micronesia all over again," Tony said. "I'd sure hate to have to do that again. It was hell on my batteries."

"Keep on joking, Tony. Twenty thousand people died that day. It's not a mistake we're likely to repeat."

Tony stood. "Nick, can the sanctimony. Yeah, I was joking, but I'm also right. The last time we decided to go in and take on the Chitauri face-to-face without Bruce, we ended up with a wrecked fleet and a hundred square miles where the fish are going to grow three heads for the next thousand years. What I'm saying, in my own inimitable fashion, is let's make sure we don't fall for the same trap again."

"The difference is, they're on the run this time," Nick said.

"And armies on the run lay traps behind them, do

they not?" Thor said. "I'm afraid Tony might be right here. How do we know what we're in for? Have we even seen this place where they're going? Do we know it exists?"

Nick pulled up a large image of Antarctica, and rescaled it to infrared. "Right there," he said, zooming in on a mountain tagged Vinson Massif, near an inlet of the Weddell Sea, "is what looks a lot like a volcanic vent. Thing is, the geologists say there's no volcanic activity anywhere near there. After Steve and the lab tracked down these invisible flights from Buenos Aires, we found others as well, from Johannesburg, Christchurch, and Melbourne. We've backtracked the manifests of those flights, and an awful lot of them had a passenger or passengers who originated in the United States but has no return flight booked. So, lady and gentlemen, I believe we have found our Chitauri stronghold. It's cold, it's isolated, and there's no telling how long they've had to prepare it or how many of them are there to hold it. We leave in twelve hours. Any questions?"

Tony, who had taken his seat, now stood again. "Just one, Nick, and I'm serious. How do we know this isn't another Micronesia?"

"Because, like I said, they're on the run," Nick said. "From what we know about their fertility rates and so forth, there can't be that many of them unless they've been cloning like crazy or they've been reinforced from off-planet." He turned his attention from Tony specifically to the group as a whole. "Neither one of those is likely, because their tactics to this point haven't squared with the idea that they're operating from what they feel is a position of strength right now. Suicide attacks, infiltrations, attempted assassinations . . . these are the tools of the outmanned force. I'm guessing they're low on manpower, but maybe not low on weapons, and they were going to be content with laying low until they found out about Hank's breakthrough with the ants. So they tried to take that out . . . ah. Maybe now is a good time for Tony to explain to us exactly what the story is with the amplifier."

"What's to explain?" Clint asked. "We got it all before."

"All except for the part about the amplifier being fake," Thor said.

Clint looked from Thor to Tony to Nick, and then back to Thor. "What?"

"Sure. Ask him. There is no amplifier. He showed it to us, then put out a distress call to get us to come save it. Only it was . . . what's the best way to put it, Tony? Would you call it instilling brand loyalty?"

"Oh, for Christ's sake," Tony said. "You and your hippie canards. It worked, didn't it? And aren't you the one who called down *lightning* in the middle of my headquarters, with my employees all over the place? You can shove your sanctimony, too."

"Let me get this straight," Clint said. "You showed off a fake amplifier in the lab, and then built your whole presentation at the Triskelion around the same fake amplifier? And then got the whole team to show up because the Chitauri were blowing up your building to get an amplifier that didn't exist?"

"More or less," Tony said. "Except you haven't talked about the reasons."

"Screw the reasons," Clint said. "You put our lives on the line for a joke."

"Clint, aren't you about the last one in the room who should be moralizing about the value of a life?" Tony asked.

"Stay on track here, people," Nick warned.

"We are on track, Nick," Tony said. "The track is to figure out what's at stake, where the enemy is, and how to fight it. That's what I did. We've got Chitauri in the Cabinet of the United States. How do I know there aren't any in SHIELD? You can be pissed about it if you want to, but from my point of view it looks like I just sacrificed my company headquarters as a decoy to round up a whole lot of Chitauri. They put all their eggs in this basket, Nick. Now it's either go back underground or rally for some big doomsday like the bomb they had before. The one that Thor teleported off to wherever."

"Niflheim," Thor said.

Tony tipped an imaginary cap. "Thanks, big man. Niflheim. And the dragon's name was, what, Bimblog or something?"

"Nidhogg."

"Okay. So Thor teleported their last bomb to Niflheim, as a result of which Nidhogg bears a serious grudge against all of us. Unintended consequences. That's fine. But we need to consider whether they might not have something similar planned right now. They know we're coming."

"If they'd had another doomsday kind of bomb, wouldn't they have set it off after Arizona?" Janet said.

"If they were thinking like human beings, maybe, sure," Nick said. "That doesn't appear to be the case, however. Now can we get back to the briefing?"

"I'd say it's part of the briefing to know what our odds are of being suckered in and incinerated, Nick. Wouldn't you?" Janet said dryly. Everyone in the room at least cracked a smile, and Tony laughed out loud.

"Our odds of being suckered in and incinerated are unknowable," Nick said. "We know they're there this time, because we've tracked them there. That's one thing that's different from Micronesia. Also, there's no place they could have gone. We've been watching that area in Antarctica since we found those first flights, and there's been a steady trickle of people—by which I mean Chitauri—coming in, but nobody's coming out. Does that make you feel better?" Nick paused to give Janet room to answer if she was going to. When she didn't, he said, "Fine. Now maybe we can get on to the actual mechanics of our operation."

"Why," Thor said, "when all of this sniping is so entertaining?"

Ignoring him, Nick said, "Estimates of the number of Chitauri in this installation vary depending on whether you think we've tracked down all of the invisible flights. If we have, there are several dozen. If we haven't, there might be a lot more. And we must assume that they have been taking care to fortify the installation and anticipate our most likely actions. Tony, your satellites did most of the thermal imaging, so why don't you tell us what this set of images means?"

On the projector screen, they saw the same heat vent, only in infrared, with the ghost of a rectangular outline visible framing it. "It looks like there's at least one level," Tony said. "The level we're looking at is a couple hundred thousand square feet, and it's definitely got warm bodies in it. Now look at the sonar imaging."

The image flipped, and the outline became more precise. "You'll see here," Tony said, indicating a sharp line of cliffs just to the west of the heat vent, "that it appears they've built a big driveway up to the surface. There aren't a ton of tracks there, but the Antarctic winds make it hard for tracks to survive more than a couple of days. Katabatic winds at the base of those cliffs are probably sixty or seventy miles per hour on average. They're at least as strong near the vent, and around the other entrance that I was able to find. See here?" Tony pointed at a crack in the ice, visible only after he had enlarged the image. "That, lady and gentlemen, is the front entrance to the Chitauri South Pole Resort and

Shape-Shifting Club. Admission, I'm sure I don't have to remind you, is very selective."

"So who goes in the front and who goes in the back?" Clint said. "Let's get this figured out and do it."

"My sentiments exactly," Nick said. "We'll be using approximately six hundred next-gens, and they'll be deployed to all three apparent entrances. We're going in hard, and fast, and without much care for whether they know we're coming or not. We'd prefer not to go in at all, but"—he glanced at Tony—"the lesson of Micronesia is that you have to go look to make sure the enemy is present. Then you can worry about whether everything is booby-trapped. So we go. We hit all three entrances. Tony, I think the only one of us who can go through the heat vent is you, so that'll be you. Heat tolerances of Chitauri vary enough that some of them can probably come out that way, so a perimeter of next-gens will be set up around the heat vent. Other next-gens will act as support and infantry for a full-on frontal assault on the other two entrances. Thor and Janet lead one, me and Clint will lead the other."

"And whenever Steve gets there," Clint said with weary sarcasm, "he'll go ahead and do whatever he wants."

"Do you want to go through this again, Clint?" Nick asked. The tension in the room, Nick thought, was enough to give even him a heart attack.

"No, Nick, I don't. But I do want to know that we can count on Steve, because if we can't, I'd just as soon he wasn't there."

That hung in the air, and Nick could feel the room taking sides. The truth was, Nick figured he could count on Steve because of Steve's shame, which was one of the most powerful motivators a man could know. The problem with that truth was that Nick could only share so much of it with the team before the disclosures tore the group dynamic into even smaller shreds than currently flapped against each other. He was about to make a decision, and even he wasn't sure what it would be, when a Triskelion warning siren went off. Quickly others joined in, including one that Nick recognized as the new alarm system built on the dock where the bombing had occurred.

"All hands on deck, people," he said, and there was a huge impact against the side of the Triskelion. Everyone in the briefing room headed for the door, and a second impact threw them off balance. "What the hell?" Janet said. "Is Bruce out again?"

Nick's phone chirped and he answered it. After a pause, he said, "Thank you. Tell him we'll be right down."

He returned the phone to his pocket and said, "Ultimates, we have a visitor. His name is Hank Pym, and I believe he's come to plead his case. We will now go downstairs and listen to what he has to say."

36

HANK HAD HIS SPEECH ALL PREPARED BEFORE HE jumped off the back of the Statue of Liberty ferry. He'd wanted to grow while underwater, but figured that the sudden expansion of his lungs without corresponding increase in the amount of air in them would create a vacuum, and the last thing in the world he needed was for his lungs to collapse while he was underwater. He'd never get Nick to listen to him that way. So he jumped, listened to the screams of his fellow passengers, and then popped his head up out of the water to shout, "I'm okay! Everything's fine! Enjoy the statue!"

Then he grew, bam, to a full sixty feet. The sounds of the transformation echoed in his newly expanded inner ears, where suddenly his anvils were the size of real anvils and the grind of his bones growing sounded like a rock slide—especially underwater, where sound was transmitted so much more intensely. He'd never grown underwater before, and for a moment he could feel the water resisting him, before the force of the Pym particles overcame the water's density. His increase in width and girth caused a shock wave that propagated outward with a receding thrum, and his tenfold increase in height momentarily stood him on a pillar of pressurized water. Shrouded in an explosion of foam, most of Hank's body burst upward above the surface, as a huge bulge in the meniscus of the Upper Bay crested and rolled away to roil the ferry's wake and slap against its stern. Then Hank sank down again, rolling over like a whale to flash his ass at the gawkers on the ferry, loving the feeling of the cold water on his skin even though he knew that he might as well be swimming through the containment lagoon at a chemical plant. That, though, was part of the point. He did it because he could. Hell, what was the point of being a Super Hero if you didn't get to do stuff like this once in a while?

One thing, Hank thought as he started swimming toward the Triskelion. He would never forget the looks on the faces of the people who had gathered around the ferry's back railing. Open mouths, wide eyes, pure slack-jawed amazement. Hank wanted everyone to look at him like that. Awe. Hank wanted awe.

● ● ●

And he got it, at least when he boomed out of the water at the edge of the Triskelion and climbed up onto its main pier. "Hey, Nick!" he shouted, his voice strong enough to send ripples through the American flag hanging above the front door. "Come on out!" Hank banged his elbow into the wall near the front door. SHIELD security people looked at him but made no move to stop him.

"Shoot if you want," he told them with a gigantic grin. "Really. Fire when ready. I won't even hit you."

They didn't, and Hank shot another elbow into the wall. One of the windows, designed to withstand explosive impact, cracked. "Hey, Nick!" he shouted again. "I've got an idea for you!"

Looking back down at the door guards, Hank said, "One of you mind going to get him? He's not answering the door."

All of the guards disappeared, and Hank sat down to wait. It was a lovely sunny day, and he enjoyed the feeling of the sun on his back. When there was so much more of him, the warming effect seemed much larger. He knew it wasn't—in fact, it was probably smaller since his mass had increased so much more than his surface area—but it seemed that way, possibly because even when he was sixty feet tall, Hank's perceptual framework still was that of someone who stood six-one. The discontinuity there made for all kinds of strange sensory effects. However the effect happened, though, Hank liked it. He basked like a crocodile on the Triskelion's

deck, between the VIP helipad and the ceremonial front
door. Someone ought to draw me, he thought. It was almost a shame when Nick showed up, followed by Clint,
Thor, Tony . . . and Janet.

"Hey, babe," he said.

The way she nodded at him made him feel kind of
like they were on opposite sides of the fence at the O.K.
Corral, but even that couldn't bring him down right
then. "So, here I am," he said. "It's about time we let bygones be bygones, right? My hit rate's gone way down,
which I'm guessing means that the ants have the Chitauri on the run. Am I right?"

Nick raised a hand as a couple of the others started to
speak. "Two things, Hank. One, we're not going to dis-
cuss things like what the Chitauri are doing. Two, you're
trespassing."

"I'll add a third," Tony said. "Isn't there some kind of
SHIELD bylaw about showing up to a meeting naked? I
mean really, Hank."

"Naked, shmaked," Hank said. "The Chitauri
headed out, didn't they? Maybe I should say bugged
out." He couldn't help but laugh at his own joke.
"Where did they go? My money's on the Himalayas.
Talk about remote. They could hide out up there forever, and by the time we tracked them down they
might have figured out something to counter the ants.
At least temporarily. I don't think there's any permanent way around the ants for them, especially if someone can cook up some way to broadcast the signals

over a wider area. Tony, you're probably working on that, right?"

"Confidential, old boy," Tony said with a wink and a grin.

"Okay, sure. I get it," Hank said. "That's not what I came for, anyway. I'm not here to talk science. I'm here to squash lizards. Let's do it."

"We are doing it," Janet said. "But you aren't."

Hank stood up and stretched. God, the sun felt good. "Jan, come on," he said. "People work together after a divorce all the time. Let's be adults about this."

"People don't work together after one of them has tried to kill the other one," she said. "Get the hell out of here, Hank."

"Well, now, wait a minute," Tony said. "Weren't you the one who was saying a little while ago that if we needed Hank to fight the Chitauri, that was more important than personal issues?"

"She said that?" Hank asked. He couldn't believe it.

Janet spun on Tony and jabbed a finger in his face. "That was a private conversation, Tony. How the hell do you know about it, and where do you get off bringing it up right now?"

Tony looked over at Hank. "Private conversation with Steve, is the part she didn't mention. And I bring it up right now, darling, because you said it and it's germane to the current conversation."

"No, it isn't," Nick said, in a tone that shut them all up. "Janet doesn't make those kinds of decisions around here. I do, and the decision was made a while ago. Hank, I'm going to tell you again. You need to leave the Triskelion, and you need to leave it now. Whatever anybody said or didn't say before is irrelevant. Get gone. You did the work with the ants, and we'll tip our caps to you for that. In fact, we managed to squash a whole lot of media interest in the way you put away your former lab assistant, so we did you a little favor, too. And now it's time for you to move along."

Hank folded his arms and looked down on the five of them. "Clint? Thor?" he said. "You guys have nothing to add?"

"They have nothing to add to this discussion," Nick said. "It's not their call. It's mine, and I made it."

"There is one thing I'd like to say," Clint put in. "I've done a lot of things I'd rather not remember, but I never hit a woman. Killed a bunch, but never hit one who wasn't an enemy in a fair fight. You're a punk, Hank. I wouldn't piss on you if you were on fire, and if you don't get the hell out of here right now, Nick's going to have to reprimand me for undisciplined use of force."

"What are you going to do, poke my eyes out with paint chips?" Hank chuckled. "Sever my jugular with your wedding ring? Give me a break, Clint. If I was worried about you, I'd squeeze you until I felt you pop."

Hank had always known that he was prone to mood swings, and long before doctors had begun strafing him with terms like *bipolar* and *manic-depressive,* he had also known when the shift was about to happen. In retrospect, it had always seemed to him that an external stimulus did it: a sound, an odor, a color. The shifts didn't seem to have much to do with his particular emotional responses to the particular actions of other people. He remembered once being moved nearly to ecstasy, from a depression as black as any he'd ever experienced, by the glint of sunlight off the surface of a car windshield—and he remembered falling into an emotional black hole because of the way *Solenopsis invicta* articulated its antennae. This time, it was the word *pop*. The way it felt in his mouth and echoed in his ears, it was like the first minute shift in a mile-wide cliff of snow. Invisibly it began an avalanche.

Janet hated him. The team scorned him. He was standing naked at the front of the Triskelion, with news helicopters probably circling overhead waiting to tell the viewers at home what a ridiculous buffoon Hank Pym had again proved himself to be.

"Piss on me if I was on fire, Clint?" Hank said. "If I pissed on you right now, bucko, you'd drown." He bent over and scooped Clint up in his left hand. "Or maybe I could squeeze you until you went pop. *Pop!* How does that sound, Clint? You going to put my eyes out with both of your arms pinned? Who's a punk now, Clint?"

He had Clint held up in front of his face, close enough that sharp consonants out of Hank's mouth carried enough punch to make Clint involuntarily flinch.

"Put him down, Hank," Fury said. Janet said it almost simultaneously, their two contrasting voices making a strange chord of disapproval.

"I don't think I will, Nick," Hank said, ignoring Janet. "In fact, maybe I'll eat him the way the Hulk was going to eat me. Remember that? Remember how he ripped the hell out of Manhattan? He's still on the team, Nick. You keep him in a box, but he's still around. Nobody ostracized him."

"Take your meds today, Hank?" Clint said.

"You go to hell," Hank said, and threw Clint as far as he could out into the bay. Janet screamed something, and Hank dropped to his hands and knees so he could get his face closer to hers. "He another one of your boyfriends, Jan? Couldn't wait until the divorce went through?" Faintly the sound of Clint Barton's splashdown reached Hank's ears. "Did you tell them you thought the team needed me back, Jan? Yes or no? I just want a straight answer."

"No," she said. "I never told them that."

And then she disappeared, and at almost the same instant Hank's eyes lit up with the pain of her stings.

"Janet!" he roared. "Don't start this again, Janet!"

He could just barely see her, as whispers of motion in his peripheral vision a split second before she stung him again. Hank flailed at the air around his head, shouting at her to stop. Once he felt the back of his hand graze her, and heard her tiny grunt at the impact. "I'm not trying to hurt you, Jan, but stop this!" he shouted.

Then a line of bullets stitched its way across his left

leg and he forgot all about Janet. Dropping briefly to one knee, Hank looked at Nick Fury and said, "Shooting me, Nick? Is this what it's come to?"

"Had to get your attention," Nick said.

"Ah," Hank said. "Of course. I understand." He took one step to his right, ripped the flagpole out of its concrete base and hurled it like a spear through the Triskelion's front door. The bulletproof glass went off like a bomb, and the flagpole buried itself at the base of the rear atrium wall after splintering the reception desk. "Now," Hank said. "Did I get your attention? Go ahead, shoot me again, Nick. I can take it."

"How about this?" a voice said from behind him. Hank spun around to see who it was, and just had time to glimpse the gleaming head of Mjolnir before it crashed into the point of his shoulder.

His arm went numb, and Hank stumbled toward the broken door. "Thor, buddy, I thought we always got along," Hank said. "Guess I was wrong about that, too." With his good arm, he swatted Thor away and returned his attention to Nick. "Tell me something, Nick," Hank said in the brief pause. "Have you ever made a mistake in your life?"

Still pointing the gun at Hank, Nick said, "Sure I have. But that doesn't mean I assume I'll always be trying to get everyone else to go along with it. My mistakes are mine—I should never have gone to D.C. when I knew what was going to happen, and I for damn sure should have played smarter by anticipating the Chitauri tactics sooner." Nick raised the gun. "But you I was right about. Stand down."

Hank saw Nick's gaze flick up and back, an instant before the back of Hank's neck lit up with Jan's stings. "Dammit, Jan!" Hank said, hunching away from the stings and swiping his arms around his head again. "Stop it!"

"Stand down, Hank," Fury said coldly. "Last chance."

"Last chance?" Hank repeated. Inside his head was a great black emptiness, a lack of hope so absolute that he couldn't even imagine what hope might feel like. He took a step toward Nick, and didn't even pause when Nick squeezed off a shot that hit Hank square on the knee. "What the hell do you know about being out of chances?"

"I know enough," Nick said, "to know that you had yours. Do it, big man."

For a split second, Hank took that as a challenge; then he realized that Nick had been talking to someone else. A crackle of energy lit up in the corner of his eye, and he turned to see Thor, Mjolnir at the ready. He got one arm up as Thor started his swing, and then—far too late—he thought, *Where's Tony?*

Simultaneously, Mjolnir slammed into Hank's jaw and a force like Hank had never felt crushed him down from behind to the steel deck of the Triskelion. He tried to get up, and heard Tony's voice, amplified through the Iron Man suit: "Stay down, Hank."

"No," Hank said. All of his anger evaporated. The impact of Mjolnir still rang in his head, and he felt as if Tony's force beams had crushed all of the air out of his lungs. Janet's stings still burned all over his skin and in his eyes. He'd never hurt like this in his life.

"No," he said again, and pushed himself up to his hands and knees.

Like a bomb going off in Hank's head, Mjolnir slammed him back to the ground. His eyes, already swelling shut from Wasp stings, wouldn't focus.

"No," he said one more time, and started to rise.

Janet's voice came to him, from near his head. "Don't," she said, but he couldn't see her and he wasn't doing it for her anyway. He got almost to his knees again.

"Stay down, Hank," Nick said. "Tony warned you."

"Tony," Hank said, and spat blood. He got one of his feet under him. No one said anything, but Hank felt the static charge in the air—the moment before Tony's force beams sledgehammered him into the deck again. Still he tried to get up again, but he couldn't make his limbs work, and he could feel consciousness slipping away.

As Hank faded to black, the last thing he heard was Tony saying, "I just heard Cap over the comm. He's found them for sure, but there's nowhere for him to land. We need to . . ."

Take me with you, Hank tried to say.

37

THE **SHIELD** HELICARRIER *ALGOL* WAS A BIG
sturdy ship, but even it was having trouble with the
storms boiling off the Antarctic coast here in the dead
of the Southern Hemisphere winter. Antarctica was the
driest place on Earth, but the wind sure did like to blow
around whatever snow did fall, and it was all blowing
right now, as Steve tried to figure out what was going on
around the Chitauri base at the edge of the Weddell Sea.
The best thermal imaging technology SHIELD could
offer had only confirmed the existence of an artificial
heat source, and because the Antarctic cold and wind
dispersed the heat so quickly, SHIELD scientists were
having trouble coming up with any kind of ballpark es-

timate of how big the heat source really was, which meant that nobody had any idea how large a space was being heated . . . which meant that there was no way to tell how many Chitauri were down there.

"You can't bring us any lower?" he asked the pilot for the dozenth time since he'd landed on *Algol* twelve hours before.

"Nope," the pilot said. "You think the wind is bad up here, try it along the face of the mountain there. We could probably handle it—well, we could maybe handle it—but we'd only get to be wrong once. And my orders from General Fury are to avoid contact with the enemy."

Which, since they didn't know what kind of surveillance capability the Chitauri had down there in their nest, meant that the captain was going to play it safe. Steve was annoyed with himself for asking, since he'd known the answer before he opened his mouth, and also since that kind of pointless repetition lacked discipline. He resolved that he'd asked for the last time.

"What's the ETA on the rest of the team?" Steve asked. General Fury hadn't shared that bit of information with him, an omission Steve attributed to the general's lingering anger and disappointment over Steve's recent actions. *And I deserve it, too,* Steve thought. *I haven't been worthy of my commission.*

"Last I knew, Iron Man should have been here by now," the pilot said. "The rest of the team is due in the next two hours, give or take."

Steve looked out through the window at the swirl of

clouds on the face of Vinson Massif. *Algol* held its position level with the top of the mountain, at about sixteen thousand feet, and maybe ten miles out over the Weddell Sea. From this high, it was practically impossible to tell where sea ended and land began. It was all ice—more specifically, the six-hundred-meter-thick Filchner-Ronne Ice Shelf, and all of the glaciers that fed it—until the black stone face of the mountain reared up. And even the mountain was mostly covered in snow and ice. In Antarctica, a surface had to be pretty steep to not get a coating of the white stuff.

I've always wanted to go here, Steve thought. When he'd been a kid, Scott, Shackleton, and Amundsen had been names to conjure with. And now he was here, after his own time spent frozen, but he wouldn't get to enjoy it much. Battling enemies of the United States and of freedom brought a certain kind of satisfaction, but it wasn't fun.

Although neither was polar exploration, to judge from most of the stories.

"So Tony's supposed to be here by now?" he said, just to be saying something. The nerves he was feeling weren't normal for him. This was a big show, for sure, but it wasn't like he hadn't been in the big shows before. The difference now was that Steve felt like he had to redeem himself. He had to prove himself worthy.

Specifically, he had to find the Chitauri who called himself Admiral Esteban Garza, and he had to settle things.

The pilot didn't answer him. Good, Steve thought. By this time, I wouldn't be answering me either. He scanned through his comm channels to see if he could raise Tony, but Tony was either out of range—which shouldn't have been possible, unless he was in outer space or under a volcano—or he was just being his typical drunken idiot playboy self. Amazing, the people brought together to be the Ultimates, Steve thought. A delusional Scandinavian nurse, a scientist who occasionally turns into a nearly invincible freak, an alcoholic with a brain tumor, a manic-depressive wife-beater . . . they make Clint look normal, and he's a psychotic assassin. Heck, they make Janet look normal, and she's a mutant.

He felt a little twinge at that last thought. His feelings for Janet ran hot and cold . . . well, hot and warm . . . and if Steve was honest with himself, he realized that the reason for that variance was that deep down inside, he felt strange about being with a mutant girl. He was old-fashioned. If he was with a girl for a while, he started thinking about white picket fences and kid-size baseball mitts lying in the yard. What kind of kids would he and Janet have?

None, was the answer. They'd never get that far. They dated sometimes, and that was as far as it would ever go. Janet would never be his twenty-first-century Gail, and that had much less to do with Hank Pym than with Steve Rogers. Another word for old-fashioned, Janet had told him once, was *bigoted*. Well, fine, Steve thought. I'm a bigot. I'm bigoted in the direction of normal, regular life, and if that's a bad thing, then put me up against the wall and shoot me. Until then, I'll keep going out there and putting my life on the line for my bigoted ideals.

Steve's comm popped. "Ahoy there, Captain Flag," came Tony's voice. "I see that you've been calling."

Steve was looking out the window, but couldn't see the ion trail left by the Iron Man suit anywhere. "What's your ETA to *Algol*?"

"Couple of minutes," Tony said breezily. "I took a turn around the South Pole, just to see it, and then I thought I should have a look at the magnetic pole, too, so that was another little detour. But I'm coming at you from the south-southwest right now."

Sure enough, there was the twinkling of the ion trail as Tony neared *Algol,* cutting through the storm like it didn't exist. "This isn't the best time for tourism, Tony," Steve said. "You know, we're supposed to be exterminating a bunch of aliens here pretty soon."

"What, you and me? Or were we going to wait for the rest of the gang and their legions of next-gens?" The ion trail grew brighter, and then Tony streaked overhead. "I'm coming down. Meet me inside so you don't catch your death of cold."

"Go to hell," Steve said. He cut the link and went to meet Tony in *Algol*'s rear internal hangar.

The latest version of the Iron Man suit had, among its other updates, a quick-exit feature. Basically, Tony gave a verbal command and the suit sprang open. This was convenient for Tony, but not so much for the support crew, since the suit's opening caused a slow-motion flood of inertial-damping gel. All SHIELD helicarriers kept a supply of the gel on hand. When Steve got to the hangar, Tony was toweling off while the hangar crew scraped and mopped up the gel and got the suit prepped for redeployment. "I'm going to need to siphon off whatever excess power there is until we head out," Tony was saying as Steve walked in. "A quick ten-thousand-mile jaunt is hell on the batteries, you know."

"No problem," one of the hangar crew said. He was already dragging an arm-thick cable from the wall over to the where the suit stood against its frame. "We'll have you topped off inside an hour, as long as we don't have to do anything else."

"And where can a guy get a drink around here?" Tony added.

"Can't help you there," the tech said.

"Barbarians," Tony said. "Steve, I'm surrounded by barbarians. Including you."

"Sometimes it's tough being a libertine," Steve said.

Tony's eyebrows shot up. "A joke from Captain Flag, so close to our final confrontation with the alien menace? A joke including the word *libertine?* Good Lord. I'm starting to think I'm having an influence on you."

Steve ignored this, not even wanting to contemplate the question of how he might influence Tony, and how any possible channel of influence might run both ways. "Instead of a drink, you ought to have something to eat.

Won't be long before *Altair* and *Alshain* are within range. I think we're going to go tonight."

"Not until tonight? I was hoping to be done by then. Ah well," Tony said. He finished drying off and got into a plain SHIELD jumpsuit. "My dissipated life can resume tomorrow."

Forty-five minutes later, as Tony was finishing a sandwich from *Algol*'s mess, word came from General Fury that *Altair* and *Alshain* were within two hundred miles. "Favorable winds," General Fury said. "We go in thirty minutes if Tony's suit is ready."

"The hangar monkeys say it will be," Tony said. "So let's get this show on the road."

"Weather being what it is," General Fury said, "we're not going to be able to land with copters. I've got Clint and Janet here, although Clint's a little gimpy from Hank's tantrum yesterday, and four companies of next-gens. We will deploy using jetpacks."

"Where's our Norse god of thunder?" Tony asked.

"No idea. He said he'd be here, and I took him at his word."

Again Steve was reminded of just how loopy everyone on this team was. "Did he say why he didn't come along with everyone else?"

General Fury rolled his eyes. "What do you think? Loki, he said. It had something to do with Loki."

Seven-thirteen p.m. local time, the Antarctic winter winds coming down off Vinson Massif at a steady gale force with gusts over a hundred miles per hour, windchill close to the negative century mark. Hell of a time to be jumping off a helicarrier, Steve thought. He imagined trying to parachute in weather like this, and just had to laugh. You'd end up floating all the way to the Falklands, or landing on an iceberg somewhere in the Southern Ocean. Thank God for technological advances, specifically jetpacks. As a temporary concession to the weather, Steve was wearing a thermal oversuit; no sense freezing before he got to the ground. The mission plan was fairly straightforward. Individual jetpack deployments would coincide with aerial bombing of the heat source, with the idea that by the time the Ultimates and the supporting next-gens hit the ground, the Chitauri nest would be blown wide open. What they knew of Chitauri physiology inclined SHIELD scientists—including Janet and Bruce—to believe that the Chitauri couldn't survive in the Antarctic, and their adoption of human form would only mean that they could go as far as an average human. Which, given the ambient conditions, wasn't far at all.

So SHIELD would hit hard, not give the Chitauri time to suit up for a coordinated flight, and go straight into the nest to mop them up. General Fury had ordered that as many Chitauri as possible were to be taken prisoner, but Steve was having a little trouble reconciling that order with the rules of engagement, which were simple. Anything that moved inside the Chitauri facility was to be considered hostile. The base of Vinson Massif was, until further notice, a free-fire zone.

Steve stood in a sheltered hangar bay facing *Algol*'s stern. The jetpack and thermal suit made him feel slow; he couldn't wait to hit the ground and get them off. His shield hung over his chest. There was no sign that the Chitauri knew they were coming, but there was also no way to know whether the Chitauri were playing possum.

We'll find out soon enough, Steve thought.

Next to him, Tony waited in the Iron Man suit. "You ever see *The Thing*?" Tony asked. "Movie about an Antarctic research station that finds an alien that can change shape. You can guess where it goes."

"Don't think so," Steve said. "When did it come out?"

"Oh. Right. After your time."

Like so much else, Steve thought. "Wait a minute," he said, at the faint spark of a memory. "I read a story when I was a teenager that was something like that. I think it was called 'Who Goes There?' Maybe the same thing."

"Maybe. You're going to freeze your ass off," Tony said.

"Already am," Steve said.

Behind them stood two platoons of next-gens. *Algol* held its position over the shallows of the Weddell Sea. *Altair* and *Alshain* were triangulating the Chitauri nest, stationing themselves at the northern and southern edges of Vinson Massif.

"Haven't heard from The Man in a little while," Tony said. "What's keeping him?"

Shut up, Steve thought. Just shut up and do your job.

Below, the landscape lit up with missile impacts. Huge white flashes walked along the base of the mountain, almost immediately obscured by clouds of steam

"Way to keep the troops informed, Nick," Tony commented dryly. "What if I'd gone to the bathroom?"

Huh, Steve thought. Wonder how he does that in the suit. Knowing him, he's figured out an instantaneous way to turn crap into energy, and he's keeping it to himself.

His comm popped. "We are go on the jetpacks," said a SHIELD officer. "Repeat, jetpacks go."

Steve lifted his right hand, made a fist, and cocked it forward. Behind him, he heard the shuffle and scrape of the next-gens getting themselves into position. Dropping his arm, Steve took three steps forward, powered the jetpack on, and stepped out into the void. For a moment he let himself fall, getting clear of *Algol*'s wash before trying to steer through the ferocious wind. Tony, who could cut through a hurricane in his suit, thundered over Steve's head and arced away toward the ground, where a second round of missile strikes was gouging deeper into the Chitauri nest. "That's your air support, ladies and gentlemen," came General Fury's voice over the comm. "There will be no further air support until all ground forces are out of the target area."

"Understood," Steve said. He glanced up and saw that the next-gens were fanning out into their formation above and behind him. It was go time. Firing up the jetpack, he followed Tony's ion trail down into the roiling clouds of steam.

38

Status Report

Relocation to the <Antarctic> facility begun before the <Arizona> event is complete. All assets previously emplaced in other locations are either eliminated, en route, or already at this location. One lesson of <Arizona> was the undesirability of allowing a broad frontal confrontation with human forces; however, given the introduction of the <Pym-Hymenoptera> technology and its next-generation improvements by <Tony Stark> and <Stark Industries>, the concentration of assets in a location uninhabited by <Hymenoptera> was an unavoidable tactical concession. The limited success of the <Polynesia> decoy, immediately previous to the <Arizona> events, is a guidepost both with respect to its successes and its failures. <Polynesia> failed in its primary goal of eliminating one or more of the core <SHIELD> operatives due to previous asset grouping's incomplete understanding of individual <SHIELD> members' capabilities. Too, <Arizona> did not achieve useful strategic or tactical outcomes due to failure to anticipate or understand the capabilities of the <SHIELD> operative known as <Thor>. It is not known whether <Thor> will be present at any <SHIELD> action against the <Antarctic> facility. If so, all effort must be expended to direct him away from the <Rogers> gambit, outlined later in this directive. Desirable outcomes following this relocation include:

Reduction or elimination of <SHIELD> capacity to perform defensive and counter-infiltration function

Retrenchment and increase of available asset strength

Maintenance of channels for future assimilations and asset placement

Development of technical and ordnance facilities unavailable in current dispersed asset grouping

Under active consideration is the possibility that the primary goal of this asset grouping should be the weakening of human resistance to a future phase of the human ordering project. The <Pym-Hymenoptera> technology, while surmountable, is a decisive tactical influence under current circumstances. In addition, the tactical situation is likely to worsen given the failure of current asset group to prevent <Stark> innovation in

<Hymenoptera> control. In view of this, recalibration of goals of this asset group has led to the conclusion that survival beyond the next .002738 solar year is unlikely.

Loss of <Bright> has hampered intelligence-coordination efforts, and discovery of <Garza>'s assimilation has compromised ability to manipulate actions of <SHIELD> and <Ultimates>. In addition, continuing losses due to the <Pym-Hymenoptera> technology further exacerbate the already prominent problem of asset paucity. It is unknown at this point when operational and asset reinforcements will be forthcoming.

A possible use for asset <Garza>, involving planned loss, is under advisement. Involved is a psychological gambit aimed at utilizing existing mental state of <Steve Rogers>, which is deemed unstable following <Rogers>'s discovery of his exploitation in intelligence and logistical work of this asset grouping. Resources and planning for this gambit are operational at this time.

Future iterations of the human ordering project would be well advised to take into consideration the peculiar circumstances involved in the interaction between human tribalism—and its more fully developed descendant, the nation-state and media-driven cultural grouping—and *Homo sapiens*' seemingly genetically coded impetus toward individual achievement and individual action. <Kleiser> and the previous iteration of this project failed to fully anticipate the effect this dynamic would have on human resistance. The current asset groups attempted a more comprehensive approach incorporating previous learning in this area, but increased understanding yielded small

39

ON A SHELF OF STONE TWO THOUSAND FEET above the storm of missile impacts, Thor closed his eyes and felt the wash of steam and heat. Now this is my kind of fight, Thor thought. Give me fire and ice, stone and smoke, air that burns coldly in the lungs, sweat that vanishes into steam. He raised both hands and threw his head back as lightning forked and crackled in the skies above the mountain. Then he said to the stones and the sky, "Loki. If you are here, I will find you. If I find you, it will not go well for you, brother."

He sensed Loki's presence the way a dog senses a threat just at the edge of the firelight. From the sky fell the embers of SHIELD troops in formation, led by the blue streak of Tony's Iron Man armor. Gods know the approach of endings, thought Thor. And an ending approaches.

He leapt from the stone, and fell into steam. Icebergs calved into the Weddell Sea at the impact of his feet on the ice. Before him, a chasm yawned in the ice, and continued down into the stone roots of Vinson Massif. Meltwater from the missile strikes ran in streams down into the depths of the exposed Chitauri complex. So very much like an anthill kicked open by a careless boy, Thor thought. The first wave of next-gens arrowed down into the ruins, and was met by a fusillade of defensive fire. In the vanguard came Steve Rogers, and Thor also saw Clint firing arrows from a rocky outcrop exposed by the melting ice. Janet would not be far away. Tony, though . . .

"So there you are," Tony said.

Thor glanced to his right and saw Tony hovering a foot off the ground. "Here I am," Thor said.

"Nick was starting to wonder if you'd show up. Enjoying the view, or were you planning to join in?"

"Loki is down there," Thor said, returning his gaze to the battle below. "Do not question my courage."

"Perish the thought," Tony said, and chuckled.

Thor took a deep breath, letting the smells of the land and the battle flood through him. As he exhaled, he said, "Here amid icebergs rule I the nations."

"Oh God," Tony groaned. "Are we quoting *eddas* today?"

Thor shot him a grin. "No, that's Longfellow. He was a big fan of mine. Gotcha."

And then he raised Mjolnir and leapt down again, blood singing with the battle to come.

From the bridge of *Altair,* Nick watched Thor join the battle. If there's one thing I hate, he thought, it's not being able to make a decision. And I just cannot decide whether Thor is the real thing or not. All of the jabbering about Loki makes me think he's a nutcase, but then he brings the lightning and teleports bombs to other dimensions. He just doesn't fit in any framework I can put together.

One possibility, Nick had to admit, was that he needed a new framework, but he was not about to admit the existence of Norse gods. If you let the Norse gods in, next thing you knew you had Kali and Ogun and Quetzalcoatl and Jesus H. Christ Himself wearing costumes and fighting bad guys. No man could stay sane for long if he took that scenario seriously.

Whatever Thor was, he sure could kick ass. That was what Nick needed right then, and that was all he was going to think about until this operation was over and they could all take a breath.

Simultaneous to this takedown of the nest, SHIELD had operatives all over the world cleaning assimilated Chitauri out of airports and other facilities used to grease the skids for the mass exodus to Antarctica. This time they were going to get them all, and if they didn't get them all today, they were going to stay on the case and hunt them down one by one for as long as it took. They had the ants, they had Tony's screener tech, and they had plain old human doggedness and ingenuity. Survival was one thing humans did as well as any other vertebrate on the planet.

Below him, the exposed warrens of the Chitauri nest were still mostly obscured by steam and smoke. Flashes of light appeared from within the clouds, mostly the little flickers of small-arms fire but sometimes much larger bursts that could have been either some kind of heavy ordnance or collateral explosions from the initial bombardment. There was no way to tell. Nick itched to be down there finding out, but he had to coordinate the bug-zapping operations elsewhere. Dammit. There were times when command was no bowl of peaches. Ah, to be a sergeant again.

At least he could follow on the comm to get the radio-play version of what was happening on the ground. Once Thor had taken the jump, Tony had boosted himself away from the edge of the blown-open next; now his force beams picked out targets in the fog, flaring to life and disappearing just as fast. The effect was almost like watching lightning . . . which put Nick in mind of Thor again.

Would Thor be able to just bring the heavens down and melt the whole Chitauri nest? Maybe he could. Nick wasn't at all sure if he would, though—especially if he was asked to. Nick's take on Thor was that the putative god of thunder was a lot more likely to come through for the team if nobody made him feel obligated. He was one of those guys—or gods—who wanted to be allowed to come to the right conclusion for himself.

Unlike Steve Rogers, who was a little too sure about his own goals and motives. That was going to be a problem if it kept up; Nick hoped that Steve would be chastened by his gullibility with Garza. Actually, no. Right then, Nick hoped that Steve would be so focused and angry that he couldn't think about anything else but taking that anger out on the Chitauri. Reflection was for another time.

"Sweet Jesus, look at the size of this."

Clint's voice over the comm got Nick's attention. "Clint," he said. "A little more detail in the report, if you don't mind."

"I'm four, maybe five levels down," came the reply. "A lot of it's collapsed, and a lot of what's farther down is flooded, but there are plenty of targets, and I just found a whole new wing of the complex that goes out into the interior of the ice shelf. I don't know, Nick. Could be they have a way out into the water. Anybody reported any submarines stolen lately?"

Just what I need, Nick thought. "Hold there, Clint," he said. "I'll be right back." He switched channels and pinged the pilot on *Alshain*'s bridge. "General Fury here. I need coverage of the open water at the edges of the Weddell Sea, where the ice shelf peters out. It's possible the Chitauri could get out that way."

"Understood," the pilot said. "We're on our way. You're picking up our next-gens?"

"I will, or *Algol* will," Nick said. "Go."

He watched until *Alshain* had made the turn and headed northwest for open water, then flipped channels again. "Clint. Can you move forward and find out for sure whether there's a way out under there?"

"Will do."

"Is anyone with you?"

"Flying solo," Clint said.

"You feeling all right? Help is on the way."

"Took some aspirin," Clint said. "And if I need help, I don't think it's going to get here in time. But thanks for thinking of me."

"Right. Team," Nick said. "Report locations."

"At the perimeter of the blast opening," Janet said. "If I knock them down out here, they die in the cold pretty quickly. It's an ugly thing, watching a Chitauri decohere and freeze at the same time."

Steve was next. "I'm dead center, on the floor of the deepest level the missiles opened up. Could be I'm on the same level with Clint. Not sure with the fog, though."

"I think you are, too, Steve," Tony said. "Nick, you can see me, right?"

"I sure can," Nick said, meaning it in two ways. He did in fact have visual contact with Tony, but each of their comms also had a homing beacon built in. So, as each of them checked in, he was also correlating their reports with a three-dimensional display in front of him on the bridge. So far it all seemed to match up, and looking at the display gave him an unsettling idea of exactly how big the Chitauri nest was. He wondered how long they'd been working on it. "Can anyone see Thor?"

"He's clearing out part of the area over under the mountain, I think," Janet said. "Was the last I saw him, anyway. And singing, my God. He's singing old Viking songs or something."

"Okay. Keep in touch with each other, and do what you can to keep the next-gens working in squads to support you."

"General," Steve said. "I'm closest to Clint, I think. Should I head toward him?"

"Good idea, Cap. Clint, hold steady until Steve gets there."

"Just like Tony's basement," Clint said. "Except maybe I get in on the real fight this time? Can I, Nick? Please, please, can I?"

"Shut up," Nick said. "We need to make a concerted push to keep the Chitauri from getting out under the ice, if they in fact can do that. Team, if Steve or Clint reports that there are Chitauri escaping that way, your new primary objective is to stop that. Let the next-gens and the weather and us helicarriers take care of Chitauri coming up. You concentrate on taking care of them when and if they head down."

Steve came back on, breathing heavily. "Oh, they're

heading down, all right. Lots of them. I think a memo went around. Janet? Tony? How's it look up top?"

"Still plenty to do," Janet said. "I think we're keeping a lid on it, though. Some of the next-gens are up on the rocks picking off the ones we miss. This would be a job for Clint, really. Where did Thor go?"

It occurred to Nick that the cold would be dangerous for a Wasp-sized Janet Pym. "Are you staying warm, Janet?"

"Sure am," she chirped. "Every so often I dip down for a steam bath. They can't see me at all down there. I only stay up in the cold for a minute or so at a time."

"Okay," Nick said. "Get out of there. Steve, Janet is coming your way. Wait for her, and then the two of you meet Clint."

"Yes, sir," Steve said, as Janet said, "You got it, chief."

"Boys and girls," Clint said then. "We've got a serious Jules Verne setup back here. I think Steve and Jan ought to step on it, and if anyone else can get here, send them, too."

40

"ON MY WAY, CLINT," STEVE BARKED INTO THE comm. He spun through a barrage of machine-gun fire from behind a rockfall and had almost closed on the shooter when the actinic blast of Tony's force beams shattered the rocks into gravel. In the swirl of steam, it was next to impossible to identify targets until they were on top of you or you were on top of them. The Chitauri apparently were solving this problem by shooting at anything that moved, unconcerned about taking out their own forces. The tactic made them seem to Steve to be suicidally resigned, which made Clint's surprise discovery a little hard to figure out.

Unless, Steve thought as he caught a Chitauri lining up one of the next-gens and broke its neck with a sweep of his shield, the ones left out here are just fighting some kind of holding action. He was sweating, more from the humidity than the heat since frigid air was pouring down into the cratered ruin of the Chitauri redoubt. "Jan, where are you?" he called out.

"Be right there," she said, and a few seconds later she was, three inches tall and gorgeous.

On the comm General Fury was trying to wring details out of Clint, but Clint wasn't talking, which Steve took to be a bad sign. He wasn't especially worried that the Chitauri had taken Clint out, but if there were enough of them around that Clint didn't think he could kill them singlehandedly, then the airstrikes hadn't done their job. It just went to prove the old military adage that you can't win a war without boots on the ground.

"Tony," Steve said. "Are you still seeing lots of bogeys from up there?"

"Not too many," Tony said. "The next-gens have them pretty well corralled, and they're organizing search-and-destroy teams to go into the parts of the nest that haven't collapsed. Man, you should see what it looks like from up here now that some of the steam is clearing out."

Steve looked around. "From where I sit, it still looks like fog and broken rocks." And dead Chitauri slowly decohering in the fog . . . and dead next-gens, too. As he looked, the steam lifted from one side of the crater, and Steve had his first real glimpse of both the size of the Chitauri installation and the damage SHIELD had done to it. He was looking nearly straight up a sixty-foot cross-section of the nest, with at least five distinct levels. Lights sparked and flared from the darkness within, and water cascaded down, catching the light. Some of it was already freezing again, walling off parts of each ripped-open floor in gleaming, sinuous sheets of ice. How long had they been at this? There was no way they could have built such a huge hideaway in the . . . what, two weeks since they'd learned about Hank's work with the ants?

"They must have been working on this since Arizona," Tony said. "Listen, shouldn't you be finding Clint?"

"Yep," Steve said, and glanced at the display of his watch, which gave him a directional bearing on Clint's signal. And, he added to himself, I need to be finding Garza. As they headed deeper into the complex, entering the part untouched by SHIELD missiles, Janet touched him on the shoulder.

He cocked an eyebrow at her and she said, "Listen."

He did, and heard it, echoing through the maze of passageways by some strange trick of acoustics: Thor, still singing as he tore a path through the Chitauri looking for Loki.

"Cap," General Fury said in the comm. "You and Janet en route?"

"Yes, sir," Steve said. "We just heard Thor, too, but nobody's seen him since we got here."

"I don't have a read on Thor, and I don't care about him right now," General Fury said. "You get to Clint and take care of what you find down there. *Alshain* is stationed out at the edge of the Weddell Sea, and if the Chitauri get out that way, we'll know about it. We've got subs on the way, too, but they're not going to get here soon. Long story short, you're on your own down there. I need to keep the next-gens back for containment topside. Find Thor if you can, but don't put too much time into it. Just go."

"Orders for me, O Potentate?" Tony asked.

"Stay put. If and when you run out of targets, we'll talk then."

"Oh, well," Tony sighed. "You two have fun down there. I'll just try to enjoy the target practice."

"General?" Steve said. "It looks like we're heading down under the ice. If we go off comm . . . ?"

"If you're off comm, you will recon the situation and Janet will report back to comm range to keep me informed. Do what you have to do in the meantime. Now go," General Fury said. "Everything's under control up here."

They went, and pinged Clint every so often, but there was no answer. Clint's location stayed steady—about two miles to the northwest and two hundred yards down—and Steve started to get worried. It wasn't like Clint to stay still for so long unless he was waiting for a shot, and the situation down there didn't sound like it could be taken care of with one shot.

Don't overthink this, Steve told himself. You have a mission. Execute it.

Except the mission didn't include tracking down Garza, and that was the one thing that still had Steve itching to go freelance. If they got down there and solved whatever problem they found, and Garza wasn't there . . .

Cross that bridge when we come to it, Steve thought. For now, just down.

They were in a sloping hallway, built at the level of the ground, which was mud and ice pressurized into water that ran out into the hall, froze, then melted again at the head from some unseen source. The bottoms of glaciers, Steve remembered, were a kind of soup; the immense weight of the ice above compressed less dense ice into more dense water, and that lubricated the glacier's movement. Then, almost before they'd noticed it, they were walking solely on ice. Steve stopped, and played a flashlight back the way they'd come. Sure enough. For the last hundred yards or so, they'd been out of the slush-and-ground-bedrock mixture.

"We're over water now," Janet said.

"We sure are," Steve agreed. He aimed the flashlight ahead. "And still going down."

They had to move much more carefully now, or at least Steve did. Janet flew near him, sometimes flitting up ahead to reconnoiter. The slope was gentle

enough that the soles of Steve's boots, and the soft-
ness of the surface ice due to whatever was heating
the tunnel, kept him from slipping. He couldn't
move too quickly, though, and ten minutes in it was
all he could do to keep from cursing a blue streak.
He looked at his watch, and saw that he still had a
bead on Clint, which meant that the comm equipment was still working at this depth. "General," he
said quietly. "We're in a tunnel through the ice. Coming up on Clint, but I'm not sure how much longer
we're going to have a signal."

"We show you a hundred meters below the ice surface," General Fury replied. Steve thought he sounded
farther away, or tinnier, or something. Maybe the
comm wasn't working so well, and the locators had a
stronger signal. "Looks like Clint's about another hundred down," the general continued. "We pulled maps of
the ice shelf, and near as we can tell he's close to the
bottom of the ice layer. Right where he is, there's about
fifty meters of water under the ice."

In other words, plenty of room for a submarine, if
the Chitauri were planning on getting out that way. Behind that knowledge hung the memory of Polynesia,
and of Arizona, where the Chitauri had left little presents for pursuing forces. If they'd had the resources to
put another little present together, Steve and Jan and
Clint would know about it soon enough. Steve didn't
say anything about it. He figured they were all riding
the same train of thought.

Jan had gone ahead to scout again. This time when she came back, she landed on Steve's shoulder. "There's another tunnel up ahead that runs into this one from the left," she said. "I could hear Thor singing again."

Steve nodded, and they approached the junction carefully. When they were even with the other tunnel, Steve paused and listened. Hearing nothing, he looked at Jan.

She shrugged. "I heard it," she said softly. "I'm going to go look."

"Jan," he said, but she was already gone. Steve stood fuming, wondering what he should do. Clint was down below, obviously in trouble. Thor would be able to help, but what if he wasn't really there? What if the sound of his voice had carried from somewhere else in the ice? Mission priority was Clint and whatever he had found. Thor was secondary.

And Steve was starting to get the feeling that Garza was down there.

That made the decision for him. "Jan," he said softly into the comm. "I'm going ahead. You catch up."

She didn't answer. That was almost enough to make him head up the side tunnel looking for her, but mission discipline reasserted itself. Maybe the comm was out. Either way, he had a job to do. Down the main tunnel he went.

From above the Mare Chitauri, as Tony had taken to calling it when nobody else was listening, things were pretty quiet. Oh, sure, there was still the occasional structural collapse, and lots of steam and smoke and water flowing and dripping here and there, but the main action was over. He was standing sentry over a graveyard. "Nick," he said into the comm. "There's nothing happening here. I'm starting to feel left out."

"Hold your position," Nick said.

"Come on. You're not still holding a grudge because of that screener gag, are you?"

"Please," Nick said.

"Nick, I'm serious. I haven't squashed a lizard in fifteen minutes. This is getting—oh. Never mind, there's one." Tony sighted in on a Chitauri coming out of a hole in the northern end of the Mare Chitauri, and let go the force beams. The Chitauri was crushed against the far wall as if it had been hit by a meteor.

Hmm, Tony thought. Was that the same hole that Steve and Janet went into? "Say, Nick," he said, and then the entire wall of ice, broken stone, and eviscerated structure exploded. The blast wave was powerful enough to rock Tony's gyros even this far away; he could only imagine what would be happening down under the ice shelf. "Nick, did you see that? Jesus!" he shouted. "They blew the tunnel Steve and Jan went into! Steve! Jan! Clint! Can you hear me?"

No answer from them. "Hold, Tony," Nick said. "We're—"

"Forget it," Tony said. One of his visor readouts tracked all of the team members. Steve and Janet were still moving in Clint's direction. "I'm not holding while they're buried down there."

He arrowed off over the Weddell Sea, still fulminating. "I cannot believe you would tell me to stand there with my thumb up my ass while the entire works down there might be collapsing. What the hell is wrong with you, Nick?"

"If you'd shut up a second, I'd tell you," Nick said mildly. "You mind?"

"No." Tony pulled up into a hover directly over where the readout said Clint Barton was, below two hundred–plus meters of ice. "Go right ahead."

"I was about to suggest," Nick said as Tony fired up the force beams, "that you take the direct route. See how we can agree?"

Tony's reply was lost in the thunder of the force beams cratering the ice.

41

"OH," JANET SAID. "IT WAS YOU."

She'd almost run smack into Thor coming around a bend in the tunnel, even though she'd seen a glow that she now realized was coming from Mjolnir. "Loki is near," Thor said.

"So is Clint, and Steve is back down this way."

"That's the way I was heading," Thor said. They turned and moved back the way Janet had come. She realized she was getting cold, her tiny size working against her even in the relative warmth of the tunnel, and she returned to normal size just to have her added body mass working for her for a while. A split second later she remembered that she was naked except for her comm, a specially miniaturized model that fit inside her ear no matter what size she was.

"If I even think you're staring at me, I'm going to sting you like I was mistletoe and you were Baldur," she said. They were at the tunnel junction, and she led him to the left and down. Her feet were freezing against the ice, but the rest of her felt a little warmer. She'd burned a lot of energy stinging today, though, and wasn't sure how much she had left.

"Not funny," Thor said. "And don't take this the wrong way, but I've seen naked women before."

The words had hardly left his mouth when they heard a rolling boom from back up the tunnel she'd first come down with Steve. Thor looked over his shoulder. "Sounds like the party's still going on up there," he commented, and they kept walking. A few minutes later, though, a trickle of water appeared at their feet. It quickly grew into an energetic stream, and then they heard a building roar.

"Shrink, Janet," Thor said.

She did, and seconds later he was swept away by a wave that nearly filled the tunnel. "Thor!" she screamed after him, but the sound of the water swept her voice away, too. The water almost caught her then, but she pressed herself to the icy ceiling until, just a few seconds later, the water receded to an ankle-deep stream. Janet put it together: the explosion must have melted a lot of ice near the end of the hall where they'd come in, and that meltwater raced through in a flash flood.

How far would it carry him? He was a god, or at least sometimes it seemed that he might be. And they were getting close to Clint and Steve and whatever the Chitauri were doing down there where the bottom of the ice shelf met the midnight sea. Janet stayed small, and raced down the tunnel, feeling the beginnings of exhaustion in her wings but knowing she had to carry on.

Tony's batteries started complaining before he'd blasted his way through fifty meters of the ice. He couldn't just go full-bore, for fear that he would collapse whatever chamber existed below—or that the shock waves would propagate and shatter the ice floor that kept Clint and Steve and Janet out of the Weddell Sea. At least he hoped it was keeping them out of the Weddell Sea. "I don't travel for funerals," Tony said.

"What?" Nick said.

"Nothing. Talking to myself." Calibrating the force beams one more time, Tony started drilling again. And he started talking again, too, but only in his head. Don't you dare collapse, ice shelf. And don't you dare die, my friends. None of us dies today.

Between the force of the water and the lack of anything to get a grip on in the tunnel, Thor was carried quite some distance before he got himself turned around and planted Mjolnir's spike in the tunnel wall. The water roared in his ears and nearly pulled his boots off, but he kept his grip on Mjolnir and almost immediately the water started to recede. A moment later it was gone, rushing ahead to its reunion with whichever ocean lived below the ice, and Thor worked Mjolnir out of the tunnel wall. He slicked his hair out of his eyes and got his bearings. He listened for the faint buzz of Janet's wings, hoping that she'd had time to shrink before the water caught her; if she hadn't, she was probably ahead somewhere, wherever the tunnel opened out into a wider space inside the ice.

Ahead he heard a sudden tumult of voices, and although he guessed that this was because a group of Chitauri had been surprised by the same mini-flood that had just given him such a carnival ride, he started to run, because the commotion might have been due to Janet arriving in the water. Or, if she'd shrunk and was still back up the tunnel, there was still Steve's presence to consider. He'd been ahead of them, and perhaps avoided the water entirely, depending on what happened in the tunnels. Thor's guess was that he wasn't too far from the chamber Steve and Janet had been heading for to back Clint up, which meant that the Chitauri were there, too . . . which in turn meant that a fight was about to start, and Thor wanted to be there when it happened. A hundred Chitauri, maybe more, he had killed today, but he was not finished.

Not until he found Loki would he be finished.

And Loki was near.

•　•　•

Three signs told Steve knew he was getting close: the sounds of machinery, the pale light that began to infuse the walls of the tunnel, and the sprawled bodies of dead Chitauri littering the tunnel floor over the last two or three hundred yards. Clint's work. Then tunnel had leveled out, and a little water pooled on its floor. Six hundred feet of ice over my head, Steve thought. I've been here before. He checked to see if he could still get Clint's location, and was surprised to find that he could; Clint was dead ahead about forty yards, and apparently hadn't moved in nearly a half hour. Steve moved slowly, staying on the inner bend of the tunnel and creeping forward to get a view of the situation before he got himself all the way into it.

First he saw steel scaffolding, reaching from the floor maybe fifty feet up to the ceiling of a huge bubble in the ice. Steel mesh covered the floor, and Chitauri nimbly ran up and down the scaffolding, some in human guise and others in their natural forms. Steve shifted his weight and leaned to take in more of the room. Looking down to make sure of his footing, he saw a trickle of water running by his right boot. He glanced back, wondering if Janet was close and whether she'd tracked Thor down, and just had time to register the wave front boiling around the previous curve in the tunnel before the water knocked his legs out from under him and spilled him out into the room. The rush of meltwater lasted only fifteen seconds or so before spreading out into a pool on the expansive floor of the room, but it left Steve scrambling to his feet on the steel mesh with maybe a hundred Chitauri looking at him the way dogs look at a squirrel that falls off a tree branch into their kennel.

Things happened fast then. Steve registered the presence of a rectangular hole in the floor, reinforced by a steel frame, and what looked like a conning tower coming up out of the water in the hole. He also registered something long and steel and gleaming supported by the scaffolding he'd seen from the mouth of the tunnel. And then the Chitauri were on him, and he was fighting for his life. They came at him in waves, and from the scaffolding they fired down on him with some kind of energy weapon that vaporized the ice in basketball-sized chunks. He caught some of the shots on his shield, and felt his forearm burning even though the shield diffused heat as fast as any material known to man.

Luckily the Chitauri on the scaffolding weren't the best shots, or maybe they were just willing to sacrifice accuracy for rate of fire, but a large number of their shots hit their own forces. Or so it seemed, until out of the corner of his eye Steve saw a glint of light and it dawned on him that some of the Chitauri around him were going down courtesy of Clint Barton, who with his typical virtuosity had turned little ice chips into lethal weapons.

"Clint," Steve grunted into the comm. "Where the hell have you been?"

"Lying low waiting for you. I couldn't get 'em all with ice chips, Cap. What do you think I am, some kind of Super Hero?"

And then something else went whizzing by Steve's head, and another of the Chitauri fell and spasmed on the floor. Janet. "Was wondering when you'd show up," Steve said. He'd started to get the rhythm of the shots coming from the scaffolding, and he angled the shield to deflect one so that it blew the guts out of a Chitauri taking a swing at Janet.

"Aren't you sweet," she said. "I brought company."

And here came Thor, scattering the Chitauri and their works with sweeping arcs of Mjolnir. Over the din, too, Steve heard some kind of booming crack in the ceiling. He wondered how much the ice shelf shifted at a time, and how stable this bubble in its bottom was.

"Thor!" Steve shouted. "The scaffold!"

General Fury's voice cut in on the comm. "Goddammit," he said. "Where the hell has everybody been? And what are you seeing?"

"We've had to be quiet, sir," Steve said. "And we're seeing a submarine, some kind of rocket on a scaffolding, and a whole lot of Chitauri."

But so far they hadn't seen what Steve was looking for. Where was Garza?

Thor cocked his arm to throw Mjolnir . . . and froze.

"The scaffolding, big man!" Janet sang out. "Let's do it!"

"A rocket under two hundred meters of ice?" Fury

was saying into the comm. "Team: the submarine is your first priority. We are trying to dig you out."

"Dig us out?" Clint said.

"The Chitauri blew the mouth of the tunnel you came in through," Fury said.

"So you want us to take out the sub? How about we just commandeer it instead?" Clint came back.

"We're coming to get you. Your objectives are to destroy Chitauri assets and prevent them from getting out. Worry about extraction later."

Tony Stark's voice came across the channel for the first time in a while. "I'm on the extraction, boys and girl. Never fear." His comm fuzzed out for a moment as another boom echoed through the ice.

"Thor!" Janet screamed. "Throw the goddamn hammer!"

"Loki, my brother," Thor said, and bared his teeth in a predatory smile. "Clever as always."

Steve tried to follow Thor's gaze, and there on the second level of the scaffolding, near an open panel on the body of the rocket, stood Garza. His vision narrowed to a laser focus, and determination to kill Garza absorbed his whole mind; he was still killing Chitauri, but the blows of shield and fist were automatic. Steve broke free of the knot of fighting and sprinted toward the scaffolding. From the corner of his eye, he saw Thor coming with him, but this was his show. The rocket, the Chitauri, the ice . . . it was all happening again.

"Cap," General Fury was saying in the comm. "The submarine first."

Steve let his shield fly, straight and true. It hit Garza square in the head, edge-on, with a sound like the seismic shifting of the ice over their heads, hammering Garza off the scaffolding with all the pent-up anger of fifty-seven years lost to a block of ice. His broken body rebounded off the wall and tumbled to the floor.

From above, another boom, sounding closer this time. A huge sheet of the ceiling sheared away and fell, crushing a number of Chitauri who were running for the submarine. The impact broke the floor into a number of shifting chunks, barely held together by the steel mesh. The water of the Weddell Sea surged up through the cracks, slopping in waves over onto the shattered floor, and the conning tower of the submarine rocked back and forth. A Chitauri on the deck slipped and was crushed against the ice. Steve took all this in, his fury momentarily blown away by the titanic sound of the falling ice in the enclosed space . . . and then, on the conning tower of the sub, he saw Garza. Again.

And next to Steve Thor was at last letting go of Mjolnir, which crashed into the base of the conning tower with all the force of the thunder god's anger. The tower buckled, and Garza teetered against the railing for a suspended moment before toppling headfirst into the turbulent water. The submarine rolled, its hull heaving up against the confines of its pen and wrecking the steel framework. Water rushed in through the gaping hole left by Mjolnir, and the submarine kept rolling until it had capsized. It settled slowly into the water and was gone.

In the aftermath, the chamber was quiet except for the grinding and crackling of the ice. "Jan? Clint? You still there?" Steve called. He was still confused.

Jan buzzed up next to him, landing clumsily on his shoulder. "Steve," she said, and he noticed she was slurring a little. "It's over, right? I'm about stung out."

He cupped her in the palm of his hand. She was so cold, he couldn't believe she was still conscious. "Yeah," he said. "I think it's over." Janet was already slipping into sleep, her tiny body having burned the last of its reserves.

Clint appeared from a seam in the ice, where he'd apparently been the whole time. He moved gingerly, and held shards of ice between all of his fingers the way a nervous woman holds her keys in a parking lot late at night. "Man," he said. "Holding still on ice sure makes the knees creaky." He scanned the room for targets, and seemed to relax ever so slightly.

"Gang," Tony's voice came over the comm. "I'm about to come through the roof. You might want to move off to the side."

"Excellent, the cavalry arrives." Clint headed toward the scaffolding, and the rest of them followed. It stood under an angled part of the wall, and seemed best protected from falling ice boulders. Plus, Steve noted as they all followed Clint, the floor was more stable in that area.

"I take it from the banter that everything is all right down there," General Fury said in the comm.

"Correct, sir," Steve said. "The submarine is destroyed. We don't see any Chitauri survivors. We'll need to take care of this rocket thing, though."

"Current plan is to let the water take care of that," General Fury said. "The amount of damage you've done to the floor, it should give way. If you want to tip it over before you head out, though, that might be a good idea."

"Yes, sir," Steve said. He looked over at the rocket. It wouldn't be too hard to knock it down once Tony arrived. "Two Garzas," he muttered to himself. He was looking at the body of one of them, in a graceless heap near one post of the scaffolding. He'd never heard of two Chitauri assuming the same human form.

"One Garza, one Loki," Thor corrected him.

Steve shook his head. "I guess."

"No guessing," said Thor. "Loki has a way of getting the last word in. This time, we thought—well, I thought—he was trying to undermine us. Now I'm thinking he decided to sabotage the Chitauri—he wanted that sub destroyed."

"I don't get it," Steve said. "I thought he had it in for you."

Thor shrugged. "What Loki wants is chaos. Every once in a while that puts him on the right side of things. Could be he doesn't like the Chitauri because of their fetish for order."

"Could be he just wants to push your buttons," Clint said. "Family. My kids do the same thing."

Thor chuckled, but there wasn't much humor in it.

An enormous crackling sound, like lightning directly overhead before the thunder sounds, rolled through the room, and a huge icefall gutted the center of the ceiling. All four of them ducked away from it, but when the collapse hit the already-broken floor, the impact knocked them off their feet. Steve took the fall on his shoulders, cradling Jan's tiny form in both hands with the shield slung over his back. Its edges cut painfully into his shoulder blades, and a wash of displaced seawater drenched him. The whole floor of the chamber was moving now, and when Steve looked up he saw that the scaffolding had begun to tilt. A column of light shone down like something out of a UFO abduction movie, and the feet of the Iron Man suit appeared as Tony slowly descended into the chamber.

"Invigorating," somebody said. Steve had a little water in his ears, and didn't place the voice right away.

"That's one word for it," he said, and got to his feet. Then he froze as he placed the voice.

"Time to go, boys and girl," Tony said. "I'm running on fumes here, but I can take two. Thor, you mind giving someone a ride?"

But Thor wasn't listening to him. Neither was Steve. They had both turned to see Garza staggering to his feet, the side of his head grotesquely caved in but his eyes still malevolently alive. He was starting to decohere in the area of the wound inflicted by Steve's shield; as he spoke, a reptilian tongue flicked out between broken fangs and one of his eyes turned over in its shattered socket, revealing a slit pupil.

"Great goals require great sacrifice," he said, gaze locked on Steve. "You are one. I am another." In one hand he held a small rectangular box, much like the sample container Tony had planted on Nick Fury back when this had all started. With a whickering sound, eight shards of ice cut through the air and buried themselves in Garza's head and the hand holding the box, but he didn't drop it, and his gaze never wavered from Steve.

"The long view," the Chitauri said, his voice gurgling around an ice splinter sunk under his jaw, "is something at which we excel." His thumb flicked a switch on the box.

Again, Steve thought. It all happens again. The rocket, the Chitauri, the ice. He remembered thinking, not too long after his encounter at Andrews, that they were a step behind the Chitauri, and now realized that he hadn't taken the thought far enough. They hadn't just been a step behind. They'd been led.

"Ah," Thor said. "Of course. Well played, my brother." He spread his arms as if to welcome what was to come.

And the world disappeared in fire and ice.

Tony sank in darkness. Around him the suit tried to repair itself, but his batteries were almost gone, and every motion of arm or leg cost him energy that he needed for the nano-sized oxygen exchangers. He nearly started moving anyway, to speed the whole thing up, because Tony Stark had failed and he wanted to die.

Over and over the loop played itself in his memory:

He looked down at the tableau of Thor, Steve, and Clint, shadowed by the looming rocket and its slowly tilting support scaffold. Knock the rocket over, hell, he thought. It'll take care of itself before long.

He saw the Chitauri get up, and zeroed in on the object in its hand, and understood.

He pivoted in midair, reaching down. Thor would save himself, and Clint was a soldier . . . but he had to save Steve. Too many people needed Steve, and Tony Stark might have been a vain, alcoholic, dying playboy with no evident moral fiber or ethical beliefs, but he would have given his life in that moment to save Steve Rogers.

He reached, and Steve was gone, and the explosion overwhelmed Tony's sensors and gyros, pinwheeling him across the room to smash into the far wall. Dampers in the suit, and the damping gel, saved his life, but at a cost of that much more precious energy. From reflex, he put his hands out, but the floor was gone, and in the next moment a million tons of ice carried him far down into the Weddell Sea.

The ice lifted away, and briefly Tony rose too, in the drag of the ice's buoyancy. Then came a moment of perfect suspension, and perfect darkness, before Tony spiraled down and came to rest with a faint grinding sound of the suit scraping the seafloor sediment.

He damped the heaters, and bought himself another hour of oxygen. The cold immediately seeped in, first at the joints of the suit and then spreading to his hands and feet. He felt himself slowly going out, guttering like a candle flame on the last strands of its wick. Above him were sounds of ice, cracking and shifting and collapsing, grinding the bodies of his friends and colleagues together with those of his enemies. Tony grew colder, and listened.

And then, after enough time had passed that he had lost track of time, and felt his limbs grow numb and his mind grow slow, came a light.

The minisub breached the surface amid icebergs, scaring a gathering of penguins who shot off into the water, leaving pale bubble trails that faded into the water's dark gray. Clutched in the minisub's robot arm, head and shoulders out of the water, was the Iron Man suit with either Tony Stark or Tony Stark's body inside. Nick gnawed on a cigar and watched as a SHIELD helicopter took up a position over the minisub. Two men rappelled down to hook the suit, and the helicopter drew Tony up to its belly before swinging over in Nick's direction, where the ice was solid enough for it to land. As soon as it was on the deck, two techs hopped out and started working on getting the suit open, while a med team stood by. Another team put up a tent over the whole scene and fired up a space heater. This was all just triage; if Tony was alive, they were going to get him in the copter and up to *Algol* pronto. Nick waited until the tent was set up, then went inside.

They'd had Jarvis send the suit specs, but this new version was trickier to open from the outside than previous iterations. Also, the dead servos and freezing temperatures didn't help. But SHIELD hired only the best, and pretty soon the techs had the helmet off, and as the air inside the tent warmed, the rest of the suit started to come off more quickly.

"He's alive," said one of the medics. "Core temp's way down, though. Get some hot blankets, and we need him on the copter yesterday."

Tony had started talking incoherently as soon as the helmet came off, and trying to move, but even though the techs had gotten the arms and torso of the suit unlocked, he didn't seem to be able to move his arms. Medics wiped the inertial gel off and got him wrapped in blankets while the techs moved on to his legs.

Abruptly, as if some kind of switch had been flipped in his metabolism, Tony started to cry and talk at the same time. "Ah, God, I couldn't save him," Tony sobbed. "I didn't quit, Nick, I just couldn't save him."

"Be easy," Nick said. He squatted down next to Tony.

"I tried, Nick, I just didn't ha—have the juice. And then—"

In a gesture so unlike him that even Nick had a hard time believing he was doing it, he put a hand gently on Tony's shoulder. "We know what you did. And everyone got out."

"Wha . . . ?" Tony's eyes rolled in Nick's direction. His skin was still terribly blue. "Everyone?"

"Yeah," Nick said. "Thor got them out."

Tony was having trouble focusing his eyes. "Thor," he whispered. "That crazy son of a bitch. He did, huh?"

Nick nodded. "Yeah, he did."

"Good for him." Tony started shivering violently. This was a good sign, Nick thought. It meant he was warming up enough to waste spare energy on shivering. Hypothermia victims often relapsed after rescue, though, as heat loss from their breathing caught up to them.

"I'm going to quit this robot suit business and become a Norse god," Tony said through the chattering of his teeth.

"The way Thor comes and goes, we could use a backup," Nick said. Thor had in fact disappeared as soon has he'd showed up on the flight deck of *Algol* with Steve, Clint, and a nearly frozen Janet. Tony was the second case of hypothermia they'd dealt with in the last sixteen hours. "But right now," Nick went on, "you're going to get into a warm bath and do nothing for a while." The techs were working the last of the suit's clamps and seals open, and Nick saw Tony's hands moving under the blankets. "Okay, let's get moving here," he said. "I've had about goddamn enough of Antarctica."

"Warm bath," Tony murmured. "Long day . . ." He fell asleep, or passed out, and the medics moved Nick out of the way.

"Respiratory loss, General," one of them said. "We've got to get him up to *Algol* right now."

"Go, then," Nick said. He stood back until Tony was stretchered onto the copter and secured inside a heated medevac tent, and then he climbed aboard and watched the Antarctic landscape recede as the helicopter powered up and wheeled away into the sky.

42

FOR A WHILE HE WOULD CALL SOMEONE HE knew at McGuire and informally requisition an F-16, just so he could see for himself. It was an eight-hour flight, with three refueling stops along the way, and Steve had a little tinge of guilt about the cost to the taxpayers . . . but he had to see for himself. He had to fly over the shallow depression in the Filchner-Ronne Ice Shelf, and tip his wings at the SHIELD personnel stationed out at the edge of the shelf where it calved into the Weddell Sea. And he had to circle the iced-over crater where SHIELD missile strikes and a perimeter of next-gens had made sure that the Chitauri had nowhere to go but down. Then, after he had seen all of this, he would know again. For a little while.

It haunted him that he had made the problem worse before he had made it better. That wasn't what soldiers did, and it wasn't what Captain America was supposed to do.

And it haunted him that he had come so close to being entombed in ice again. He dreamed sometimes that he was waking up in the year 2249, or 3188, or 9999; the year didn't matter. Every time he had the dream, he awoke in an unrecognizable future, and was never able to become part of it.

Then, every morning, he woke up and did everything he could to make a lie of the dream. He went out to the movies instead of staying up with Turner Classics; he read a book once in a while if the *Times Book Review* suggested he should; he kept up a desultory kind of relationship with Janet until she told him one morning over eggs benedict that she thought they'd both be better off trying to find someone who really made each of them happy, instead of just keeping a place warm for someone else who was really never coming back. He'd argued at first, but only the way you argue when you know that the other party will be angry if you acquiesce too easily to what's obviously the right thing to do.

And so they didn't talk much anymore.

It was all fine, it was going to be fine. The Chitauri were gone completely, as far as anyone could be certain. Tony had succeeded in buying his radio stations, and along with a steady diet of top-40 hits and boilerplate talk, each broadcast alerted all the ants within range to attack and destroy a certain alien invader. So far—and it had been three months since Antarctica—not a single confirmed hit had been reported. Steve was beginning to let himself believe that they'd really gotten rid of the Chitauri this time, which also meant that everything he'd said about the triumph of human ingenuity was, for the moment, vindicated.

Until the next threat came along, which was where he still had a problem. If he got up in the morning and looked at himself in the mirror with the kind of ruthless honesty he expected of himself, Steve Rogers had to admit that he'd been seduced by the idea that he knew better than the people he was sworn to protect. He wanted to believe that he'd never fall for the same scam again, but how did you know?

General Fury had no answers.

How did you know?

The answer, perhaps unsurprisingly, had come from Gail. Bucky was in the hospital again, and although the doctors said he would get out, every time they signed Bucky in, Steve confronted the cold fact that the world was too damn full of people he was going to outlive. One night, not too long after he'd found himself on the flight deck of SHIELD helicarrier *Algol* with his eyebrows singed off and one of Thor's meaty arms draped around his neck, he'd confided in her. "I blew it, Gail," he said. "They used me, and I let them, and I let myself think that I was bigger than the flag. Now everyone in SHIELD knows I did it. How do you . . . I mean, why should anyone ever trust me again?"

"Because you did it for the right reasons," Gail said without hesitation. It was late fall, three full months after Antarctica, and for some reason she'd wanted to walk from Mount Sinai down through Central Park to the petting zoo. They were feeding two Vietnamese potbellied pigs, all by themselves in the late afternoon chill.

"Everyone thinks their reasons are the right reasons," Steve said. "That wasn't good enough this time."

"It might be next time," she said, and moved on from the potbellied pigs to a pen full of various goats.

Petting zoos, Steve thought. What are we doing here? I'm the one who's lost in time, and Gail's acting like a ten-year-old. "And it might not," he said.

Gail fed the goats the rest of the feed they'd bought from the vending machines near the entrance to the bird enclosure, which was closed for some reason. "Steve," she said. "We've both had way too much time to think about what might have been different, and all of that time to think hasn't done either of us a lick of good. You were wrong? Fine. You were wrong. Let it be the lesson it is, but don't let it change the things about you that made Nick Fury want you out there in the first place. If there's one thing I can't stand, it's a wishy-washy man. Now take me back to the hospital."

And he did, walking her back up Fifth Avenue in the

Acknowledgments

Thanks first of all to Millar and Hitch for giving me such a rich field to work with. Also to Jen Heddle for thinking of me, and to the ever-anonymous copyeditor for some excellent catches. And thanks to P and t. and L, for superhero conversation and for being the people I can count on.

About the Author

Alex Irvine is the author of the novels *The Narrows; The Life of Riley; Batman: Inferno; One King, One Soldier*; and *A Scattering of Jades*. His short fiction, published in Salon, *Vestal Review, The Magazine of Fantasy and Science Fiction, Trampoline*, and elsewhere, is collected in *Unintended Consequences and Pictures from an Expedition*. He has also written comic books and online narratives. He has won the Locus, Crawford, and International Horror Guild awards for his fiction, and has been nominated for the Pushcart Prize and the World Fantasy Award. His fiction has been translated into French, Spanish, Italian, Czech, Polish, Hebrew, Russian, and Chinese. In 2005, he was awarded the New England Press Association's top prize for investigative journalism, and that same year was part of a writing team that won a Webby and the International Game Developers Association Innovation Award. He is an assistant professor of English at the University of Maine.